The Testament of Jessie Lamb

Jane Rogers has written eight novels including *Her Living Image* (winner of the Somerset Maugham Award), *Mr Wroe's Virgins* (shortlisted for the Guardian Fiction prize), *Promised Lands* (winner of the Writers Guild Best Novel Award), and *Island* (long-listed for the Orange Prize). She has written drama for radio and TV, including an award-winning adaptation of *Mr Wroe's Virgins* for BBC2. Her radio work includes both original drama and Classic Serial adaptations. *The Testament of Jessie Lamb* was long-listed for the Man Booker Prize in 2011.

She is Professor of Writing at Sheffield Hallam University, and has taught writing at the University of Adelaide, Paris Sorbonne IV, and on a radio-writing project in eastern Uganda. She lives on the edge of the moors in Lancashire.

Praise for *The Voyage Home*:

'Jane Rogers' new novel is extraordinarily bold . . . It is also powerfully imagined, a real web of forces. What a book. What an astonishing achievement'

Adam Piette, *Scotland on Sunday*

'Beautifully constructed and controlled . . . an absorbing, nuanced drama about moral choices and personal responsibility'

Katie Owen, *Sunday Telegraph*

'A voyage of self-discovery that is eloquent, lucid and entirely enthralling'

Hephzibah Anderson, *Daily Mail*

'A startling and gripping exploration of love, grief, responsibility and power that moves effortlessly from the personal—the pain of a woman who has recently lost her father—to one of the most hotly debated and emotive issues of the moment, the plight of asylum seekers . . . A wonderfully humane and vividly written story that will keep you entranced until the last page'

Alex Clark, 'Must Read of the Month', *Red*

Praise for *Island*:

'Nikki is a triumphant creation . . . There is indeed a house-style: one of economy, accuracy and controlled passion. But the authorial voice has a chameleon quality; she speaks with tongues. And the tongue here is persuasive indeed'

Penelope Lively, *Independent*

'There is a lot of delicious black comedy here . . . Then, there is the magic. This book reminds us of the power of stories, of their possibilities. It is the song Jane Rogers sings, and it is triumphant'

Sunday Telegraph

'Heart-breakingly lyrical . . . It takes you into the heart of a dark wood, where there is no hope at all, and brings you out the other side, ready, if not to live happily ever after, then at least to begin to live'

Julia Blackburn, *Guardian*

'Weaves a spell that glimpses another world'

Sunday Times

Praise for *Promised Lands*:

'Ambitiously conceived and brilliantly realised'

Sunday Times

'This story of lost innocence is rich in itself and beautifully imagined from Rogers' researches. In air that 'waves and wrinkles with heat' we see Dawes' moral labours translated into physical terms—sweat, stickiness, pinched flesh. White buttocked convicts rut in the mud; a debonair surgeon plays Mozart in a tent thick with insects …. Marvellously intelligent'

Observer

'Ambitious, brave, and beautifully crafted'.

TLS

Praise for *Mr Wroe's Virgins*:

'An engaging, serious and gleefully ironic novel, one that leaps headlong into the most ambitious and risky territories: faith, love and existential meaning'

New York Times Book Review

'There is a rich vein of comedy in this beautifully written book which deals so profoundly with the attractions of idealism and the confusion between sexual and religious feeling'

Guardian

'A delight from the first page to the last'

Observer

The Testament of Jessie Lamb

JANE ROGERS

For Heather,
It's been lovely to meet you
& I really hope you have success
with your
own writing —
best wishes,

SANDSTONE PRESS
HIGHLAND | SCOTLAND

CANONGATE
Edinburgh · London

Jane Rogers

Moniack 2016

Thanks
I am grateful to Hawthornden Castle for a writing retreat, and to
Arts Council England and the Banff Centre Canada, for a Fellowship
Award which allowed me to work uninterrupted for 10 weeks in
an amazing setting. JR.

This paperback edition published in 2012 by Canongate Books,
14 High Street, Edinburgh EH1 1TE

2

Copyright © Jane Rogers 2011

The moral right of the author has been asserted

First published in Great Britain 2011 by Sandstone Press Ltd,
One High Street, Dingwall IV15 9WJ

British Library Cataloguing-in-Publication Data
A catalogue record for this book is available on
request from the British Library

ISBN 978 0 85786 418 5

Typeset in Sabon by Palimpsest Book Production Limited,
Falkirk, Stirlingshire

Printed and bound by Clays Ltd, St Ives plc

www.canongate.tv

For Wendy

'Another kind of light and life
Are to be mine . . .'
Iphigenia at Aulis, Euripides

Sunday morning

The house is very quiet now he's gone. I get up
carefully without falling over and shuffle to the
window. The light is partly blocked by gigantic
leylandii in next door's garden. No one lives in this
row any more. I lean my forehead against the window
and peer down into the overgrown garden. The cold
pane mists up straightaway with my breath, but I
know it's too far to jump. Anyway, there are window
locks and no key. I shuffle around the room, keeping
my left hand on the wall for balance, until I reach the
door. I try it again, just in case.

He's left me cheese sandwiches and a plastic bottle
of orange juice in the corner. He must be planning to
be out all day. Well at least I don't have to listen to
him saying the same things over and over, or see him
crying, or hear him pacing around the house in a
restless fit. At least there's space for my own thoughts
now, and I have nothing to worry about but myself.

I test the bike locks again. They are the clear blue plastic coated type, inside the plastic you can see silvery wire. He's wound one three times around each ankle and locked it, like bangles. And threaded the third through the other two then looped it round and locked it. The circlets round each leg are too tight to slide over my ankles. I can only move my feet six inches apart. It makes me shuffle like a prisoner in a chain gang. I have to keep adjusting the circlets otherwise the one the joining-lock is fixed to pulls wider and the others get tighter and bite into me.

He's left me a bucket with a lid and toilet roll, but it's hard to use because I can't get my feet wide enough apart to squat properly. He has left me a pad and pencil for entertainment. And my sleeping bag and pillow are scrumpled against the wall. The wonky heating's come on at last and I'm not so cold any more.

My brain has finally stopped behaving like a rat in a trap. It's stopped hurling itself in all directions and chasing its own tail. After all, he can't keep me here forever. All I have to do is sit it out.

I have that strangely pleasant ache above the bridge of my nose from all the crying and now I don't feel as if I shall ever cry again. I'm a bit stiff from sleeping on the floor, but all in all it's not so bad. It could be worse. I shuffle all round the walls again, then over to the picnic table and chair he has placed in the middle of the room. I shuffle into position and sit on the chair. I write my name on the first page of the pad: Jessie Lamb.

He wants me to think about what I am doing. Not that I am doing anything, now. I am suspended;

stopped in my tracks. It almost feels like I'm not here any more—I'm not that Jessie Lamb who was busily rushing towards her goal. If I spotted the bike lock keys, dropped there, say, on the floorboards—would I pick them up and unlock my ankles? Would I figure out a way to get free? Maybe I'd just pretend I hadn't noticed, and stay captive. In a way it's a relief to be prisoner and to not have to think. To be passive, instead of active.

He's trying to give me a way out. So that I can blame *him* if I don't do it, instead of facing up to being a coward.

Is that what you want?

What else could explain me so stupidly jumping in the car with him when he suggested going to check Nanna's house?

You thought he was making a friendly gesture; you wanted to make up.

Yes. But he had already threatened to do 'whatever it takes to stop you'. So, did you get into the car *knowing* you would be imprisoned? Is that secretly what you wanted?

Oh, I can't be bothered with all this. Isn't it bad enough to have him going on at you, without doing it yourself when he's not here?

The logical thing is to do as he's asked; to *think* about it. Indeed. Write it down. Remember it, re-imagine it, gather it together. Because it'll be proof—won't it?—proof that you really are doing what you want. Proof that I, Jessie Lamb, being of sound mind and good health, take full responsibility for my decision, and intend to pursue it to its rightful end.

I underline my name on the pad. The question is, where to begin? Where does my story begin? With my own beginning, I suppose; the day I was born.

No way am I writing sixteen years!

No, but it needs to begin at the beginning. Before that terrible feeling of pressure came into my head insisting that I must do something, I must do something, I must do *something* or else explode. That I must find the thing I was destined to do.

I'll set it down exactly, everything that happened, I'll set it down perfectly honestly, so there can be no doubt in anybody's mind, least of all mine, about what I want to do and why.

The testament of Jessie Lamb.

One

I used to be as aimless as a feather in the wind. I thought stuff on the news and in the papers was for grownups. It was part of their stupid miserable complicated world, it didn't touch me. I remember sitting on the fence at the level crossing above Roaches one evening, with Sal and Danny and some of the others. It was dark, especially either side of the railway, because of the steep banks of burnt black heather. We looked down at the bright windows of the pub in the valley bottom, and the small yellow eyes of cars running along the road. Everyone except us was indoors and we were up there in the windy darkness, facing the black mass of the moors rising up on the other side of the valley.

A train roared past, going to Huddersfield, and the hot draught of it almost blew us off the fence. Danny said we should try walking along one of the rails, like balancing on a tightrope, and see who could get the furthest. 'Just jump off if a train comes,' he said, 'there's only one an hour.' Sal climbed down from the fence and began to teeter along the rail, arms outstretched. I could barely make her out, she blobbed into darkness as she moved and I couldn't tell if she was really overbalancing or if my eyes were just joining her up to the rest of the dark. She swore so I knew she'd fallen off, and then each of the others tried, and we were counting loudly in a chant. 'One *and* two *and* three *and* OUT!', seeing who could be the first to make it up to ten.

When it was my go I realised I couldn't even see the rail, only feel it through my soles, and I got my balance and looked up at the green signal light far ahead along the track. There was a kind of roaring filling up my ears. I don't know if it was the wind up there or my own blood, or the way the others were yelling and laughing. But I felt as if I could do anything, anything at all, and nothing would have the power to hurt me. I told myself if I could do twenty steps that would prove it. On twenty-one I jumped down from the rail and as I climbed onto the fence a train came hurtling out of the darkness behind me and gave a deafening blast on its whistle. And the thought just popped into my head: I could fix it, MDS. I could make everything in the world OK again. But because no one asked me to, I simply wouldn't bother.

That's almost like the daft things you believe when you're really little, like I used to believe I could fly. I believed it for years, but it had to be kept secret. I knew if I ever told anyone or showed it off to anyone, I'd lose the power. And if I doubted it, and tried it out just to see, I'd lose the power—so I didn't. I believed in it.

I knew I would be able to fly when there really was a need. Which, fortunately for me, there never was.

I remember things that make me ashamed now, like driving home from the caravan at Scarborough with Mum and Dad, and all the roads around York being clogged up because of a mass funeral at the Minster. Dad had forgotten to check online. And I was impatient to get home and call for Sal. We were stuck behind the traffic for two hours. I remember staring at all the miserable people in their cars and saying 'Why can't they just stay at home to mourn? The women who're dead won't care!'

I thought it was normal, that's the thing. When you're little you think everything is normal. If your mother had a pointed head and green ears you'd think it's normal. Only when you grow up do you realise that not everybody is like that. Gradually you can even come to learn that the time you are living in is strange too, that it hasn't always been like this. The more you feel uncomfortable and unconfident and want to find a way to be like everyone else and fit in, the more normality runs away from you because there isn't any such thing. Or if there is, you have to find someone else who'll agree with you what it is. Which I seem singularly unable to do.

Back then, before, Sal agreed with me. Together we knew all the answers. And we thought it was normal for women to die. Or, even worse than that, almost that they might have deserved it, because they'd done something shameful. I thought that if you died it must be at least a tiny bit your fault. There must be something bad in you, to attract such a fate—and especially with MDS, because you had to have had sex.

The first person we knew who died fitted that exactly. Caitlin McDonagh in year ten. I'm not counting teachers from primary school or women Mum and Dad knew, because they were adults, and adults (to me then) were all old and liable to die. But Caitlin started crying her eyes out in History, and they took her to the office and she never came back. Her best friend told us she was pregnant, and we imagined her with her sleazebag boyfriend who was about twenty years old, and it seemed like just deserts. Except they came into school and gave us all Implanon implants a few weeks later, even though most of us hadn't even got boyfriends, so that no matter what bad thing we did, none of us would get punished like Caitlin.

Sal and I were curious but it didn't touch us. Not until—well, not until the day she heard about her aunty. We were in her bedroom with her clothes scattered across the floor and both of us trying not to listen to her mum's anxious voice on the phone downstairs.

'Did you see those doctors on the news last night?' Sal asked.

'I don't think so.'

'They showed what MDS does to the brain. It kind of makes holes come in your brain. They said women who get it, their brains will look like Swiss cheese.'

'That's disgusting.'

'Yeah, they gradually lose bits of their brain, they stop being able to balance, and they forget stuff.'

'D'you think it hurts?'

'They didn't say. Some of them die really fast. After only three days of being ill.'

We agreed that knowing it was coming must be the worst part. Who wants to know their brain will turn into Swiss cheese? We sat in silence for a while. Sal had lots of clockwork toys in her room, she used to collect them—and we wound up a nun and a Lisa Simpson and raced them across her desk. The nun won. We entered a letterbox pencil-sharpener and a toy car as well. It's harder with four because you have to wind them up and hold one ready in each hand without it unwinding. I told myself if the nun won again then they would find a cure to MDS. But Lisa fell off the edge of the desk and the nun and the letterbox collided.

'Maybe we'll never have children,' said Sal.

'When the youngest people who're alive today get old—'

'They'll be the last people on earth.' It had been on the news for ages, but it was the first time I could really see it. 'As we get older, there won't *be* any children.'

'They'll have to close the schools.'

'All the things children need—they won't make them any more.'

'Nappies, baby clothes, pushchairs.'

'It'll be so weird.'

'And when we're old, everyone'll be old. There'll be no one going to work.'

'No shops or bin men or buses.'

'Nothing. It'll all just grind to a halt.'

Sal turned on the telly. There'd been a riot at some

holy place in India. Too many women had tried to go there to pray and someone had panicked, and lots of them were trampled to death. She turned off the sound. 'There doesn't seem much point in doing our homework, does there? If we're about to be extinct.'

We thought of all the things that would be pointless; university, work, getting married, building, farming, mending the roads.

'There'd be nothing to do but try to keep ourselves amused until we died,' said Sal. 'It wouldn't matter what we did. Nobody'd care.'

I started to worry about how there'd be no one to cremate or bury the last corpses. Then I realised animals would probably eat them. 'The world will be really peaceful. No more cars or planes or factories—no more pollution. Gradually, plants will take over cities—'

We thought about our houses slowly falling to bits, the doors blowing open, the roofs caving in, birds and animals nesting there.

'Some other species will dominate,' said Sal, and we began to argue about what it might be. All the animals in zoos etc would have to be let out before the last people died. Which would probably kill off a few of us even sooner. And those animals that could adapt to life in their new territory might take over. There might be wolves again in England, and bears. Tigers might live off untended herds of cows. Tree branches would spread out over roads, and hedges would grow huge and wild, and weeds burst through the tarmac. After a hundred years the world would be one great nature reserve, with all the threatened species breeding again, and great shoals of cod in the sea, eagles nesting in old church spires. It made me think of the garden of Eden, how it was supposed to be so beautiful before Adam and Eve messed things up.

'But just imagine never holding a baby in your arms.' Sal turned up the TV; that advert for dancing yoghurt pots was on, we always sang along to it in high squeaky voices, so we did.

Then her mum came upstairs in tears and told Sal it was her aunty. I didn't even know her aunty was pregnant. All I could think about was the smell of burning which wafted in when her mum opened the door. A harsh burnt sweet smell that caught in your throat—it was the chocolate cake we'd made which her mum was meant to be keeping an eye on. I said goodbye awkwardly and went downstairs. Their dog Sammy was whining at the back door so I let him in, and I turned off the oven. There wasn't any point in looking, you could tell it would be cinders. I didn't feel anything about her aunty. I simply didn't *care*. I thought, I wonder what will happen next? As if the human race and its fate was nothing at all to do with me. As if I was on a bicycle, freewheeling very fast downhill, in the smooth blackness of night.

Two

At that time Mum and Dad bickered constantly between themselves and when they got a chance they'd snarl at me as well. I suppose they must have been worried about MDS but I don't remember them talking about it much. What I remember are endless petty rows. You'd wake up in the morning and there was this mood right through the house like the smell of gas. They'd manage everything without speaking, politely moving out of each other's way, talking to me with exaggerated friendliness. They'd keep it up, sometimes for days on end, and then stop for practically no reason. Dad'd do something, pour Mum a glass of wine and hand it to her with a little bow, or ask her if she wanted to watch a DVD. And suddenly everything was OK again. Because *they'd* decided. The only night of peace was Tuesdays; Mum had an evening clinic and Dad and I always had tea together.

Tuesday night in the kitchen.

Dad's got all his ingredients out, in a neat row along the counter, and he's weighing and measuring them onto separate plates. He's got one of those old-fashioned sets of balancing scales with a metal dish on one side and little brass weights that you add in a pile, on the other. Mum gave it him for Christmas and he loves it. The weights are smooth and chunky and fit together in a neat tower. Mum says he cooks like a scientist. He won't cook something if he hasn't got the exactly right ingredients.

He's standing there measuring, with his shoulders hunched forward, he looks a bit like an ape! He's hairy like an ape too, with a furry chest. When Mum used to take me swimming I stared at the strange men with bare chests. He's got broad shoulders and a thick neck but short legs, and when he turns round to smile you can see he's got bright brown eyes and two deep smile creases carved either side of his mouth in a really monkey-ish grin. When he grins at you you can't help yourself, you have to grin back. Except he hasn't grinned for a long time now. Which I suppose is my fault.

I used to do my homework on the kitchen table on Tuesdays and we'd think up perfect crimes that you wouldn't get caught for and make each other laugh. Things like, if your victim is allergic to bee stings, put a drop of honey on his collar and let loose some bees. When they sting his neck it'll swell up and suffocate him before he can get help. Or, if you need to dispose of a corpse, put it in your car and drive to a safari park. Chuck it out for the lions when no one's looking. They'll eat it up and leave no trace.

There was a Tuesday when Dad properly explained Maternal Death Syndrome to me. The news was saying it was everywhere. Rumours about unaffected tribes deep in the Amazon rainforest or amongst the Inuit of the frozen north, all of them were untrue. It wasn't just the West, or the First World, or cities. There *were* some pregnant women left, but only ones who were far on in their pregnancies; women who must have got pregnant before MDS arrived. Once these women gave birth, it seemed there wouldn't be any more babies.

'I don't understand,' I said to Dad. 'Why is it only pregnant women who get it?'

'Well,' he said, settling down to peel some potatoes. 'Up till a hundred years ago, pregnancy was the most dangerous experience in a woman's life, and the one the highest percentage were likely to die from.'

'Father of Wisdom,' I said, and rolled my eyes at him. That's what I call him when he goes off on one. But he didn't smile.

'D'you want to know or don't you?'

'I want to know.'

'Right then. There are all sorts of reasons why pregnancy is dangerous—obviously. The baby can come too early or too late; it may not present head first, the placenta may not come away properly, etc. But once you take away all the physical, *mechanical* things that can go wrong—there's something else, which is even more disturbing—because they think it's what these guys have latched on to.'

'These guys?'

'The terrorists. Bio-terrorists, who've engineered this virus.'

'What is it?'

'Well you know what your immune system is?'

'Yes, it fights diseases.'

'Exactly. It knows what *you* are, and it attacks anything that is not *you*. Anything foreign in your system, it attacks, in order to defend you. Now spot the problem. When a woman gets pregnant, what's the problem?'

I sat and puzzled my brain. 'Is it the baby? Because the baby's a different person?'

'Nearly. What's the baby made of?'

'Doh. Blood, bones—'

He shook his head at me. 'In the very beginning.'

'An egg.'

'And?'

'A sperm.'

'Thank you. Which comes from someone else. And for the baby to grow, that sperm needs to survive, and all the cells that grow from the union of the sperm and the egg need to survive. But the woman's immune system should attack it. Because it's a foreigner in her body.'

'OK.'

'But it doesn't. In most normal pregnancies, the woman's immune system does not attack the sperm or developing foetus. Her immune system takes a step back, in order to let the baby grow. And while the woman's not being defended against the sperm, she's also not being completely defended against various other nasties that might want to invade her system.'

'And that's why she gets MDS?'

'So they think. The blip in her immune system, which allows her to remain pregnant, seems to make her vulnerable to Maternal Death Syndrome. That's when it kicks in. It's a freakish chance—whoever worked it out is either a genius or very lucky.'

'So when they say it's full-blown—'

'They mean it's triggered CJD. Prion disease. They've married the AIDS virus with CJD, that's what researchers reckon. So the AIDS gets a hold and makes the woman vulnerable to everything going, and the first thing that's going is CJD. For which we have no cure in sight—never have had, not since back in the days of Mad Cow disease.'

'A scientist must have done it.'

'Well it hasn't happened by accident.'

'But *why*?'

'Power? Religion? Your guess is as good as mine, Jessie.' He'd cut the potatoes into chips and now he lowered them into the pan, and they hissed and fizzed. The smell of hot oil filled the kitchen. 'Set the table, love, these are nearly done. And let's change the record, shall we?'

I shifted my books off the table.

'Come on,' he said, 'how about a perfect crime? You have to use an ostrich feather and a safety pin. I'll give you three minutes.' That's what we used to do. Give each other a clue, or a weapon. We could always make each other laugh. It's like remembering another life. 'Come along,' he said, 'my nut brown maid.'

The next thing that happened was that Sal's aunt in Birmingham died. She was ten weeks pregnant. Sal's aunt and uncle already had three children. 'Mum says we might have Tommy, the little one, to live with us,' Sal told me.

'Is your mum very upset?'

She pulled her face.

I felt clumsy and thick and miserable but I wanted to talk about it. 'Why do you think this is happening?'

'Doh.'

'No, I mean, what's behind it?'

She blew out through her lips. 'Someone wants the human race extinct.'

'But *why*?'

'How should I know?'

'I've been thinking about it.'

Sal started picking up clothes off her floor and flinging them into a heap in the corner. 'Go on, wonder-brain.'

'Maybe they've done it for a reason.'

'Like?'

'Well they must hate everyone.'

'Brilliant.'

'They must—they must be really angry.'

'What about?'

'Anything. Wars. Injustice.'

'This isn't exactly going to fix anything, is it?'

'Yes. It'll make all the bad things end.'

'Why are they targeting women? Of all the people in the world, why women and their babies? If you want to wipe out bad people why not start with politicians— or paedophiles?'

'Because—I don't know.'

'Why are you thinking about whoever did it? They're a monster—they're evil, they should have holes drilled in *their* brain and needles stuck all over them and boiling wax poured in!' Sal wiped the back of her hand across her eyes. 'I don't know why you care about who did it.'

'I'm sorry. Shall I make some cocoa?' Sal likes cocoa, we always used to have it at her house. When we went down to the kitchen Sammy got excited and started barking, and we ended up throwing the ball for him in the garden.

That was one of the first times I argued with Sal. I didn't really know what I wanted to say but I didn't just want to talk about how bad the terrorists were and how they should be punished. Yes, of course they were wicked, but it was more I wanted to know why this had been *allowed* to happen. Or, what it was about now, about us, that made it able to happen? I felt outside all that blah about isn't it terrible and shocking, as if there was something I knew that no one else did.

Three

Then came the public information announcement. They trailed it all week on TV and in the papers; it was when they officially stated that MDS was world-wide and everybody had it. They compared it to being HIV positive and said most of us would live out our lives without ever getting ill; the trigger for it to become deadly was pregnancy. They wanted to reassure us that governments across the world were co-operating in research blah blah blah.

I remember watching it with Mum and Dad and staring at them afterwards. They had the disease. I had it. We all had MDS. It was like knowing you've swallowed slow-acting poison. I didn't want to sit with them so I went up to my room and texted Baz. (How ridiculous. Just writing his name makes me happy. Baz, Baz, Baz. And now there are stupid tears running down my cheeks.)

Back then he was just a friend. We were at primary

school together. I went to Sunday School for years because of him—his dad was a vicar and Baz always went, so I tagged along too. Sometimes when you're talking to him it's as if he's still practising piano in his head, you wonder if he's even heard. Then when he speaks you realise he's been thoughtfully considering, instead of leaping in and babbling. When we started secondary we both made other friends and avoided each other in school, as if we were embarrassed. But we still used to go round to each other's houses.

That night he rang me back and said his parents were out, get Sal and some of the others and come round. I didn't want to get Sal. I felt like talking to him on my own. I had thought he was the only boy I knew who didn't fancy Sal, but clearly I was wrong. I looked at myself in the mirror and thought how much better my life would be if my legs were longer and my tits were bigger and closer together. I wondered if I should dye my hair blonde, like everyone does, but then I thought how my dad at least really liked it brown. He called me his nut brown maid, hazel eyes and chestnut hair. And hairy brown caterpillar eyebrows, he forgot to mention that. There was no point in straightening my hair, I looked revolting and who cared?

So Sal and I went round and everyone was in a weird mood. Rosa Davis was there, who Baz'd sort-of gone out with the year before. It hardly counted, he'd dumped her after two weeks. She was pretending to be really drunk. Baz was wearing a black T-shirt with a blue whale on it the exact colour of his eyes. After we'd been there half an hour Sal rang Damien and got him to come round. The two of them smooched together for a while then went off upstairs. I asked Baz where his parents were. His dad was working with the bereaved, there was a residential weekend of counselling and faith, and his mum'd gone too, to help. We laughed about how MDS is great for business—for vicars and undertakers. I asked him if he'd watched the TV announcement and he said ye-es, slowly, as if there was more.

'What?' I asked him.

'I was thinking that maybe we deserve it.'

'MDS?'

He nodded.

'Why?'

'Well something bad was bound to happen sooner or later. People have messed up the world so much—'

'You mean, like global warming?'

'Sure. And running out of oil, and water, and food. The point is, a bad thing was ready to happen. The ground was prepared.'

'Not by us,' I said. 'By our parents. And their parents. They're the ones who've messed things up.'

'Right. But now this has happened everyone can blame someone else. Instead of being mad at the government for giving scientists money to make hideous weapons, or at themselves for polluting the entire world, they can put all the blame on some unknown monster.' Baz tapped a little rhythm on his beer bottle, then blew across the top a few times to hear the sound. 'People always think there's enough time left to change,' he said.

'Well they're stupid.'

Someone turned up the music and we raided his parents' booze cupboard, and Kaz passed round a spliff. I remember feeling very cunning when I thought of phoning my parents to say I was staying over at Sal's. I remember snogging Danny who I don't even like, and the next thing I remember is sitting propped against the bath feeling sick. Sal told me to put my fingers down my throat and I did puke a bit, but not as much as I needed to. I went down to Baz's room in the cellar after that. He was there on his own playing his piano, he didn't take any notice of me. I curled up in the big armchair and tried to doze, while the notes ran on and on like water pouring from his fingertips, and every few minutes I had to open my eyes to stop the room going round. I must have dozed off eventually because when I woke up there was a rug draped over me and Baz had vanished. I felt terrible in the morning of course, and even worse when I went upstairs and found Rosa helping Baz to tidy up. I asked her where she'd slept and she grinned and said his parents' bed was kingsize. I went home and stayed in my room all day, telling my mum I had a headache which was true.

But during that evening, before I started feeling ill, when we were all madly dancing and making the world spin around us, I had this fantastic sense of freedom. I thought I could be free of my mum and dad and their petty squabbles. I could soar. No one could say a thing to me, especially not anyone older than me. Because it was them who had messed things up.

The feeling that I had was power; like when I went to help my aunt Mandy at the theatre. As well as making puppets and masks for the children's theatre company, she did lighting. Sometimes in the holidays she'd let me help and I'd do follow spot. There's a metal frame like a handle around the big hot spotlight and you twist and tilt it so the beam follows the actor and he's always standing in a beam of light. You get to know his moves so you can predict where he's going and move the spot exactly with him. For a while I thought I'd like to have the same job as her, sitting up there in the dark with the lighting desk and all the controls, softly turning the pages of her marked-up script. Giving light to the characters who needed it, making the sun shine or darkness fall, making the stage into a firelit cottage or a bright summer morning. Giving them light brings the characters to life. That's the kind of power I felt I had.

We heard Caitlin was dead, and some people from my class went to her funeral. I didn't because it seemed a bit hypocritical, I hadn't even known her that well. Rosa Davis disappeared and there was a rumour that she'd been pregnant too. Nobody was bothered, she'd always been weird. She never had any real friends among the girls, she used to hang around on the edges of groups. I was glad she'd gone.

The next time I went to school I was feeling a bit schizo. Part of me was panicking about my GCSEs, and part of me was going, 'So what? This stuff is meaningless.' I was afraid Baz thought I was a drunken idiot. Then he rang and asked if I was interested in a meeting. 'It's about what we were talking about the other night,' he said. 'How people have fouled up the world.'

I said yes because I thought he was asking me to go with him—then it turned out he had a piano exam in Manchester and his mum was dropping him off after that. I felt stupid, and stupid for feeling stupid. I asked Sal but she didn't want to come.

'It'll be boring,' she said. 'It's one of Baz's greeny things. Who needs to save the planet now?' Sal didn't have space in her head for anything but Damien. They were just at it whenever they got the chance. I ended up going to the meeting on my own.

It was in a grotty area, the west end of Ashton, a low redbrick building like a fort with hardly any windows. It smelt of food and sweat inside, and I could hear a babble of voices. There was an office to my left, with its door open—no one there—and straight ahead a big low-ceilinged room where the voices were coming from. I went to the doorway and saw Baz's long black hair straight away. He was talking to a boy I didn't know. There must have been about thirty kids there, but only three other girls. One lad was in a wheelchair. A skinny youth with a plait in his beard—studenty type—faced us all and said, 'Quiet please.' He began to mutter about how human beings had the earth in trust and have abused that. The kids in front of me looked at each other then gradually began to whisper. An Asian boy in the front row stood up and asked everyone to listen. People began to call out, 'Get on with it!' and 'Shut up!' and a slow handclap started up. Beardy Plait soldiered on about politicians being useless, then a pale boy with floppy brown hair started shouting at us. He looked like he was about to burst into tears, and everyone suddenly went quiet. 'This isn't a joke! The experiments scientists are doing are against nature. Because they attack nature, nature's attacked us. They mutilate animals—'

Beardy Plait was asking him not to interrupt, the Asian boy was shouting 'Wait your turn!' and a girl in front of me was screaming, really screaming, 'Women are dying! You want to talk about animals? Women are *dying*!' No one was listening to anyone else.

Some people got up and left, and I was happy to see Baz uncurl his skinny self and come round to the end of my row. 'Want to go?' he mouthed, and I moved along to join him. There was a man with bristly-short blond hair sitting there. He stood up to let me pass, then quietly asked Baz and me to hang on a minute. He walked to the front of the room and held up his hands, then he clapped them and called out, 'Friends! Friends!'

It was like at school; Mr Clarke comes in and everything goes quiet. Very calmly he asked us all to move our chairs into a circle. He stood there patiently waiting for us to settle, then he introduced himself— Iain—and started talking about how we need to make our voice heard because young people are the future. The wheelchair boy, Jacob, called out, 'There isn't any future!' and the angry girl, who was Lisa, muttered under her breath but loud enough for everyone to hear, 'Who asked you anyway?' Iain glanced at her.

'I should tell you about myself,' he said to all of us. 'I'm an activist. I've been living in a solidarity camp opposing a high-pressure gas pipeline. Before that I was involved in airport runway protests. I know how these things work, alright? I'm not here to put words in anyone's mouth.' There is something about Iain that is very careful. He doesn't fidget, he's always still, his voice is calm and steady. He keeps his grey eyes fixed on you, like you would if you were trying to recapture a frightened animal. It's as if he chooses every word, as if he's steadily and constantly deciding how he will speak to you, and everything's under control. It used to almost hypnotise me. Lisa looked down at her hands as if it was nothing to do with her.

'OK,' said Iain. 'Why don't we start by going round the circle again each naming one important thing we want to change? Then we can discuss which ones we want to start with.' A red-faced boy sitting near me pushed his chair back loudly, and said it was just like fucking school. He went out and slammed the door. Iain said, 'Anyone else?' and no one moved. He got the flipchart and asked Ahmed to make a list of each person's change. Lisa said she wanted more money putting into MDS research, and for scientists to be allowed to do *any* experiments that might help lead to a cure. She was staring at the pale faced animal liberationist—Nat—as she said it and of course he said, all experiments on animals to be stopped immediately. Other people wanted the usual stuff, carbon rationing, no nuclear power, ban arms sales, stop wars, no to GM crops. Jacob when it was his turn said, 'I can't believe you people. Haven't you listened to the news? We'll be extinct in seventy years and you're fussing about organic farming?' Iain asked him what was the change he wanted and he said, 'I want to show those bastards, man. I want to blow up parliament!' And someone called out 'Guy Fawkes!' and everyone burst out laughing, Jacob included.

Iain held up his hand now and then to stop some people butting in, but we were all picking up on what each other said. It was about being angry, about seeing how all the old people, parents and politicians and business men had messed up the world. *We* wanted power. It was us who were going to have to live with the catastrophe they had made. MDS was the worst of it but there was everything else too—wars, floods, famines. People had just carried on pleasing them-selves—but now they would have to stop. 'They can't tell us what to do any more,' said Jacob.

'No,' said Lisa, 'they owe us.' Her little brother Gabriel was sitting next to her. When she spoke he began to cry, and she put her arm around his shoulder and pulled him close, but she went right on talking. 'They owe us compensation,' she said. 'Our mother's dead. There are thousands and thousands of us. Our mothers are dead, they have to listen to us, they have to give us money.' There was a shocked silence. I didn't know anyone my age whose actual mother had died. Mostly it was mothers of younger kids. Then the clamour started up again; that we needed to get ourselves heard. To have meetings, rallies, where masses of kids could listen and decide what they wanted to do. Iain said we should meet again next Friday and he would draw up an agenda.

Baz and I walked home together. We joked about starting a revolution in Ashton. When I turned off at the end of my road he said, 'Goodnight Comrade.' In bed I thought about how it might be interesting to be part of a group that was trying to make things better. But I still quite liked the idea of it all falling to bits and coming to an end. MDS was like a punishment, and I thought people did need punishing—especially old people—and serve them right.

Four

It was seeing my aunt Mandy that began to change my mind. It's true, what happened to her has been an influence. *Influence* isn't the right word: a pressure. Wanting it to be different, and not being able to make it so, was a headache that grew inside me slowly for weeks, like a hot-air balloon swelling and swelling until there was no space for anything else at all. I think this was the day it began.

Mum and I went to tea at Mandy's. And all her brightly painted walls, and the puppets and masks, looked somehow dim and scruffy. Mum said Mand needed to replace her light bulb, but it wasn't just the light. The papier mâché on the big table was dried up and stuck to the insides of the bucket, the clay was rock hard, the scraps of fabric lying around were curled up and dusty. It looked as if she hadn't made anything for ages, maybe even since Clive left. Her black and grey hair was pulled back off her face and twisted round a big wooden knitting needle, and her skin was papery. She looked a bit like a witch. She didn't really look younger than Mum any more. Mum never let her grey hairs show, and her skin's the smooth kind you want to stroke, 'like a baby's bottom!' my dad used to tease her, when they were in a good mood.

Mand had an open bottle of wine by her chair and she poured some for Mum and herself. She asked me about school and everything but I could see Mum's eyes darting round the room looking at the state of it. Then she ran to open the oven, and said the pizzas were more than ready. After we'd eaten and they had moved on to their second bottle of wine, Mum asked her if she'd been down to Penny Meadow. There was an overflow MDS hospital there, where she volunteered.

'I've been there every day this week,' said Mand.

'Aren't they tailing off now?'

'There aren't as many. But it's still heartbreaking—some of them thought they'd escaped—'

'Don't they sedate them?'

'Of course. But their relatives—'

'Joe said there's no point in people visiting.'

'It helps it to sink in, I suppose. People can't believe it.'

'Is there anything you can actually do?'

Mandy shrugged. 'They come in the main doors on a stretcher and go out the back in a box.'

Mum glanced at me. She and Dad used to stop talking about stuff like this if they thought I was listening. As if MDS would vanish if we all stuck our heads in the sand. Mand noticed the look, and spoke directly to me. 'The worst part is the guilt, actually.'

'Because they're dying and you're alive?' I knew she was still sad about her miscarriage.

'There is that—why should innocent people die. But it's more complicated—'

'Mand—' said my mum.

'Don't be ridiculous, she's not a child.'

Mum didn't say anything.

'I decided to have a baby on my own, by artificial insemination. I had the appointment lined up at the clinic. And then . . .'

'You heard about MDS?'

'No. It was them that cancelled. They cancelled everyone's appointments, even before it was on the news.'

'It was obvious something was wrong,' said my mum. 'Thank God they acted quickly.'

Mandy sat still, staring down at her long thin hands. Her forehead was wrinkled in a strange frown and I realised she was trying not to cry.

'Mandy?' I went to sit on the arm of her chair and put my arm around her. She pressed her face against my shoulder and I could feel her damp hot breath through my T-shirt. Mum sighed and went into the kitchen, I heard her filling the kettle.

'It makes me feel so bad,' Mandy whispered.

Mum came back. 'Why don't you help out with some older kids instead? Look online, there's a register of bereaved men looking for help with childcare.'

Mandy laughed as if it wasn't funny. 'There's one in the newsagents. Local families where the wife . . .

Babysitting, school runs, cooking, there's a whole grid of stuff you can fill in for. Everything bar wifely sexual services.'

'Wouldn't helping with children make more sense?'

'How can I go and help look after someone else's children?'

'You looked after me!' I butted in. 'You were brill.'

She gave me a watery smile. 'That was then, sweetheart.' She turned back to Mum. 'How can I do that, when the woman who had them is dead? And all I can do is envy her? They shouldn't let me near children.'

It was Mum's turn to get up and go to Mand. She knelt by her chair. 'Come on, love,' she said. 'Shush now.' She tore a new piece off the kitchen roll. 'Have you got any hidden fags?'

Mandy laughed in the middle of her crying and said, 'Bedside cabinet, top drawer.'

Mum nodded at me to get them. I went into Mandy's bedroom, that used to be hers and Clive's. The curtains were drawn and it smelt fusty. I opened the window to let in the evening air. I could hear wood pigeons burbling in the tree behind her house, and the air had that first spring smell of earth and leafiness. I thought about how kind Mandy used to be with me, when I was little. She used to plait my hair in a special way; and she and Mum used to make my dancing costumes together and really laugh about them, they were giddy like Sal and me. I wished it could have stayed like that. I wished we could still be happy together.

I turned back to the bedroom. On the purple wall opposite the window Mandy'd done a mural of two stone windows, copied from a room in the Alhambra in Spain. She and Clive had visited it together. The painted windows were latticed, criss-crossed black like lace with little dabs of pale yellow showing in the gaps, like sunlight. I used to think it was beautiful but when I looked at it today it looked like a prison. I opened the jumbled drawer by her bed. The cigarettes were right on top.

As I came out of the room I heard the murmur of their voices. They'd shut the door, they were obviously trying not to be heard. I thought they must be talking about me so I crept to the door and listened.

'I think you're mad,' Mand was saying.

'Joe doesn't care if I'm there or not.'

'Yes he does,' said Mand. 'You know he does.'

'He talks to Jessie more than he talks to me.'

'So you think it's alright—'

'There aren't exactly any angels in the case, are there?'

'Look, if you were madly in love—'

'It's not about being madly in love, it's about being visible. He *looks* at me—'

'Sssh,' said Mand, so I pushed the door open. They each took a fag and lit up. I cleared the table, wondering about Mum and some other man. Then I realised she had distracted Mandy, and I thought that must be why she'd said it. I felt sadness like a stone in my tummy for Mandy, and for how her flat which used to be my favourite place in the world had turned into a smelly prison.

Mum drove home slowly, she'd had way too much to drink. I asked her what had happened to Mandy's theatre group.

'They haven't got any bookings,' Mum said. 'It would be good if she had a project to work on, but no one's thinking about children's plays.'

'What about the other things she does?' Mum and Dad used to call them her fads. She joined a circus skills group, and an all-women choir. Before that she did guitar lessons and Italian classes. She'd done half an Indian cookery course. After a few weeks she always got interested in something new. She wasn't that different to Dad, really—back then he was always going off on some new branch of knowledge, reading up on ancient civilisations or learning Esperanto. But Mum took him more seriously. She thought what my Father of Wisdom learned was proper, and Mandy's just a craze.

'She's dropped all her fads,' said Mum. 'Did you see the state of the kitchen?'

I agreed that it was bad.

'It's all or nothing, with Mand. She's been like that ever since we were kids. When she's happy she does 20 things at once, and when she's sad . . .'

'But how can she be happy, if she's not allowed to have a baby?'

'That's a good question, Jess.'

I wanted there to be an answer. I guess it was the first time I ever took MDS seriously.

Five

At the next meeting Iain brought his laptop and showed us a bunch of websites. They were all about the things people'd said the week before—climate change, animal lib, carbon-rationing. 'OK,' he said. 'So how are we going to be different?'

Nathan said, 'It's through airports that MDS spread. We need to stop planes from taking off.' Everyone started laughing and suggesting more and more drastic things, but Nat was deadly serious. His face was white and strained, like he had to put a huge effort into making himself speak. 'We have to *do* something, that's the only point of this. It's not a game.'

Baz was nodding and drumming on the side of his chair. 'Everything that's gone wrong is connected. Scientists think they can do what they want, just muck about with anything.'

'We shouldn't have to live with adults,' said Lisa suddenly. 'We can look after ourselves.' Everyone stared at her. 'We're not stupid. Why should we be kept like—like *pets*? By them? Why should we let *them* tell us what to do?'

As people grasped what she was saying they began to nod.

'They've killed our mothers,' she said. 'We should have the right to decide what to do for ourselves, not be dictated to by them. They've *lost* their rights. Because they abused them.'

'Where will you live?' asked Ahmed.

'Anywhere,' she said. 'We can take over some houses. And not let any adults in.'

'Like a Wendy house,' sneered one of the boys, and the others laughed.

Lisa fired straight back at him. 'No other animals keep their young for eighteen years! Kids of six can fend for themselves. Why do we let ourselves be *imprisoned* by them?' I wondered about her dad. It must have been awful for him.

'We've got more sense than adults,' piped up Gabe. 'We don't start wars!'

'Never mind animal lib,' said Lisa to Nat. 'What about kids' lib? What about *us* telling *them* how to run things? We are the victims of every stupid thing they do.'

'We are the best!' yelled Gabe, and everyone laughed.

Lisa's a year younger than me but she's not afraid of anyone. She has long fuzzy brown hair and a pointed face hidden in the middle of it, and when she gets going her cheeks flush pink and a deep frown-crease forms between her eyes. Her idea about kids living separately was the best one at that meeting. It was easy to feel a bit futile when you saw how many protest groups there already were in the world.

'But every individual can make a difference,' Iain said. He told us about the trees in China. In the 20th century it had lost nearly all its trees, causing terrible erosion. The Chinese decided that every person must plant three trees a year, and up to now they've planted 45 billion! Forests flourish where deserts were. Even if we couldn't turn back the tide, and wipe out MDS—we could still *show*. We could show that we weren't just interested in grabbing as much of the earth's resources for ourselves, as our parents. We could create less waste. We could stop air travel. We could live together in groups, without the dead weight of adults' lives pressing down on us. And maybe, if we could get enough people to join us, trying to create a different way of living on the planet, maybe that in itself would start to produce an answer to MDS. A solution we couldn't even imagine yet.

I tried to explain this to Dad when he asked why I was so keen on these meetings. Since we don't know why MDS started, why should he assume that the only way to stop it was through scientific research? Maybe the person or being who invented it was actually trying to make people change their lives?

'And will reward us with a cure if we recycle our bottles and stop using cars? Magical thinking, nut brown one. You'll be telling me next about the power of prayer.'

'I'm not saying stop the research, I'm just saying why not try living on the planet in a less greedy destructive way?'

'Better *not* stop the research, or I'll be out of a job!'

I said he was typical of his generation—cynical, complacent, couldn't-care-less. Then he grinned and said true enough, and he was glad I was getting political, everyone needs to change the world when they're young.

I wonder if he remembers that now?

There were meetings twice a week after that, and I went to as many as I could. We called ourselves YOFI— Youth For Independence. A rubbish name, but it took about ten hours even to agree that. We got a constitution (thank you Iain) and we elected calm sensible Mary to be treasurer. We were an official group. *New World London* set up a website in April and different actions got co-ordinated through that. We joined in the Manchester Rally, at the end of May on a beautiful hot Saturday. Two thousand kids in Piccadilly gardens, and loads of press and TV. Our speaker was Lisa. That was where she made contact with more motherless kids who wanted to live with her and Gabe or to found kids' centres of their own. She demanded compensation for kids of MDS mothers. The papers loved it, and offers of support poured in, including two buildings that could be used for kids' centres. Mary said our bank account was swelling nicely.

Mostly, Mum and Dad seemed to approve of it all. I remember when I went home and told them about the Chinese tree planting (which, of course, my Father of Wisdom knew all about), my mum actually said, 'We should do that.' And one Sunday the three of us went to one of the memorial services at Old Trafford, and Mum and Dad gave money towards the Women's

Forest of Remembrance. Those memorial services were amazing. I'd seen them on telly but to be in the middle of a crowd that size, all singing, all standing in complete silence, all piling our one flower on the flower mountain—it was electrifying. In the car coming home Dad told us about a belief they used to have in Korea, that the souls of women who die in childbirth go to live in trees. And passers-by leave offerings of food and wine on stones under the trees. I like the idea of the women in the trees. I'd much rather think of them there, flickering in the moving leaves, than buried in the dark earth.

Nat and Baz wanted to campaign against scientists; I had an argument about that with Baz. We were walking to YOFI and he suddenly said, 'I think we should focus our energies on closing research labs.'

'Why?'

'Because that's where MDS has come from. From scientists researching more and more complicated, horrible things which nobody needs.'

'They do research to find the cures for diseases!'

'Some do. But most of them are researching microbes or sub-atomic stuff, or genetic mutation. Just for the sake of knowing more—trying to control everything.'

'It's good to know more.'

'You think? Like splitting the atom? Einstein said if he'd known what they were going to do he would've become a shoemaker.' Baz tapped a triumphant little *ta-da*! on the letterbox we were passing, and grinned at me. I liked it when he grinned.

'What about penicillin?'

'You're just in favour of scientists because of your

dad. Even apart from weapons, why should they invent more and more diet pills and tranquillisers? It's because they think they're God, that MDS has happened. And that's why they're arresting scientists.'

'You really think that's alright?'

'Well why should they go on messing about with everything, scot free?'

I did say that because of my dad. He worked in a fertility clinic, in the lab where they made embryos. After all the pregnant women had died, they carried on making embryos for MDS research. He believed the more scientists could find out, the better. But now he doesn't want me to act on that belief. In his book, it's fine to *say* you agree with something, but not to *do* it.

I keep coming back to that, that tackiness of Mum and Dad's lives, which is like treading in chewing gum. They say they believe things, then they don't act upon them. Everything's impossible because of something else. It makes me feel as if I'm suffocating. If there is nothing I can do, then what's the point of being alive?

Back then, Baz argued his case at the next meeting and it was agreed; one of our aims would be to stop all pointless scientific research. And since my dad's wasn't pointless, that was fine. We also started our carbon self-rationing scheme, and everyone agreed not to over-spend our personal quota, including at home, which meant we had to convert our parents. Mum and Dad went yes yes you can plant veg in the garden, yes we can stop the supermarket run, if you've got time to go to the market. Transferring the effort to me, and then niggling if they thought I hadn't spent long enough on my homework. I was doing GCSE coursework and there was never enough time. One evening when I came home from a meeting Mum and Dad were sitting side by side at the computer booking an online holiday. The human race facing extinction, and my parents comparing web prices for a summer break on the Spanish Med. Mum asked if I preferred the idea of a hotel near the beach, or a villa with a pool up in the hills. She said we'd take Mandy, it would give her something to look forward to. I stared at her and watched her face turn red.

'What d'you want us to do?' she said. 'We've got to get on with our lives.'

'*Why?*' I said it sarcastically, in the way I know she hates, and my dad said 'Jessie—' in a warning voice. So I went to my room and slammed the door. They thought it was alright. A plane filled with people like them who all thought it was alright would burn up tons of fossil fuel and pour carbon into the sky, so they could lie by a Spanish hotel pool and get skin cancer. When they called me to tea I didn't go and when my dad knocked at my door I shouted at him to go away.

I lay in bed and thought about the holidays we *used* to have. We went to Scarborough and stayed in Nanna Bessie's caravan. I loved it, sleeping on a bed like a shelf with the wind rocking the caravan, waking up to look out of the porthole at the bright morning light; going down the caravan steps and over to the shower block where you had to pick your way among the snails who crawl in there at night; helping Dad dig fortifications in the wet golden sand. Sand in your shoes, in your pants, in your bed; sand in your sandwiches. Mum and Dad laughing and splashing each other. Why couldn't we have holidays like that any more?

Or the summer days out, at home? We used to take a picnic up on the moors, above Dovestones, we called it Kingfisher valley. The ferns were taller than me and we used to play hide and seek for hours, till the air was full of the green smell of crushed fern. Dad saw a kingfisher, he said it was electric, the bluest bird in all the land, better than a peacock. We used to sit very still and watch for it. We were happy then, the three of us. Now it was the two of them against me. The way they lived was horrible.

Later on Dad came back and knocked again. He'd got a toasted tea cake for me. I let him in and he sat on the end of my bed. 'I heard some good news today,' he told me.

'Right. About trashing the planet.'

'No actually. About surviving MDS.'

'It wouldn't even have spread if it wasn't for people like you.'

'What d'you mean?'

'The virus was released at airports. If everybody stopped flying—'

'It would be shutting the stable door. What d'you want, a return to the dark ages?'

'Yes. Imagine, when there was bubonic plague, if everyone had flown around spreading it instead of staying in their village. The human race would probably have died out then.'

He laughed and I told him to get out of my room,

but then he said, 'Seriously, Jess, they think there may be some new babies within the next year.'

'What d'you mean? There's already some top-secret cure that only scientists know about?'

'No. But there are some patients at the clinic now—and at other clinics and hospitals round the world—who may, just possibly, have a chance of giving birth to live babies.'

'And how can they do that, when being pregnant kills them?'

'They've agreed to be given drugs early on to lessen the MDS symptoms and—and put them to sleep, so the babies can survive.'

'What d'you mean, *put them to sleep?*'

'Well, they're in a drug-induced coma. They call them Sleeping Beauties.'

'Can they ever wake up?'

'No. Maternal Death Syndrome destroys the brain during pregnancy. But the baby could survive.'

'You get a live baby out of a dead mother?'

'When the pregnancy nears its end, the doctors can do a caesarean.'

'And the baby doesn't get ill?'

'The disease attacks the mother, not the baby. The baby can still take what it needs from the mother's body.'

'It sounds gruesome. Everybody's mother would be dead.'

He smiled. 'Well it's not a long-term solution, Jesseroon. But it is a start.'

After he'd gone I lay on the floor under my window, staring up into the beech tree as the light began to fade. They were always threatening to chop that beech down because it's too big to be near houses. From the floor you get the sky through the bare branches in winter and spring, and the light is always different. And when the leaves start to come out they're floppy and damp like new-hatched chicks. Then they harden off and darken, but on a sunny day you can still see the sparkle of the sky coming through them. After I've been staring at them for a bit it's like I'm a leaf too, seeing fragments of the bright sky through the other leaves above me, fluttering in the wind with all the others, or bending under drips of battering rain. It's a sort of trance, I'm not Jessie any more, I'm not this awkward separate object, I'm part of the tree, and there's nothing in my head but wind and sky,

I lay staring at the beech and I thought. If my dad was right—if the doctors could get out babies who were OK even though the mothers died—then everything would carry on. We wouldn't be extinct. There would be a future world and if we worked hard to change things, it would have the chance of being really really different, and better, than this one. I got up and started making a list of the ways we could save energy around the house.

Sunday evening

I keep thinking about what I'll do. Twisting and
turning in my mind to find a way of behaving that will
convince him. There isn't one that I can imagine. We
are in opposition. I will always want to do this, and he
will always want me not to. Day will always be light,
and night dark.

When he comes in he's got a pizza although he
knows I don't eat that crap—in a cardboard box on a
circle of polystyrene. And a carton of orange juice. I
was sorry for him when he wasn't here but now the
sight of him makes me shake with rage. 'Get out! Get
out! Get out!' I swipe at the pizza and send it spinning
to the floor. He looks surprised.

'I thought you'd be hungry.'

'I don't eat that!' I shriek. 'You can't keep me
here.' I want to run at him and hit him but I trip
because of the bike locks and he bends to try and
help me up so I twist round and bite his hand as hard

as I can. I'm grabbing at his arms, digging my nails in, trying to swing my feet round to kick him. He yelps and scrambles up away from me, nursing his hand. 'Let me go!' I scream. 'You can't keep me prisoner, let me go!'

'Stop it,' he says. 'No one can hear you.'

'You going to keep me here forever? Living on junk food and going to the toilet in a bucket? You think you can do that?' I crawl as fast as I can towards the bucket and knock it over, the pee slopping across the floor. I roll in it so my clothes are wet and when he comes towards me again I lash out with my feet together and catch him on the shin.

He backs away. 'I don't want to do this. I only want to stop you.'

'You'll never stop me. Never. I hate you!' I grab the pizza box and try to hurl that but it flops open and falls. The carton of juice nearly hits him, though. He goes out quickly and locks the door behind him.

If I smashed the window and cut myself he'd have to take me to hospital. He wouldn't let me bleed to death, he'd have to do something then. I'm trying to get to my feet when he comes back in and grabs me; I overbalance and we both go crashing to the floor. I'm kicking and scratching at his face but he's stronger and he's got my arm and is twisting it behind my back. I scream. I keep screaming but he's got the other one and he's kneeling on my arm and he's tying something round my wrists. Tying my arms behind my back.

'No no no!' I roar. He pulls it tight and knots it then he crawls to his feet and stumbles away from me. I can't get up because I can't use my hand to push myself up. I wriggle around on the floor like a fish on the riverbank. He goes into the corner and squats down with his back against the wall and his face in his hands, crying.

After a bit he stops. He speaks in a slow flat voice. 'I don't want to tie you up. I want to undo your hands and legs and let you go into the bathroom for a bath and to put on some clean clothes.'

'On my own?'

'Of course.'

'Then can I go?'

'No. Then I'll fix the leg locks again.'

'Fuck off.'

'This is for your own good.'

'No it isn't.'

'You are deluded. You are temporarily deranged. I am keeping you safe until you can think sensibly.'

'Your definition of thinking sensibly is *me* thinking what *you* think. *You* are deranged. You should be tied up till you agree with me.'

He stares at me bleakly then he suddenly laughs. I'm lying on my side in pee-soaked clothes with my cheek on the gritty carpet and Dad's squatting there in the corner laughing at me. I burst into tears. He crawls over to me and helps me to sit up.

'I'm sorry, Jess. Please, please, don't make this more horrible than it has to be. If you promise to behave I'll undo your arms.'

'Why should I promise?'

'There's no point in you fighting. It's not going to change my mind, and you're the one who'll be hurt.'

'If you heard of a father locking up his daughter

because he didn't like what she thought, you'd say it was an outrage.'

'It is. I would. But I don't know what else to do.'

'Let me go. It's *my* life.'

'Not to throw away it isn't.'

'Hypocrite.'

'Stop it Jess. D'you want a bath? The water's hot.'

'Hypocrite! Hypocrite! Hypocrite!' I scream.

Six

Mandy got more and more depressed, and Mum tried to get her into hospital. But they were closing wards because of nursing shortages. Then she found a daycare centre. The trouble was, it was run by the Noahs. The night Mum came home early and told us about it, Dad and I were going through my options for college. I was still dithering about whether to do biology AS, or start a new language. Dad said, 'If ever we needed scientists it's now.' But I didn't fancy having to admit to Baz that I was taking Science. There was a grid thing so you could work out what subjects you could take with what, and we were sitting at the kitchen table trying to figure it out, with the radio burbling quietly in the background.

We got distracted with a perfect crime which would involve telling your victim he didn't look very well, and keeping a graph of his temperature morning and night. You'd check the thermometer with a worried look, then put an x on the graph one square higher than the previous day's. The graph would show the temperature going steadily up and up till it was at an incredibly dangerous level. Dad insisted that simply being told he was at death's door would be enough to finish someone off. 'You know the Roman cure for fever? Cut the patient's nails and stick the parings with wax onto a neighbour's door. The fever passes from the patient to the neighbour. I'm cured and you're ill instead. The mind is a powerful instrument!'

I was asking Father of Wisdom about voodoo when Mum came in. There was one of those massive summer thunderstorms and the rain drumming against the kitchen window made us feel cosy. We didn't hear her until she came right into the kitchen, still in her mac, dripping everywhere.

'Good grief,' said Dad, 'Why didn't you ring for a lift?'

'I felt like walking,' she said. 'If that's alright with you.'

Dad shrugged. The cosy mood of the kitchen teetered on a knife edge.

'Anyway, there was a road block.' She pulled a damp yellow leaflet out of her coat pocket. It said in big letters GOD'S SIGN TO HIS PEOPLE, then there were paragraphs of small print, and across the bottom, CHILDREN OF NOAH. 'Take a look at this.'

My dad rolled his eyes at me. 'Religious loons!' It said God had tried to warn us through all the natural disasters but people are so hardened they take no notice. When the world was as depraved as this before, God sent a flood to drown it and only Noah and his ark were saved. Now the whole human race would die out unless we could prove to Him that we were turning away from evil.

My mum came back in with dry clothes on. 'What d'you make of it?' she asked Dad.

'The usual fundamentalist nonsense.'

'Mandy's really into it.'

'You've been to Mandy's?'

'Yes. She's going to this meeting on Sunday—she wants me to go with her.'

'I wouldn't go near them,' said Dad.

'More to the point, she's started to tidy her house. She says God likes cleanliness.'

Dad handed her a mug of tea. 'If they want converts why not target healthy people? Why are they going for patients who are unstable? And frankly, open to abuse?'

'You think they'll abuse her?'

'Don't a lot of these sects abuse people? They take their money, or they expect the women to be sex slaves to the leader.'

'She says there *isn't* a leader. They have to try and improve the world so that God will change his mind and *send* a leader.'

'And what will they do if God ignores them? Commit mass suicide? Heard of Jim Jones' People's Temple? Or The Branch Davidians—the Waco bunch?'

'For goodness sake—' Mum bent so her forehead touched the table, as if she was giving up, then she straightened herself and faced my dad again. 'Look Joe, Mandy's depressed. She only has a shower when I force her. And now—'

'They've grabbed themselves a sick vulnerable woman—'

'And now—' my mum went on as if he hadn't spoken, 'she says, at last there's something she can do.'

'What does she have to do?'

'Harmless stuff. Reject alcohol and sex outside marriage. Follow the commandments.'

'Cath, she's brainwashed.'

'You and I agreed she should be on antidepressants. The whole purpose of which is not to change your depressing life, but to make you think it's OK anyway. How can it be worse, to *actually* change her life?'

Mandy joined the Noahs. There was nothing they could do to stop her.

A few days later it was still raining and I borrowed Mum's mac to take the compost out. In her pocket with the old tissues I found a folded-up note. It was written in cramped handwriting I didn't recognise:

> 5.30 Tues, I can pick you up. Don't ring, I'm at home. Txt me early tomorrow. X

Why would you say *don't ring I'm at home*? Because someone else might answer the phone? Because you have a sick grandmother who mustn't be disturbed by the sound of a ringing phone? Or because you don't want to talk to Mum while anyone else is listening? I remembered the conversation between Mandy and Mum, where Mum said there were no angels. But Tuesday was her evening clinic, she was always late on Tuesday. I put it out of my head.

*

I guess the spitting was the next thing. It wasn't a big deal, I'm not trying to pretend it was, but it still makes me go hot and sweaty with shame. It's nowhere near as bad as what happened to Sal. The thing is, they're both part of the same pattern: the pattern that has led me here, to this dim room where I sit with my feet locked together, listening to my dad pacing the floorboards in the room below.

I was walking back from YOFI with Nat. It had been one of those hot August days, when the roads get so warm that it's still radiating back out of the tarmac at ten o'clock at night, and the sky stays light and clear. It was lovely to be outside after the stuffiness of the community centre. The shops on the main road were closed with metal roll-down shutters covered in graffiti. There were empty houses with broken windows, and odd men about. I was glad I was with Nat. Then he told me he was leaving.

'But why? The airport protest plan you guys did is really good.' Lots of people were supposed to buy tickets for consecutive flights and check in luggage, then fail to board. All the flights would be delayed, as they unloaded the unaccompanied luggage. It would clog things up for hours.

'I don't like Iain telling us what to do.'

'But nothing would happen if he didn't. People'd just argue all the time.'

'Iain is on a power trip. He's got his own agenda.'

'Like what?'

'That crap about the vote.' Well we do live in a democracy. We had spent hours discussing it. Why shouldn't anyone over ten should be able to elect representatives and have them stand up for us in parliament? How else could kids have power? But Nat and Lisa said why would you want to join their stupid system. And Lisa said why did Iain care, he already had the vote and it'd done a fat lot of good. I actually thought we *should* get the vote, like the suffragettes. But they made it seem tame. It turned into one of those endless arguments that made precisely nothing happen.

I was working out how to reply to Nat when we reached the main road, and had to wait for the pedestrian signal. A car full of lads came past and slowed right down when it was level with us. There was music blaring out and they were shouting something. Then one of them leaned right out and spat on me. A horrible big glob of white slime sliding down my bare arm. I screamed. I wasn't hurt, it was just the shock. Nat grabbed a handful of leaves from a dusty little garden behind us, and quickly scooped it off. I asked him what they were shouting.

'Just crap.'

'What?'

'Rubbish. They're dickheads.'

I knew he'd heard something he didn't want to tell me. I felt like scrubbing my arm until the layer of skin they had polluted was scraped right off. I was furious but there was another feeling too, like a dog that slinks back towards you after you've yelled at it, looking up at you with his eyes ashamed and hopeful. I wanted them to come back so I could prove to them that I wasn't the sort of person you should spit at. I tried to pull myself together. 'What are you going to do?' I asked Nat. 'If you're leaving?'

'Animal Liberation Front. I'm going underground!' He looked extremely pleased with himself.

I remembered what Lisa'd said at the first meeting. 'You think what happens to animals is more important than what's happening to women.'

'No, I think MDS came out of this kind of research, and scientists should be stopped before they invent something even worse. D'you really think it's OK to torture animals?'

I didn't but bashing scientists just wasn't the most important thing. It seemed childish, cloak and dagger stuff, *underground*, breaking the law in the name of the ALF. I thought we could achieve more inside YOFI.

Then the next day Sal said she wanted to start coming to meetings. I was surprised because she was usually busy with Damien. But she came and had tea with me and we walked down to the community centre together. I asked her what had happened to Damien.

'Football.'

He worked at the leisure centre so that wasn't very surprising, but she said, 'He's obsessed with it.'

'What d'you mean?'

'His football mates. They meet up every night.'

'Every *night*?'

'Well. About four times a week. For a practice and a drink, he says.'

'You think he's seeing someone else?'

She shrugged. 'He's an arse.' But she didn't say it as if she couldn't care less, in the usual Sal way.

'Sal?'

'Oh, he's just being weird.'

I knew it must be something embarrassing, because

she used to tell me most things. Then she suddenly said, 'I think he might be gay.' I couldn't help it, I just went 'Ooh ducky!' and we both burst out laughing. I thought about the times I'd seen him, when he was all over her.

'He's changed,' she insisted, 'I can't explain it, but the way he is now, he's impatient, he's kind of contemptuous.'

'Well sack him. Plenty more fish in the sea.' Sal'd been going out with lads since we were eleven and not one of them had ever dumped her. It was hard to see why she was making such a fuss over Damien.

'He wants me to go out with them, him and his football mates.'

'Well can't you?'

'I can. But they drink themselves stupid and only listen to each other.'

'Haven't *they* got girlfriends?'

'On Friday I was the only girl. He changes when he's with them. It's like he's bored with me.'

With everything that was happening in the world, all Sal could do was obsess about a stupid man. 'Forget him,' I said.

I wish she had. Or I wish I had taken her more seriously. But I took over organising the airport protest, and I was so busy co-ordinating that, and helping set up the Recycle Fashion shows, I didn't even stop to think. It's one of the things I regret most in my whole life.

Seven

There was only one ray of hope that whole autumn. Baby Johnson was delivered by Caesarean section. The first post-MDS baby! His picture was on the front of all the papers, shops put up flags, and people went round with huge grins on their faces. Even the suicide rate dropped. His grandmother's street was full of flowers, and the news showed her holding him, crying, thanking everyone. Baby Johnson's mother was fifteen and they held her funeral in Westminster Abbey. She was called Ursula. Her mother told the story. Back when Ursula's pregnancy was confirmed women were still having abortions, in the hopes of saving their own lives. It was the first time in Ursula's life she ever had sex. She believed that because her baby had been conceived, he had the right to be born. Her parents tried to dissuade her but Ursula must have known how important her baby would be for the world, because she had this amazing faith in him.

Her doctor knew that researchers were working on putting women into a coma and helping the babies survive, and he told Ursula about them. She was one of the first to volunteer for the Sleeping Beauty experiment. Her mother described how they had stayed awake all night before they signed the consent forms, crying and praying for guidance. But Ursula had never wavered, and the last thing she had done before they gave her the injection was to smile at her parents and thank them for her beautiful life.

'And I believe in fairies,' said Mum.

Dad said, 'Still—good for her!'

What I loved was that Ursula decided she wanted to save her baby, and she made it happen. She chose what to do. By then they had some Sleeping Beauties at my dad's clinic and I asked him if they were like Ursula. He said he didn't know, it's the doctors who deal with them, he only does technical stuff. Then he grinned and admitted that two of their babies might be going to be delivered soon.

And in the days after Baby Johnson there were new babies delivered all around the world. At my dad's clinic, Baby Jill was born one week later, though the other one who was due at the same time, who they called Jack, died. Dad was saying there wouldn't be many more pregnancies after this wave, because these babies were all like Baby Johnson, conceived before girls knew the consequences of MDS. 'Since then, everyone's taken care not to get pregnant. We've hardly got any other pregnant women coming through. Our ward's nearly empty.'

The sadness attached to these wonderful new babies

was that they had MDS just like the rest of us. It was in their cells from their parents. In the papers there was a flood of statistics calculating the future population. To keep it stable, every woman has to have 2.1 children, which means ten women should have twenty-one babies between them. But now a woman dies to produce just one baby. And obviously, since pregnancy is death, most women would choose not to have a baby at all. Experts said the population would shrink to nothing.

Dad was wrong, though, about there being no more pregnancies after this batch. Because once it was proved that babies really could be delivered from the Sleeping Beauties, and that they were healthy except for dormant MDS which everyone had anyway, a stream of girls started to volunteer. You could see why they did, even then. They were following Ursula Johnson's example. They did it for their husbands, or their families, or their religions. They did it for the future. What better single thing could a person do with her life?

But naturally people fussed and objected like they always do when someone tries to do something positive. 'The girls who volunteer are too young to know their own minds, blah blah blah.' Or, 'the programme is too expensive, families should pay for the life support of a Sleeping Beauty'. Or, just for a change, the opposite; the family should get compensation for their girl's sacrifice, and no girl should volunteer until that's agreed. OK there are bad things, like the Chinese who sold their daughters to clinics—*OK*—but because there are bad things does it mean nothing new should happen? That nothing can be done?

It was like a wave of energy washing over the whole

world, the way babies could be born again—even when it was bad, it was good. I knew the world would be different when they grew up, because the population would be so much smaller. Everything really could be better. I began setting my alarm for 5.30 so I could get more done. We were trying to persuade more kids to join us—I had this dream that we might get everyone, one day, everyone under twenty—and simply root out all the bad old ways of consuming and spoiling and wasting. The world was changing so quickly no one could guess what would happen next!

After the Manchester rally YOFI was offered a big old pub, the *Rising Sun*, to turn into a centre where Lisa and Gabe and other motherless kids could live. I went along to help clear it out. Lisa and Gabe had their sleeping bags spread in one of the bedrooms, and were working on the room next to it, which would be theirs when it was finished. Other kids were stripping walls downstairs and ripping out the seats. They had music on and it was noisy down there, with people shouting across the room. I asked Lisa if I could help her upstairs and she gave me a pot of white paint and asked me to start on the woodwork. It was all stained dark tobacco brown. The floor was covered in shrivellings of paper they'd scraped from the walls. I crawled round sweeping a clear path by the skirting boards.

'You and Gabe here permanently now?' I asked.

She nodded.

'What does your dad say?'

'My Dad's an alcoholic,' said Lisa.

'Oh.'

'He's not fit to look after children, and the joke is

he knows that himself. *I* was looking after *him*.' Neither of us said anything for a bit, there was just the sound of our brushes slopping and swishing, and the music and hollow voices from downstairs.

'I did feel bad at first,' she said suddenly. 'Leaving him on his own. But Gabe and me have to survive. And now I just think, you're sick. Lots of adults are. I mean, if they don't drink they take drugs or medicine, or they're addicted to some crappy routine. They're like those horses in the olden days that used to walk round in a circle to turn a mill wheel. They keep on walking in a circle even when the mill wheel's gone. That's why so many of them are killing themselves. They don't know how to change.'

I thought about Mum and Dad and their package holidays. 'They're all mad, our parents' generation.'

'Mad and useless. The world will be a better place without them.'

'But it's hard for you, if you have to look after Gabe as well.'

'Gabe can look after himself. Anyway, looking after people is easy.'

'I guess I've never had to.'

'Taking responsibility for things is easy. That's how they infantilise us. They make us think that if you decide to do something and take responsibility for your decision, you'll have a really tough time. But it's not true. What's hard is being in someone *else's* power.'

'Aren't you ever frightened?'

'Look, we don't have to be trapped in our parents' lives. How will we know what we can do unless we try?'

Lisa's right. You can choose to do something and plan your own destiny. It's never as hard as you fear. You can make yourself free, you can be responsible for yourself. The only difficulty is other people. And I don't just mean Mum and Dad.

The difficulty is also other people like Baz. In the beginning I went along to the meetings because of him. He and I did some really good things together there. The YOFI website, for example; I wrote the content and Baz created the site. We'd sit side by side together at that big desk in the office, trying different versions, making it more user-friendly, putting in the links, selecting graphics. We'd work on it till everyone else had gone home, and it was quiet and peaceful in the building. We turned off the light to cut the glare, and sat muttering to each other and making suggestions, both sets of our eyes fixed on the bright screen. I could feel the warmth of him next to me. Once he looked up and said, 'Why're you smiling?' and I pointed to his jiggling leg. He jumped as if it didn't belong to him, then after a couple of minutes the jiggling started up again. We didn't *do* anything, we didn't *say* anything, but it was a lovely feeling, that it was all in reserve. I thought we were both waiting till the urgent business of getting YOFI to a point where it could really make a difference, was achieved, and then—then there would be the time for the two of us.

But instead of growing and blossoming into what I had hoped, everything went wrong. YOFI was already going wrong, with people bickering endlessly about priorities, and about what we should do next. The airport protest became a nightmare. People had to buy their own tickets—obviously. It would have been a bit of a giveaway if the airport noticed one purchaser buying tickets for 60 consecutive flights. We agreed to reimburse them from the donations that came in after the Manchester rally. Some people didn't have enough cash so Mary gave them the money upfront, but then they didn't buy tickets right away. Some who had agreed to participate dropped out after their flights and times had been agreed, so there were time gaps: they realised you have to give your details when you book, which meant they could be traced by the police. Since the point of the whole thing was anti-flight publicity, and YOFI was going to claim it at the end of the day, I couldn't see the problem. It got into more and more of a mess—a scattering of tickets bought, too much money handed out, recriminations. Iain said he'd help me sort it out.

He began to notice me more and more. At meetings I didn't have to keep trying to interrupt the boys, he'd glance at me and raise his eyebrows to see if I had anything to say, and if I nodded he'd tell them to shut up. He used to put his rucksack on the next chair in the circle and when I came in he'd lift it off and indicate the seat was for me. I liked it at first; it made me feel important. But it all went pear-shaped.

We'd been painting banners and everyone else had left. Iain was in the office emailing publicity to other groups. I was finishing off the tidying up. The banners were on sheets spread on the floor and I didn't want to move them till the paint was dry. I was in the little kitchen washing the brushes when Iain came in. I knew it was him so I didn't turn round. I just said, 'All done?' and he said, 'Yes,' surprisingly close behind me. Then he took another step and I could feel his breath on my neck. I turned the tap off. I kept my eyes on the brushes I was washing, slowly rubbing my fingers through the bristles to get them clean, staring at the little clouds of faint red that came puffing out of them into the water. He was right against me, I could feel the heat of his body. I twisted my neck to try and see his face and he took a tiny step back so I could turn round. Then he was pressing me against the sink and kissing me and my heart was galloping with the surprise of it. I noticed his hands. He was holding his hands out to the sides—holding his hands away from me as if I might burn him. The weight of him was squashing me against the sink. I jerked my head away and he opened his eyes then straightened up and moved back. There was a little gap between us and I could breathe.

'No,' he said. 'Not a good idea.'

He turned and went into the office and shut the door. I got my things as quickly as I could and let myself out, leaving him to roll up the banners. My heart kept pounding madly all the way home. I hadn't thought of him like that. For a moment, for that moment when he was squashing me against the sink, I was scared. But then how contradictory can a person be? There was a strand of my mind that kept going back to that moment by the sink, imagining; if I hadn't jerked my head back. If he'd put his hands on my hips. If . . . It was a hot shameful excited feeling.

Nobody else knew what had happened but it made things different between me and Iain. We were

64

hyper-aware of each other. I could feel myself blushing whenever he came near. And Baz picked up on it one night. He fell into step beside me as I was heading for the bus stop and asked me how I was getting on with Iain.

'OK.'

'You like him.'

'I didn't say I liked him. I said he was OK. He's good at keeping meetings in order.'

'Nat's group are managing without him. Without some *adult* telling them what to do.' He was fidgeting about with a stick he'd picked up, twitching it from side to side.

'You in touch with Nat? What's he doing?'

'There's an animal research lab near Chester that they're trying to infiltrate. They've already targeted some of the scientists.'

'You're not—'

'I might join them. I'm not really interested in all this bickering, or in recycling.'

'But what about the website?'

'It's done, isn't it.'

'But will you go to Chester too? What about piano?'

He didn't reply.

'Baz? You still playing?'

'For what it's worth. I'm entering for a scholarship.'

'Where to?'

'Salzburg. There's an under-seventeen's piano scholarship.'

'You'd go to Austria? When?'

'January. If I get it. Which I won't.' There was a silence then he suddenly said, 'Has Iain kissed you?'

And like an idiot I blurted, 'Yes.'

'Uh huh,' said Baz. 'Uh huh, uh huh,' and he began to run the stick along the railings, backwards and forwards, making it into a demented rhythm.

I started to say 'It wasn't important' and at the same time he quickly said, 'My Dad's lost his job.'

'Why?'

'The Noahs. People from his church have joined the Noahs. Now they're going to all these happy-clappy the-lord-will-save-us meetings.'

I wanted to explain about Iain but it seemed as if it would be making it more important than it was. 'Wasn't your dad helping the bereaved?'

'He had a fight with some high ups in the church. About what to do about the Noahs. He fell out with everybody and he told them to get stuffed.'

A laugh burst out of me, it was embarrassment as much as anything. Baz carried on with his tapping. He said he was sick of YOFI, he was leaving.

Monday morning

I sit on the floor beneath the window, looking up at
the sky as it begins to get light. The days are getting
longer now—it's earlier every day. The purplish-blue
patch I can see looks clear, maybe the sun will shine.
Last night I heard him on the phone for ages, I guess
to Mum. Maybe she reasoned with him, because when
he came upstairs he untied my arms. Neither of us said
anything, he went straight out again and locked the
door. I crawled over to the radiator and sat against it
while my clothes dried. I almost like the smell, now.

I still can't believe he's not going to come in and say,
'God I'm sorry, Jessie. Let me undo those stupid locks.'
I'm still waiting for him to see how completely mad
this is. Today, surely, he'll give it up.

Yes! Sunlight hits the top of the leylandii, a fantastic
glowing reddish-orangey-green against the purple sky.
I stare and stare, as gradually the sky lightens, and the
sunlight pales to watery whiteness and it all turns

ordinary. I waft my arms up and down and wriggle my shoulders to ease the stiffness. Today, surely, this will end.

After Baz told me he was leaving YOFI, I decided to leave too. The bubble burst. I remember sitting in my room and feeling as if I was sitting in the ruins of my life. Why was I trying to get Mum and Dad to compost their potato peel and give up their flights? What difference would that make to anything? Greens had been campaigning for decades, I knew that perfectly well, and what did they ever achieve? Why on earth did I imagine a bunch of kids under the leadership of a perv like Iain might suddenly change the world? Everything I had been working for and believing in collapsed into dust, and I couldn't make sense of anything any more.

I remember I thought about dying then; but in a childish, furious way. Since everything was going to rack and ruin and nothing could be done to make any of it right, the most ecologically useful thing anyone could do would be to die. Then at least you'd stop consuming resources. I wished I was dead. I thought about Iain creeping up behind me, his hot breath on my neck, and I was boilingly angry. What right did he have? And then saying, 'Not a good idea'—like it was me who'd suggested it! I should tell the police. What if he tried it on someone younger?

Slamming stuff around in my room I managed to smash the clay owl mask that Mandy made me for my tenth birthday. It shattered into crumbs, it couldn't be saved.

I was in a rage at all the time I'd wasted. But

looking back, if I hadn't done all that—the meetings and arguments and petitions and demonstrations, the hours hunched over the computer—if I hadn't done all that in good faith, and then been so totally frustrated—then maybe I would never even have found the next thing to do. If I'd never felt the thrill of imagining we could change things—perhaps I wouldn't have looked for it again.

It's light enough now to crawl to my table and chair, and write there. But I don't want to go into all that, how I felt when I left YOFI—bad, stupid, hoodwinked. I remember telling myself only an idiot would dream of trying to make anything better. I was angry with everything. Stupid YOFI. Iain. Baz. Myself. I wished I was a giant so I could stamp across the town, smashing their little houses to smithereens.

He's tapping on the door. He's locked me in, and he's tapping on the door! 'Jess?'

'Yes?'

He doesn't open it, he just talks through the wood. 'I'm sorry. What would you like for breakfast?'

I pause to think. 'A boiled free-range egg. Brown toast and damson jam.'

'Tea?'

'A glass of milk.'

'OK.'

I hear him going down the stairs. And then out of the house. Good, I feel easier when he's not here. And good! A lovely breakfast. But he wouldn't go out to buy me breakfast if he was planning to release me. The opposite. He's trying to win me over—to bribe me with food. Fine: he'll soon see how well that works!

It was soon after I left YOFI that the bad thing happened to Sal. I can see now that was the turning point for me as much as for her. But it turned her one way and me another. It turned us in opposite directions, friend against friend. Oh Sal. Because it helped to set me on the track that led me here.

Eight

It was Friday night and I was already fast asleep when my mobile rang. It was Sal's phone but she didn't speak, there was a jumbled noise like she was striding along fast, and muffled distant music and voices. I guessed it had gone on accidentally. It was half past one, so I tried to go back to sleep. But ten minutes later I was still wide awake. I didn't know what she was doing. Something with Damien, obviously—I guessed she had gone out drinking with him and his mates. She was probably really bored. I decided to ring her back. She didn't answer the first time, so I tried again a few minutes later. Her phone does eight rings before it goes to answer, but she got it on the eighth. 'Sal, it's me.'

Now it was so quiet at the other end that I could hear her breathing. It was like she was gasping for air.

'Sal? You alright?' Then I realised she was crying. 'Where are you?'

Her voice was croaky. 'Can you come round? I'm at home.'

I knew it was bad. Sal doesn't cry. I dressed, let myself out as quietly as I could, and ran down the empty street to her house. The hall light was on, and she let me in as I got to the door, and slammed and locked it quickly after me. She was all wet. She had her dressing gown on but she was dripping wet and shivering. Her face was a mess, not just from smeared mascara; her bottom lip was bleeding, and there was a reddish-purple mark across one cheek. I went into their sitting room to get the shawl off the back of the sofa. The room was trashed. Cans and ashtrays and takeaways, furniture all anywhere, spilt drinks on the carpet. It smelt awful. I found the shawl and wrapped it round her. I realised I could hear Sammy whining and whining from the kitchen, and I let him out. He ran to Sal but she pushed him away. 'Where's your mum? Sal?'

She shook her head.

'Was it Damien?'

'His mates,' she whispered.

'His mates? Here?'

She nodded.

'Shall I call the police?'

'No.' She gasped for breath again. 'They raped me.'

'They . . .'

'Three of them. The. The others watched.'

'Why are you so wet?' Stupid question but it's all I could say.

'I got in the bath—' She began to cry again.

'Shall we go upstairs?' I said. 'Shall I help you Sal?' We struggled up to the bathroom. I let out the cloudy

72

water and ran more hot, and squirted bubble bath in it. It was lavender scented. If I smell lavender now it makes me feel sick all over again. I made sure it wasn't too hot, and helped her take off her dressing gown and step in. She was slow squatting down into the water, I could see it hurt her to move. There were marks on her shoulders like dirty handprints. 'I should get a doctor. The police. We should—'

Sal shook her head.

'But—'

'I don't want anyone to know, OK?' Her voice had come back, suddenly. She sounded tough again and I was so relieved I finally started to cry myself.

'Shall I bathe you?'

'I'm OK.' She got the flannel and scrubbed herself all over, then lay down in the water so it covered her, face and hair and all. After a moment she got out abruptly and stood under the shower and washed herself all over again. I let out the bath water, and got her a clean towel. We went in her bedroom. She put on pyjamas and I got into bed beside her in my clothes.

She told me what had happened. Damien had begged her to go out with him and his mates and she agreed. They went drinking till late then got takeaways, and Damien asked if they could bring them back to her house. He knew her mum was away. She said OK because she was fed up and she wanted to go to bed by then, she thought they'd just eat their takeaways and go home. They were making jokes about sex, one of them rubbed himself against another's arse and they all acted as if it was hilarious. Damien hardly spoke to her, she said, all he was interested in was being one of the lads. She told him she was going to bed and asked him to lock up after them when they'd gone. Two of them who were on the sofa had their hands down each other's jeans, she wished they'd just go away. But as she was going upstairs to her room one of them was coming down from the toilet. The big one, the goalie, Gerrard. 'Come on love,' he said, grabbing her by the arm. 'Don't you want a bit of the action?' He dragged her down into the sitting room again, and ripped her skirt off. She slapped him but he knocked her to the floor, and when she tried to get up one of them knelt on her legs and another held her arms. Her mobile was in her jacket pocket—that must have been when I got the call from her phone. She could hear Damien shouting and the others telling him it was only a bit of fun.

'They were saying things,' she said. 'About not having any pussy for a long time. *Now they've got all those diseases up there*, they said. They were egging each other on, telling me it was my lucky day.'

She fought as best she could, and she was aware of Damien somewhere fighting too, then another one got onto her and some of them seemed to leave. She heard the door bang and Damien wasn't there any more either. Her phone started ringing (that must have been me) then they were shouting at the last one to hurry up and they were calling her dirt and slag and then in a rush they were all gone and she was lying alone in the mess. She was trying to have a bath when I rang again.

'Damien didn't come back?'

'No.'

'Maybe he's gone to the police.'

'I don't think so.'

'Shall I call my dad? He'll take us to hospital.'

'I'm OK.'

'But Sal—'

'What? What good would it do? The only thing it would do is upset my mum. Forget it.'

We sat in bed in silence for a long time, then I'm afraid I was so tired I just snuggled down next to her and fell asleep. When I woke up it was nearly five and she was still staring into space. 'Don't ever tell anyone,' she said. 'Promise.'

'OK.' I didn't know what else to say. It was her decision. I offered to help her clear up, and she had another bath then we binned all the rubbish and cleaned the house till there was no trace left. Poor Sammy was skulking about with his ears flat and his tail drooping, as if he thought it was his fault. I made Sal some cocoa. She was pale and quiet but she seemed OK. She said she hated men and to forget it, and I left her sitting on the sofa with Sammy beside her, his head resting on her knee.

At home I went quietly to my room and lay down. Then when Dad called me at seven o'clock I got up again. I pretended I was going to college. Sal didn't answer the door so I phoned her from her own doorstep and she said her mum would be home from Birmingham by lunchtime. She wanted to be alone. As I walked away I phoned Baz. It didn't matter what he thought about me and Iain. I wanted to see him.

'You OK?'

'Can I come round?'

'My Dad's here,' he said. Then, 'Fine.'

I walked to his house. I was in a daze, everything went past me at the wrong speed. He let me in and his dad was sitting in the front room staring at the wall. He'd grown a dirty grey beard. I said hello but he ignored me. Baz took me down to his room.

'What is it?' he said. 'What's happened?'

I swore him to secrecy and told him. 'D'you think I should tell the police?'

'Not if she doesn't want you to. What good will it do?'

It helped to hear someone else say it. Baz told me to get into his bed and have a kip. He watched while I pulled the duvet up. Then he sat at his piano and began to play, a soft complicated running tune that seemed to weave in and out of my head. A couple of times I opened my eyes to watch him, sitting hunched over the keyboard, arms spread and taut, fingers delicately tapping the keys, notes rippling from them. The music was so clear and clean. Then I fell properly asleep. When I woke up it was the afternoon and Baz'd gone. I put on my shoes and went upstairs. His dad was still sitting there in his dressing gown and he looked at me fiercely. I was afraid he was going to be angry with me. But he didn't speak, he didn't even answer when I said 'good afternoon'. I could hear someone moving about in the kitchen but I didn't know if it was Baz or his mum, and it seemed easier just to quietly let myself out the front door.

It was the strangest day, for a while after I felt as if I'd dreamed it. The way he listened to me, then played, the way I slept and woke feeling soothed. I wished I could give that feeling of peace to Sal—but I couldn't. I couldn't do anything to make her feel better.

Nine

I texted Sal all the time but the only reply she sent was 'x'. When I called round her mum said she wasn't well and was in bed. I was pretty sure her mum didn't know what had happened. I was getting to the point of thinking I had to tell her when Sal finally sent me a message: 'U want 2 com 2 wimin only protest meet? Thur 8pm xS'.

We met at the bus stop. She was hidden under a mask of makeup and when I asked how she was she snapped 'Fine. Don't talk about it.' So I rattled on randomly about college. She'd heard about this group through a friend of her mum; they were called FLAME. Feminist Link Against Men. They met in Glossop in a big old house that a group of women shared. The living room was like a doctor's waiting room with chairs and sofas pushed against the walls. There were about twenty women there. Everyone was older than me and some looked older than Mum. They were all a bit hippy-ish,

77

with layers of old clothes and shrunken cardigans or ponchos on top. I wished I'd had another layer, it was freezing.

Compared to YOFI, it felt serious. There was something almost deadly about it. The woman running the meeting was called Gina, she was quick and fierce and she never smiled once. She talked about the war against women. She said the introduction of MDS is the logical outcome of thousands of years of men's oppression and abuse of women. Women's sexuality disgusts men and they're jealous of a mother's ownership of an unborn child. That's why they want to marry virgins and keep women subservient, because they can never be certain that a child is their own. And women used to just be men's possessions, and only men could inherit, and no one wanted daughters. Millions of baby girls have been killed or aborted. She kept bringing it back to having babies. How it used to be women's business, helped by wise women, and then men said these midwives were witches and insisted on male doctors. And when some women couldn't get pregnant, male scientists started working out ways to make babies outside women's bodies. Which was what they'd always wanted to do, so *they* could own the mystery and power of creating babies. She talked about the first test-tube babies and men stealing control of the process and turning women into passive cows. 'Mad cow disease is no mistake, believe me, that's what we are to them.' She called MDS the atom bomb of the sex war. 'By turning pregnancy into a death sentence they can take it away from us forever. They can insist there is no other way but the man-made child.'

I glanced at Sal but she was intent on every word. Another woman talked about sex, and how men prefer to have sex with other men but they were obliged to have sex with women in order to make children. She said that was at the root of religious laws against homosexuality, because it was in the interests of religion to create as many new babies as possible, to boost membership. But now sexual reproduction was over, all those old commandments against homosexuality were melting away and millions more men were coming out.

Other people broke in, talking about men treating women like lepers because of the disease. Sal was staring straight ahead but her eyes were glittering. I gently put my hand on her arm and she didn't take it away. I remembered that carful of lads and the one who spat on me. I thought about Sal sitting in the lavender-scented bath scrubbing at her skin.

Then they talked about the way MDS women had been treated across the world, how some had been left to die in the streets like dogs, or how they had been rounded up, misinformed, pushed about by police—how none of this would have happened if the victims had been men. They argued that if the disease had hit men, scientists would have found a cure by now. I sat there with these awful things swirling round in my head like leaves in a storm. I couldn't quiet it. What they said about men preferring to be gay reminded me of college.

The thing is, there *was* a change. Back before MDS, if you said a boy was gay, it was an insult. Everyone knew there were gay people, and that it was legal and everything, there were loads of gay celebrities on TV. If they met a gay couple in real life of course they'd be fine and act normally, but still in school it was an insult. If they called a boy *gay* it meant he was pathetic. And the boys and girls who really were gay kept it hidden. In fact, you wouldn't have known that anybody was. But in the months after MDS, that changed. It happened so gradually you almost didn't notice.

Boys started to cluster together with boys, and girls with girls. Some girls became frightened of boys—even though we were all on Implanon it was still a terrible thought, especially for those girls who knew a woman who'd died. Sex didn't seem worth the risk. And the boys—well, I didn't really know what they were thinking, but the atmosphere changed. They got more involved in their own conversations, and less interested in trying to make us laugh. In a way they were more shy with us. It wasn't everybody; there were people who behaved exactly opposite. Like the gangs, where you often saw boys and girls together—or even, like Sal and Damien had been at the beginning. People bounced from one extreme to another, as if we couldn't find out the proper way to behave.

But I was remembering one particular sunny afternoon, soon after the beginning of term. I had a free period before French. I stuck my nose in the library and it was like a greenhouse with all those floor-to-ceiling windows. There was no one there but the red-faced librarian, her hair stuck to her head with sweat. I went out the back, thinking I'd find somewhere to sunbathe while I revised my vocab. I was just going to sit on the steps behind the gym, but looking across the playing field I could see bodies sprawled on the grass along the line of the hedge. I hoped there might be someone I knew, and it would be a sheltered spot to soak up the sun. The playing field had been mowed that morning and the smell of freshly cut grass lured me on. As I walked across I was scanning the sunbathers, but when I got closer I realised they were all boys. They'd taken their shirts off to get a tan. I started to feel embarrassed; I kept my eyes on the corner of the field I was aiming for, and walked as fast as I could, as if I hadn't noticed they were there. I lay on the grass facing away from them, with my vocab book open in front of me. I could hear whispering and laughter. They were urging someone on, trying to get them to do something. I concentrated on my book and when a shadow fell across the page it made me jump. I looked up and there were two boys holding hands, silhouetted against the sun.

'Excuse me,' said one, and the other laughed. 'This is private sunbathing.'

'Gay boys' beach,' said the laughing one.

'No girls allowed,' said the first. I could hear the others laughing. As I picked up my things I couldn't help glancing towards them, and seeing their mocking faces and their bare chests pink in the sunlight, and a glimpse of bare legs and buttocks too. I marched back across the playing field wishing the earth would swallow me up.

A strange thought crept into my head. About Baz. About why nothing ever happened, through I always thought it would. But then why had he asked if Iain had kissed me? Why would he care?

On the bus home Sal told me she'd decided to join FLAME.

'They're a bit extreme,' I said.

'Don't you think it's time to get extreme? Millions of women dead and still no cure. If we don't get extreme now, when will we?'

I thought of telling her about the women doctors who work at my dad's lab, and about all the infertile women who used to go to the clinic, who were *glad* about IVF, who *wanted* it. The thing is, I could hear my dad's voice in my head, arguing with every single thing Gina had said. I didn't think anything she'd said was true. But maybe it was. Why did I always have to believe my dad?

I felt ashamed, as if Sal was older than me and knew more, because of what had happened to her. As if I didn't have the right to argue or stop her. I knew she knew how I felt and was furious about it; she didn't want sympathy or anxiety, she simply wanted nobody to know what had happened. She was angry with me for knowing, but we both knew that wasn't my fault. Neither of us could behave normally.

What the FLAME women said seemed to burn itself into my brain, like when I used to wake up and hear Mum and Dad arguing. You can't ever unknow things once you've heard them. They become part of you, they work inside you like yeast in the dough Sal and I made one weekend. You leave it on a board with a tea-towel over it, and it starts rising and changing its shape. It swells until it's become something else altogether.

Tuesday

Each time he comes into the room he looks at me expectantly. As if he imagines I will have changed my mind.

I've decided to stop speaking to him. When he brings food or drink he says things like, 'Come on Jess, stop it now,' and 'Let's talk the whole thing through again, shall we?' And I either look away or stare at the top of his head, like we used to at school when we wanted to really annoy a teacher. This time he says, 'You know this makes it easier for me? You behaving like a sulky kid. I can just play at cross Dad.'

I am itching to retort, 'You do that anyway.' But I won't give him the satisfaction. When he goes out he stops on the landing and listens to see what I'm doing. I sit very still, listening to him. I hope he is ashamed.

He always turns the light on when he comes in, and when he goes out, I shuffle over and turn it off. Without the light on, the room is bigger, with shadowy edges, and the soft grey that falls through the window can even make a paler rectangle on the floor. It shifts as the day passes, from near my sleeping bag, across to the middle of the carpet. My eyes adjust to the dimness. I feel as if I'm drawing on whatever rays of light there are out there, sucking them in greedily; using them, like a fire sucking in air to feed its flames.

I know everything in this room. The dry wooden boards down the right-hand side, where the bed and wardrobe used to be. (The bed has left imprints of two of its feet in the dusty rose carpet. The imprints are deep and rectangular, and the carpet there is dark pink like inside your mouth.) In the doorway the carpet is worn nearly bald, to the yellowish weave underneath. The light bulb dangling on a brown flex in the middle of the ceiling is an old-fashioned energy guzzler. When it's off I can see the metal attaching bit is speckled with age and rust. I thought they only lasted a few months, but it can't have been changed for years.

Above the window there's a white plastic curtain rail. I wonder why Mum took down the curtain. I remember it had a pattern of little pink and yellow flowers. What did she do with it? I wish she had left it here.

The wallpaper is a faded creamy colour, once it was yellow. It has a faint blotchy pattern which you can't really make out. But this morning for a few minutes the sun shone, and then the pink carpet and yellow walls really glowed, and I thought, my prison is beautiful!

The obvious way out is to lie. That's what I keep

thinking. Next time he comes in, say, 'OK. You win. I won't do it.'

Obviously, embroider it a bit. Sound regretful, or as if you've just had an epic revelation, or as if you're heartbroken but resigned. Simply persuade him you've changed your mind—and he'll let you go. And once you're free, well, you can do what you like.

I keep turning it over in my mind and I don't know why I can't do it. Is it because I know he'd see through me? Like when we used to play *Lie Detector*. Sometimes I would look on Wikipedia for outlandish facts; a silkworm's cocoon contains one thread a kilometre and a half in length. True! A snail travels at 15 metres an hour. False! (Too slow). Father of Wisdom knows all the answers. But he knew things there were no answers to; I've just eaten a chocolate cupcake at Sal's. False! He could tell when I was lying.

I'm not a child any more. I could make a lie convincing.

But I don't want to. As soon as I try to make myself plan it, in detail, something stubborn blocks me. I don't want to lie. Why should I have to lie? If he forces me to lie, he's winning. I want him to *understand* what I am doing, and agree with me.

I go round this loop as often as I shuffle round the walls, from the window heading left to the corner, along the wall where the darker yellow outline of the old mirror stands like a second ghostly window; round the corner to the door and the grubby light switch, avoiding bumping my toe again on the plug socket in the skirting board, and on to the bare boards; round that corner and shuffle more carefully in case of splinters, down to the next corner and round onto the carpet and towards the window and the radiator again. I shuffle round as much as I can, to keep my blood moving and so I'll be capable of making a dash for it when I can.

Why is it alright to run away, but not to lie?

I shouldn't *have* to lie. It annoys me. I hear him unlocking the front door and going out. His footsteps on the paving stones of the little front garden. The clank of the gate. It is so quiet here, and still. In a funny way he's preparing me. Slowing me down; restricting me; forcing me in on myself.

Maybe it's necessary. That's an underlying thought. Maybe it's necessary for me to go through this, maybe it was meant. So that I actually do everything in full knowledge, instead of rushing into it pell-mell.

Maybe I shouldn't struggle or resist at all, but just accept each stage as it happens, and trust where it's taking me.

Ten

I came home from a college science evening to find Dad telling Mum all about a wonderful new breakthrough. I could hear their raised voices as I opened the front door, Mum was saying it wouldn't work and he was saying she didn't understand. There was wine on the table, he offered me some.

'Have a glass with us to celebrate, Jesseroon!'

'Celebrate what?'

'There's a vaccine!'

'But it's no use—' broke in my mum, and he said 'Shush' to her sternly. She burst out giggling and after a moment he joined in. I didn't like it when they were drunk and I told him he could explain it to me in the morning. As I went upstairs they were laughing like a couple of hyenas.

In the morning he was still happy. Mum had already gone off to early theatre, and he was dancing around the kitchen with a porridgy wooden spoon. He gave me a bowl of porridge and said did I want to hear the good news? They had discovered a vaccine against MDS.

'But what's the use of that? Isn't everyone in the world already infected?'

'It can be used to vaccinate embryos.'

'Embryos?'

'There are hundreds of thousands of embryos stored around the world—millions, that predate Maternal Death Syndrome. Pristine, healthy, disease-free embryos, stacked in freezers.'

'Why?'

'In IVF treatment, a woman is given drugs to make her super-ovulate, so you can harvest quite a few eggs at once. You can't freeze eggs so we fertilise them all and pop one or two embryos back inside her. The others, if they look good, get frozen. They're backup in case the implanted one fails, or to get a sibling.'

'OK.'

'Since most women only used a couple of their embryos, fertility clinics have freezers full of them. Which haven't been touched since MDS.'

'So now you vaccinate these embryos.'

'Bingo! There are only two possible ways for them to contract MDS, either through the placenta, or once they start breathing: and we prevent both by early vaccination.'

'Then why was Mum saying it was no good?'

'Oh, she's imagining all sorts of arguments and complications, but they'll certainly want to try it at the clinic and I would imagine at a lot of other places round the world.'

'The women who have these babies—the first ones—'

'Yes, they already have MDS. At least they'll die in a good cause. And there are all sorts of other possibilities; the frozen embryos could be gestated in artificial wombs, or in animals—all these alternatives become much more interesting, once we know we can vaccinate the embryos.'

'What are artificial wombs?'

'Incubators. Machines babies can grow in.'

I thought it sounded disgusting.

'More porridge for the nut brown maid?' He shared the remains between our two bowls. *He* was happy. *I* was the one who couldn't see it in a good light. It's true, he was happy about it from the start-off. All I could think was that the scientists were meddling more and more. If there was going to be a cure I didn't want it to be like this, with frozen vaccinated embryos and artificial wombs or even worse, animals. I thought they'd end up creating a race of half-human monsters for all we knew. What the FLAME women said flared up in my mind: the (male) scientists would always be in control, because they would be the only ones who could make it happen.

I wanted to talk to Sal about it, but she wasn't in college and when I texted her to find out why, it turned out she and her mum had gone down to Birmingham again. 'Bad news' she put in her text, and I texted '?' But she sent back 'L8r'. I was in a black clumsy furious mood. I couldn't see the good in what Dad told me, and I certainly couldn't see any good anywhere else. I hadn't spoken to Baz since the day after Sal's rape. I hadn't even told him I'd left YOFI too. I was waiting to see if he would get in touch with me, but he didn't.

Then coming home from college I took a shortcut through the car park in front of Blockbuster and noticed two youths staring at me. It was one of those moments where someone's watching you and you accidentally look them in the eye, and then they feel they have to do something. I'd got really good at avoiding weirdo demented men, but this time I just blew it. I told myself that if I kept walking steadily for twenty steps they'd go away. Before I'd done ten they were in front of me. They had long hair tied back, and the taller one had a backpack. 'Wantae come wi' us?' he said.

'No.'

'There's lassies wi' us an all,' he said, nodding towards the bus station; and I could see there was a gang of thirty or more, standing in a huddle in one of the parking bays. The bus station was otherwise deserted, everyone had melted away.

'No thanks, I'm going home.'

'Och! She's goin' home, tha's nice. Gie us yer bag.'

'There's nothing worth—'

He snatched it off my shoulder.

'Please don't! There's Coursework in there—'

'Coursework?' He unzipped the bag and tipped it upside down. My History ring binder fell out and sprang open, and pages splayed across the ground. 'She's studyin'!' he said in tones of amazement to the small one. 'D'ye not know it's all over?' And he made a slicing gesture at his throat, with the side of his hand. Then he picked up my iPod and purse, stuffed them back in the bag, and slung it over his shoulder. He kicked at the ring binder so it went spinning through the air, shedding pages as it went. I must have shouted because he swung back round to me and put his face right close to mine, close enough for me to see the dirty pores at the sides of his nose, and he whispered, 'Fuckin' stupid bitch!' and gave me a shove.

By the time I'd crawled to my feet they were gone. I had to go stooping round the car park trying to collect soggy pages of my work. I didn't realise I was crying till a woman came out of Blockbuster and put her arm around me. 'Come and get cleaned up, love. The bloody police, we called them half an hour ago. They're never here when you need them.'

There were three staff in Blockbuster. I realised they must have locked up and turned off the lights to make the place look closed when they first spotted the gang in the bus station. I think they felt guilty, because one of the women drove me home.

I was more scared afterwards than I had been when it was happening—I realised he could have had a knife. It was in the papers all the time, about girls getting abducted by gangs. It was one of the things the road-blocks were meant to stop—terrorists, suicide bombers, and gangs. But mainly they just stopped the traffic. Mum and Dad made a fuss of me, and I had a bath and tea, then watched telly with them and took a hot water bottle up to bed. But I had to leave the light on. I was thinking, how much worse can this get? I felt so futile, so absolutely powerless, it was as if I was transparent.

Sal rang me as I was lying there staring into space. She said things were bad there too.

'Where are you?'

'I'm still in Birmingham. My cousin Tom's been kidnapped.' Tom was the littlest, he was just two. His dad—Sal's uncle—had gone to pick him up from crêche after work, but Tom had already been collected by someone else.

'Who was it?'

'We don't know. A young woman with red hair. She told them she was his father's girlfriend.'

'But didn't they check?'

'There's a password system. If you're not picking your kid up you have to get the day's password from nursery staff and tell it to the picker-up.'

'And this woman had it?'

'Yeah. Which makes it look pretty suspicious for the nursery. It's the second time it's happened.'

'But why?'

'Why? Why d'you think? People want babies!' She went raving on about how the police were questioning all the staff and going to search their homes, sounding more like her old self than she had for a while. I tried to say yes and no and I'm sorry in the right places, but I was filled with numbing tiredness, like someone had poured grey slushy ice water into me and filled me to my eyeballs, and it was freezing my body from the inside out. I was tired. I was afraid. I was deathly cold.

Wednesday morning

I can still remember that feeling. I never want to feel it again. I never will feel it again: no matter what he does. Never again will I lose all hope, I swear. Never again will I feel there is nothing in my power to do.

Back then it was Dad who got me out of it. Here's the terrible joke of all this. What Dad said helped me to crawl out of that pit, and gave me the ray of light to follow. It was Dad who made me see there *was* hope.

He gave me freedom and now he wants to take it away. On a day like today when I'm not in a rage with him, I feel so sorry. I feel so sorry for him and Mum that tears spring to my eyes. But how can I let them know? Last time I tried with Dad it made him furious. Maybe that's the best I can do. If he's furious at least he's not sad. I admitted I hadn't got the right to be angry—well, I haven't. I'm the one doing the damage. The way he's reacted is only natural. But then he told me I was a pious brainwashed fool.

Today when he comes in I say again, 'I'm sorry.'

'What are you sorry for?'

'All the upset I'm causing you and Mum.'

'If you're sorry, don't do it.'

'I'm sorry but I'm still going to do it.'

'Then I shall keep you locked up.'

'There's no point, but I understand why you're doing it. I forgive you.'

'Forgive me? Who do you think you are? Jesus fucking Christ?'

'What I mean is, I know you're doing this for good reasons so I shouldn't get mad at you. I'm sorry I bit you.'

'Jess what is the point of this drivel? I'm sorry I tied you up—we're both sorry for everything we've done—but the point is, we've done it. Because every other method of resolving this difference of opinion has failed. We are reduced to violence, which is the last resort.'

I laugh. 'You can't hold me captive all my life.'

'I won't need to.'

Suddenly I see. He is actually contemplating keeping me here till I'm too old. 'You can't do that.'

'Why not?'

'Keep me here a year?'

'Why not?'

'Because you can't.'

'Watch me.'

There are things I can do. Hunger strike. Injure myself so I need medical attention. But both of those involve a risk to my health, which is my one really vital asset. My mind is racing now, because I have to

94

find a way of outwitting him. I can, I will, I don't feel any doubt about it. I will beat him, because what I'm doing is right, and what he's doing is only negative—blocking me, stopping me. It's like him trying to dam a river, trying to hold back the tide. The force is with me, because I'm in the right.

I shuffle my chair around so I am sitting with my back to him. He says 'Jess?' I ignore him. After a minute I hear him moving to the door, he goes out and locks it.

Once I know he's gone I start wriggling my feet. They keep going to sleep, even though the plastic loops aren't tight. Last night when I was lying in the sleeping bag they felt enormous, and I sat up in a panic, thinking they must be swollen. They felt huge, and tender all over. But when I looked they were perfectly normal. I would have given anything for someone to rub and massage them. All I wanted in the world was a person to stroke my feet.

I keep thinking about my feet when there are more important things to concentrate on. But he doesn't know that. I won't let him know that any of it is getting to me. I'm strong and he's weak. That's the way round it is. And I'm not going to let him imagine he can ever break me.

What's funny is, back then *he* was trying to cheer *me* up. He was trying to cheer me up and he succeeded; what a pity he's not happy with the result.

Eleven

He and Mum must have been as shocked about the gang as I was, because they became ridiculously protective, and offered me lifts all over the place, until it finally sank in to their heads that I had given up car travel. I knew I'd been attacked because I had stupidly walked straight into something; if I kept my eyes and ears open I could avoid trouble. I knew how to make myself almost invisible on the street. I felt as if I could actually control my own visibility, and when girls at college talked about the men calling out to them or following them I laughed in my heart and felt superior.

I asked Mum and Dad to respect *Buy Nothing Christmas*, and they agreed. I said I didn't want anything for my birthday either. Then Dad said but at least let's have an outing to celebrate, just the three of us—a proper outing, like in the old days. Wouldn't that cheer me up? Sal'd been to this fantastic aquarium in Birmingham, so I asked if we could go there.

I love aquariums. I love the brightly lit tanks like windows in a dark street, where you look in to the private strangeness of the fishes' homes. The *SeaLife* centre has one part that's a glass tunnel through a gigantic tank where sharks and turtles swim over your head, and shoals of fish dart past. It has creatures so strange you can't believe you're seeing them. Best of all, it has a special collection of sea horses.

With their dragon heads and fragile mermaid bodies, moving upright through the water, they look so brave! Dad and I watched them for ages, there's a whole wall of tanks with different species, like the Big Bellied Seahorse and the Spiny Seahorse and the Weedy Sea Dragon which looks just like a drifting piece of seaweed. In one there was a pregnant male who was due to release his babies any day, and in another a pair who were doing a courtship dance, their tails lovingly twisted together.

Dad and I wondered why the male carried the babies—I asked if that could be an evolutionary response to something that threatened them millions of years ago. Like maybe pregnant females got attacked or ill. Dad told me with the male seahorses it's not exactly pregnancy, because their eggs are ferti-lised externally, like most fish eggs. The father just keeps the babies in his pouch to grow. They must have a better chance of survival because of that.

I knew Dad and I were both thinking about those frozen embryos which can be put in a surrogate mother and vaccinated against MDS. It's exactly the same thing. It gives us a chance of survival. And quite suddenly it struck me how amazingly clever that was. I was thinking about the extraordinariness of the way sea horses must have evolved over thousands of years, and then about how humans know so much that within a space of *days* they can use their brains to *choose* to incubate their babies in a different way. The shining sea horses hung like question marks in the water, staring at me with their sideways eyes. I remember staring back at them and realising that human beings are beautiful and clever and ingenious.

It was like walking out of a dark tunnel into sunlight. It was like my brain just did a flip and turned itself inside out, and I could *see*, all of a sudden I could really see, what a hopeful thing the vaccine was. I could see Dad was right to be happy! Scientists had found a way for us to survive.

After the seahorses we looked at the rays. They lie there flat as plates then they ripple their fins and glide though the water like birds through the air. Their bodies undulate as if they themselves were waves. And they've found not just one but two ways to protect their babies; some keep their eggs inside, and give birth to live young; others produce eggs in those rubbery brown cases that I always used to think were seaweed. Mermaid's purses. They float across oceans, drifting in the currents. A time capsule, carrying the babies to a safer place.

Dad and I were still staring at the rays when Mum appeared and asked us if we knew what time it was. She'd finished going round ages ago and had been waiting for us in the café. Dad suggested she go shopping while he and I checked out the rest of the tanks, and she was really offended. 'Why didn't you two just come on your own? Why drag me along?' She walked away from us fast, clicking on her high heels. Dad started to hurry after her but she went right out through the barrier.

By the time we'd been stamped for re-entry she'd vanished. It was cold and grey outside, the light glared off the concrete buildings and pavement. Dad moved away to the side of the canal and rang her. I stood in the doorway staring back longingly into the dimness.

But we had to go and join Mum for lunch in the pub on the other side of the canal. It was new and nearly empty, with a sad tinsel tree and a heap of gift-wrapped boxes. Mum'd combed her hair and put on new lipstick; she looked miserable. I ordered a mozzarella and tomato and basil baguette; seeing *prawn* and *tuna melt* on the menu nearly put me off eating anything at all. 'What did you find that was so fascinating?' she asked at last.

'The seahorses,' I said.

'What about them?'

'The father hatching the babies. It's like those frozen embryos being born by surrogate mothers.'

'It won't work,' she said.

Dad came back with our drinks. 'What won't?'

'The frozen embryo surrogacy thing. Even before MDS, it was a legal and emotional minefield.'

'Yes, when someone's paying a woman to have their baby,' said Dad. 'But isn't this a bit different?'

'How?'

'For a start, the surrogate mother dies. That's one complication out of the way.'

'Which leaves the biological parents holding one end of the baby, and the surrogate's parents the other. Look at the shenanigans over the Sleeping Beauties.'

'That's exactly my point. The Sleeping Beauties are giving birth to a child where the genetic father is part of the process. The child has been conceived and brought to term by its biological parents. That's why you get these horrible squabbles between the father and the dead mother's parents.'

'Maybe,' said my mum, 'but here's another thing. Like you say, those Sleeping Beauties are choosing to have their own genetic baby. The biological motivation for reproduction is in place. Whereas the frozen embryo girls would be expected to give up their lives for *alien* genes.'

'But the girls who do this will know they're helping the survival of the whole race.' Thus spoke my father.

'The girls who do this will be poor brainwashed little things. The Noahs will put up girls, and dress them in white and fill their heads with stories about rewards in heaven. They'll marry them off to all the rejects who can't attract girlfriends.'

'They don't need to marry them to anyone, actually, since the pregnancy will be by IVF.'

'Right, I forgot. Virgin births. Won't the churches love it. We'll be worshipping them in the streets.'

'Don't you think these girls will deserve all the razzmatazz they can get? Really, they'll be heroines,' said Dad.

'They'll have been *tricked* into giving up their lives.'

'Think of it as a suicide mission—or, no, a sacrifice . . . Like the Khond.'

'Here we go,' said Mum.

'The Khond of Bengal. Heard of them?'

'No. Surprisingly enough, no.'

'Well they used to have a tradition of human sacrifice, to ensure good crops. And they treated their sacrificial victims like gods. That was what made it possible. The victims had a role to play, and they were important.'

'They knew in advance that they were going to die?'

'Yes. They were called Meriahs, and they were practically worshipped. They were given everything they needed. They could marry other Meriahs and have Meriah children. But all Meriahs lived their lives knowing they were destined for sacrifice. Their deaths meant everyone else could live. So they had this status.'

'You think that's good.'

'I think it meant they lived knowing they were special and died believing they were saving the lives of others, and that that was their destiny. And if girls who volunteer for surrogacy think that too—wouldn't it be good?'

'It's like Jesus,' I said.

'Yes my Jesseroon, exactly right. There was a long tradition of human sacrifice before Jesus appeared on the scene. The best thing a king could do to get his country out of trouble, was to sacrifice a son.'

'There you are!' said my mum. 'A *parent* sacrifices a son. Or in this case a daughter. What right does a parent have to tell a child to die?'

'There'd be a proper process. Counselling.' Dad laughed. 'They missed that bit out of the Bible.'

'And what about those girls who don't even *think*? Who volunteer on a whim, because they crave attention?'

'Well I don't know,' said my dad. 'But since it seems the only way forward, I think we have to embrace it. Golding's already setting up.'

'You'll have them at the clinic?'

'He's got a volunteers' meeting scheduled.'

'But Joe—healthy, strong young girls!'

'What else can we do? At least until there's a break-through with transgenic wombs.'

'So the end justifies the means. They'd be taking these girls' *lives*.'

'Like recruiting young men for a war? Asking them to make the ultimate sacrifice for their people?'

'It's not *certain* a soldier will die. He's not *simply* a passive victim.'

'They often are. Have you heard of—'

'No,' said my mum. 'And I don't want to.'

'Girls who volunteer would be heroines. We have to honour courageous self-sacrifice.'

As we rode home on the train I stared through the layers of reflections on the window, out into the dark countryside. I knew my dad was right. It would be a wonderfully courageous thing to do, to give your life for a child who would be disease-free. To offer yourself as a gateway for the future. He said it and he was right. In black and white.

But there was a while to go before I thought any more about it. At that time I imagined some distant, shining, heroic girls. Girls that my dad would praise and honour, girls who were helping to save the world. They were as bright and faraway as stars.

And close up, I had my own busy and annoying life to live. There was Baz. I knew he liked me from the way he reacted about Iain that time. The way he looked after me, after Sal's rape, was lovely. I knew he wasn't gay, it was a stupid thing to think. But now we weren't going to YOFI we hardly seemed to see each other. I waited for him after college one afternoon and asked if he wanted to walk home together. He told me what'd been going on at his house. Since his father'd lost his church he'd spent every day sitting in their house glaring, just like he was the day I went there. He forbade Baz's mum to go to church, which upset her because she was religious, and he told them that God wanted the world to end. He said the end was coming very soon and the only thing to do was to prepare for it by cleansing your mind. He wanted them both to sit there all day and wait with him. Baz's mum's a teacher, she had to go to work. But he shut her in the bedroom and she had to climb out the window; once he tied her to the towel rail and she was stuck there till Baz came home from college. In the end she phoned her school and said she had to take time off for family reasons. He shouted at Baz for going out or even for practising in his room.

'But he doesn't try to push me around, like he does my mum,' Baz said. 'Maybe he thinks I'll hit him.'

His mum had talked about getting the doctor and his dad said, 'if a doctor steps through that door, I'll kill him.' Baz and his mother tried to work out what to do in whispered conversations, but his dad followed them around, watching every move.

'He doesn't even sleep,' Baz told me. 'If you go into that room at night he's sitting there in the dark like a filthy old spider, staring.' The only things Baz's mother was allowed to do were to read the Bible aloud to him or to clean the house. Baz was afraid to go out in case anything happened to her.

'You have to get help. He's mentally ill,' I said.

'Yeah, but—' Baz stopped to tap a little dance with his fingers, as if that would help him find the words. 'It's *him*. It's like essence of him now, it's just he's stopped caring what people think of it.'

'What d'you mean?'

'He's always told her what to do. Us. Both of us. You *have* to go to Sunday School, you *have* to creep about while he communes with the Lord, you *have* to jump when he says jump. And if not he turns nasty.'

'Violent?'

'No. But even before, if my mum was late back from school, or if she didn't drop what she was doing quick enough when he wanted something, he'd be furious. Not just irritated, but furious. For hours.'

'Before MDS?'

'He's always been like it. He's spent his whole life expecting other people to do what he says. That's why he's lost it, because his congregation didn't lie down and let him walk all over them.'

'You need to tell someone.'

'He's cunning. He wouldn't forget. And he could take it out on my mum any time.'

What could I do? Baz promised to phone me if things got worse.

Twelve

My parents weren't as bad as his but they were bad enough. They had a particularly idiotic row at the weekend. Mum asked if Dad minded her going out for the day on Sunday for some colleague's birthday. He went, 'Sure, fine,' in the distracted way he does when he's trying to read and you're pestering him. But instead of saying 'good', she attacked him.

'You really don't care if I'm here or not, do you? As long as you've got your books, I can prance naked down the street for all you care.'

'What have I done?' he kept asking. 'I don't know what I've done! I thought you *wanted* to go out.'

'I'm sick of being invisible!' Mum yelled. On Sunday she dressed up in a shocking pink top and black wool trousers that were clearly new, although they'd both signed the Compact, and didn't come home till after I'd gone to bed.

And then Mandy nosedived. She rang up one

afternoon just as I got in from college and I dashed to answer it. She said she was getting married. I stood in the kitchen with my coat on staring out at the cold dark garden while Mandy babbled away in my ear. 'It's in March. There'll be an open air ceremony in Platt Fields with hundreds of people. I'm going to design my own dress, it can be any style as long as it's white. I've got some beautiful antique lace—'

I didn't understand who she was going to marry. I didn't even know she had a boyfriend.

'They'll give us the names on Sunday,' she said.

'Who will?'

'At meeting. At the Noahs.'

'Give you whose names?'

'The names of the men we're marrying!' The more she told me the madder it was. Fifty couples all getting married in the same ceremony, and they didn't even know each other's names. I was impatient because Sal was coming round later to watch a DVD for the first time in ages, and I wanted to sort out my room before she came. I was also supposed to be cooking tea for Mum and Dad.

'Does Mum know?' I asked her.

'Of course not. I've only just volunteered.'

'D'you want me to get her to ring you?'

'Sure.'

After I put the phone down I felt mean, because I hadn't actually spoken to her for ages. I quickly scrubbed some jacket potatoes and put them in the microwave, then I called her back. She was excited all over again.

'The Noahs are organising three big ceremonies in

different cities and only women from clean and sacred areas can apply.'

'What's a clean and sacred area?'

'We've converted over fifty per cent of households in the streets between the library and the co-op, bounded by Manchester road to the north and the playing fields to the south.'

'OK.' She was clearly demented.

'The old couple next door were the worst, you know the ones who used to complain about Clive's music? I spent hours trying to explain it all to them— but they finally cracked and came along to meeting last Sunday.'

'I still don't really under—'

'Look,' she said patiently. 'You know how we've made it possible for babies to be born?'

'The *Noahs* have?'

'Yes. Through prayer and intercession.'

'You mean the Sleeping Beauties?'

'Yes, yes. The Noahs have started to turn the tide of evil, and Sleeping Beauties have borne children.'

'Isn't it because the doctors put them to sleep?'

'You have to look at root causes, Jess. You can't just take things at face value. If you look at the Bible—'

I heard the car pull up outside. 'You mean, the doctors can only do this because of the Noahs' prayers?'

'Exactly.'

'But the Sleeping Beauties aren't all Noahs.'

'You'd be surprised how many are. And even those who aren't have been found to come from clean and sacred areas. So they've been helped by the Noahs' prayers.'

My mum came into the kitchen. I handed her the phone and began grating some cheese. Mum seemed to get the point a lot quicker than I had.

'You don't even know who?' she asked. 'Mand, it could be anyone—some dirty old perv, some religions nutter—'

I could hear Mandy's voice rising and falling, arguing away at the other end.

'Joe's right,' said my mum. 'You've been brainwashed. Listen to me. A man you don't know—in your house. In your *bed*—'

The voice at the other end was getting louder. Mum held the phone away from her ear and shook her head at me. When there was a gap she said, 'Look Mandy, you can't do this. I want you to ring them up and—no, no, stop it—no, I do want you to be happy, of course I do . . . that's not fair—' There was a silence then Mum put the phone down. She stared at it miserably for a moment. Dad came into the kitchen, still with his coat on. 'Hello, nut brown maid,' he said. He was going out for tea, no need to make anything for him. I told him it was only baked potato and he grinned and said he must've known.

'Joe,' said my mum. 'Just stop it for one minute, will you. Mandy says she's getting married in one of those big Noah weddings.'

'Stop it?' said my dad. 'It wasn't me that started it!'

'Please—'

'You want to heap abuse on me one minute and ask for my help the next—'

'I'm sorry,' said Mum. She rubbed her face. 'Sorry.'

'What am I supposed to say?'

There was a silence. Mum shook her head as if she was trying to get rid of an annoying insect. 'Look, about Mandy,' she said. 'Can we get her into hospital?'

'You've got to be joking. They'd have to classify all the Noahs as insane, which they patently are, but I can't see anyone rushing out with the straitjackets.' He kissed me on the top of my head and went back out to the car without even saying goodbye to Mum.

Mum went to Mandy's on Saturday and ended up bringing her back to our house that night. Dad had to help drag her out of the car. Mum gave her a sleeping pill and sat with her in the spare room until she went to sleep. Then she told me and Dad what had happened. When she got there Mandy had her sewing machine out, and was busily making a wedding dress. She'd got hold of some lace curtains and cut them into panels, she was planning to layer them over a flesh-coloured silk underskirt. My mum tried to find out who was organising the wedding, and Mandy just laughed and said, 'The Noahs have set me free!' She was completely hyper, whirring away on her sewing machine and giggling at Mum for being so serious. Then the phone rang and she ran to answer it: and she collapsed like a burst balloon.

They told her she was too old, they only wanted young women in the mass weddings. She was heart-broken—it was like Clive leaving all over again. Except that this time she didn't even *know* the man she wasn't going to marry. But as my dad pointed out, it wasn't the man she was interested in. He said the Noahs knew hospitals and clinics would only accept young volunteers to be Sleeping Beauties. They were the only ones whose babies survived. Mum had brought her back to ours because she was afraid Mand might do something daft. Dad took all the pills out of the bathroom cabinet and hid them.

Mandy stayed in bed all week. She wouldn't eat and she would hardly drink; she just lay there stony faced. Mum was worried about leaving her on her own but she had to go to work. Dad took a couple of days off and after that I looked after her as much as I could. It was pitiful; I'd go in with a drink and she'd just be lying there with her eyes closed and tears trickling down her cheeks. When I begged her to drink she slowly turned her head from one side to the other without even looking at me. I ended up going in and kneeling by her bed, holding her hand and crying myself. She half opened her eyes, like the lids were too heavy to raise, and muttered, 'They promised. God hears your prayers, he will give you your heart's desire.'

'Mand, nobody can give—'

'They promised.'

The doctor prescribed a load of pills and Mum managed to find someone qualified—he was called Paul—who could care for her at home. It was expensive and Mand didn't have any money. If Nanna Bessie's house had sold it would have been fine because it was left to Mandy and my mum; but no one had even been to look at it.

If Nanna Bessie's house had been sold . . . where would I be now, I wonder? Would he have been able to find anywhere else so perfect for a kidnap?

Mum and Dad had a brisk not-quite-row where

she said the only way to pay for Mand's care was to not replace the car and to not go on holiday. And he said fine by him. Two good decisions for the earth; but at night the vision of Mandy's crying face was haunting me.

Everything kept churning round in my head. All the women like Mandy, who wanted children, crying in their beds around the world. The suicides. The gangs, roaming through and grabbing whatever and whoever they fancied. And what Sal was thinking—the things the FLAME women said, the way MDS was driving a wedge between women and men. And all the silly chattering little protest groups, achieving nothing.

I thought, there has to be something we can do, before everything fractures and shatters into pieces. I had an image of our windscreen when we were driving on the motorway one time. A stone flew up from the car in front and we heard it ping against the windscreen. It chipped the glass and from that chip a crack slowly spread along the middle of the screen towards the driver's side. My dad pulled onto the hard shoulder, to turn off at the next exit. The crack in the glass kept moving, slowly, as if it had a life of its own, snaking across the windscreen. As we reached the turn-off it got to the other side and a new crack began, slanting upwards from that point. It was as if someone was doodling lines on the glass. Dad stopped at the slip road roundabout, and when he started again there was a little jerk with the gears, and the whole window suddenly shattered. Dad had to bash it out with the road atlas. And I thought, that's what's happening to us. MDS was a crack but now it's breaking the whole world into fragments.

The only ray of hope I could see was through those frozen embryos, whose births would kill their mothers.

Thirteen

I began to think about them quite a lot. They would simply float into my head. At different times, in different moods, I would think of those girls volunteering.

Sal was getting involved in the FLAME group—her mum went too. I wasn't up for that, and I was lonely, so when Mary phoned to ask if I'd help sort out a big YOFI clothes recycle, and told me Iain was away in London, I didn't mind saying yes. I wasn't going to get involved again, but an evening catching up with everyone would be fine. There weren't that many people there, actually; it seemed lots of others had drifted away too. I reckoned YOFI was on its last legs.

Jacob brought some beer because it was his birthday. The clothes had that manky musty smell of old clothes that've been put away. The smell got into everything, even the taste of our beer. They were saving the decent stuff for a Really Free stall, and the rest would be used to pack suitcases for the twice-delayed airport protest. Someone put on a tape and the beat of the music began to speed us up.

'I bet loads of it belonged to dead people,' said Mary. I thought about the women who'd died from MDS and wondered if their husbands had given away their clothes. Imagine going through your wife's wardrobe and just putting it all in binliners—the T-shirts, the jeans, that you've seen her wearing every day.

I thought about what Dad had said about the frozen-embryo Sleeping Beauties, how they would be helping the survival of the race. I tried to work out how many lives one of those volunteers might create. If she gave birth to a daughter, and that daughter had children, and *they* all had children . . . over a few generations, it could be hundreds of people. But it would make a difference sooner than that. It would make a difference to people kidnapping and trafficking young kids. To the Noahs. The suicides. The men who think women are dirty. The FLAME women hating men. The scientists doing awful experiments on animals, the ALF attacking them. It would make a difference to the way everyone looked at the world, because they'd be able to see there's hope.

Mary threw me a silky blue dress. It was heavy and slippery, the colour of the sky on a clear summer evening. I took off my jumper and pulled the dress on over my T-shirt and jeans. It was an old design, tight over the bust then flared, hanging in beautiful folds down to midcalf length. 'Wow!' said Mary, 'look!' The others all stopped to look, and someone wolf-whistled and the others clapped. I gave them a twirl. I loved the cool feel of the heavy silk swishing round me. I found a brown skirt with cream embroidery and passed it over to Mary. Ahmed was pulling on an orangey-golden kaftan. Everyone began scrabbling through the heaps to find things they liked. The old song that came on next seemed to echo through me. *Love, love will tear us apart again.* It was the saddest song I had ever heard.

'Jessie! Jessie! Here!' Mary found a little black hat with brilliant blue feathers round it. They were beautiful, curling round the curve of the hat making a lacy blue pattern against the velvety black. We all began admiring one another, stretching out our arms and necks to display our finery, striding about and striking poses, like models on the catwalk. I wondered who had worn my dress, I wondered if she went dancing in it. I had the strangest feeling, almost as if the dress was a body. I'd put the dress on and in doing that I'd put on another body. A light, twirling, dancing body. And after me, someone else could wear the dress. And someone else. And they would all have a sense of that, the light twirling dancing body. But of course they would be themselves as well. I was thinking, if that much can be passed on just in a dress, how much of every living person lives on after they die? Feeds into everyone else, in different ways, through what they've said, and done, and made. All these dead clothes could come back to life as soon as we put them on. I thought, death is really no big deal. I could die and I wouldn't mind at all.

Who will the volunteers be? I remember asking myself. Mary had put on a leather waistcoat and some black evening gloves. She came up and bowed to me and we sauntered round the piles of clothes arm in arm, bowing and curtseying to everyone we passed. The volunteers will be girls like me, they have to be young. The younger the better. I unhooked my arm from Mary's and went to sit on the stage steps. I stroked the silk of my skirt, smoothing it over my denim thighs. I thought about those tribesmen Dad was talking about, the sacrifice ones, Meriahs, who live knowing they are special and die believing they are saving the lives of others. They think it's their destiny. It *is* their destiny. And I thought, how could anyone have a better life and death than that?

I wasn't drunk but I was up above the room, high above it, looking down on the mountains of clothes with all their departed lives, and on the energetic YOFI members hurling clothes from one pile into another, or putting them on and dancing about, and it was nothing to do with me because I had something more important to do. I knew that I could take on the knowledge of other sacrificers. Other volunteers who have died for their people. Suicide bombers, strapping on their bomb belts. Young Japanese kamikaze pilots, winding their silk scarves around their necks. Just like putting on the silk dress. Putting on their strength and certainty. Donning my destiny.

I don't remember my dreams that night but I do remember waking and feeling as if I'd been right down to the bottom of something. Down into the very deep blue water, the sea, going down down down through layers of darkening blue like all the shades on a paint chart, turquoise, teal, aquamarine, royal blue, navy blue, French navy, midnight blue, ink, darker and darker but not scared, just marvelling at the depth and intensity of colour. I knew that whenever I wanted, soon enough, I'd come popping backup to the surface like a cork.

Which is what I did, waking up. And I felt surprised and dizzy to see my ordinary room around me. I remembered that I had thought about volunteering.

I made myself imagine volunteering to be a Sleeping Beauty. Being put to sleep and never waking up. I still didn't know how anyone could volunteer for that. I felt spacey inside my head, as if there was easily room there for lots of contradictory ideas. Spacey and excited. I wondered if I would talk about it with Baz. I felt as if something extraordinary was going to happen that very day.

Fourteen

Something extraordinary did happen but it wasn't good. In the evening when I was watching BABIES OF THE WEEK I heard Mum and Dad's raised voices in the kitchen. I turned up the telly, because I love that programme. It's organised by *Mothers for Life*. They show photos of the babies, and of their mothers before they were pregnant. Someone, usually the Sleeping Beauty's mother, reads a poem or from the Bible or the Koran. You can choose your own poem but there are also some purpose-written ones, this is my favourite:

> *Sleep well, dear _____, in the cool dark earth.*
> *You gave your life for this new birth.*
> *The radiance of your sacrifice*
> *Shines like a star in your infant's life.*

Some people chose to have their favourite song. I tried to imagine myself on there, and wondered what photo of me they'd use. I watched all the babies. There was one like a little monkey with wispy black hair and solemn eyes. And another had a bald head and fat hamster cheeks. I love it when they're staring at you with that dazed look, like they're wondering 'Where on earth am I now?' After the babies came more news: arson, suicides, wars, famines and fighting as usual; coup in Malaysia, state of emergency in Pakistan, riots in Washington; attacks on the homes of UK animal-research scientists; terror suspects appealing against imprisonment without trial; new Chinese Sleeping Beauty programme recruiting 5,000 volunteers a week; voluntary redeployment into vital services; floods in India; and of course a story about a healthy pregnant woman in Nigeria, kept alive by her followers at a secret location. There was always a story like this, but most mysteriously they never showed the woman on screen, and you never actually heard about it when her baby was born. There were endless rumours about things which were supposed to have helped women survive pregnancies: diets, special herbs, round the clock prayers to the Virgin, cannibalism, sterile environments, living underwater, meditation, hypnotism, voodoo, acupuncture, fasting, staying at high altitudes, making blood sacrifices to the mother goddess. Strange how all those healthy pregnant women were invisible, though!

I tuned out and then I could hear Mum and Dad weren't just having a standard row. Mum was crying, so it was hard to make out what she said. *I didn't need to tell you?* I muted the telly. My ears latched onto my own name; Dad in a low voice, *something something*

Jessie knows? Then the shocking sound of a dish smashing against the tiles. I crept to the door and pressed my ear against it.

'You never even looked at me—'

'Oh it's *my* fault. Whichever way you spin it, Cath's the victim—'

'No—listen—Joe—'

'Why should I listen? Why should I listen to another word of this self-serving shite?'

There was an awful silence and I stretched and strained my hearing but couldn't get anything—then the kitchen door being snatched open, steps in the hall, the front door slamming shut and the car roaring into life.

I froze, waiting for the next sound, but there was nothing. Dad had gone. As quietly as I could I tiptoed upstairs. I knew what this was about and I didn't want to see Mum. When I reached my room I shut the door without a sound and put on my headphones so I wouldn't hear if she called. I sat at my desk and stared at the wall. I had known for weeks. I could have stopped it—I could have told Mum I knew, threatened her I'd tell Dad. But I'd been merrily going along in my own life blanking it out (the note in the pocket? The new trousers? The day out with 'colleagues'?) as if it was nothing to do with me. And now Dad had driven off into the night in rage and misery, going I didn't know where, at risk of crashing and never coming back. *Something something Jessie knows?* Was he asking, did I know? What if he thought I knew and was keeping it secret from him, that I was conspiring with Mum?

Of course he would think that. Driving along the icy roads, with blackness swooshing past the windows, he'd think about all the things I was thinking—the late clinics, the smart clothes, the supposed teas with Mandy—and he'd think I must have been in on it, helping to cover up her lies. He'd think I was as bad as her.

I had to listen for him coming back. I took off the headphones, turned off the light and got into bed. After a long time I heard her coming upstairs. She stood still on the landing for ages, then used the bathroom and went into their room. She left the landing light on. I lay rigid straining my ears for the car, willing it to turn in at the end of the road. I lay like that for hours, and my head kept flashing with images of Dad skidding off the road, of black water swirling over the roof of the car, and the wavering headlamps shining on astonished flickering fish, down in the murky depths of the river.

I thought about texting or phoning him but I was afraid of causing an accident if he was still driving. I lay awake all night and in the morning when Mum knocked quietly on my door and then opened it, I pretended to be asleep. Eventually I heard her leave the house. When I crept down she'd left a note saying she'd be back from work by seven and that she'd cook. No mention of Dad. She'd probably left it hoping he would come back and see it.

I had a shower and put on some clean clothes. I didn't know if they'd split up. Part of me didn't want to know and didn't in the least care. I stared at my empty phone for a bit then I texted him, 'Dad r u OK? xoxoJ'. There hadn't been any reply by the time I got to college so I switched it to silent. There was no reply all day. And no Sal at college.

When I got home, it was exactly as I'd left it. I didn't want to eat with Mum so I made a sandwich and took it to my room. I rang Dad's lab but there was no reply. After a bit I rang his mobile but it went straight to answer. Which was weird, I'd never know him turn it off.

When Mum got in I called down that I'd had my tea. She came and tapped on my door and I told her I didn't want to talk. She opened the door anyway.

'Have you heard from Joe?'

'No.' I couldn't bear to look at her.

I stayed in my room all evening. I could hear Mum moving around downstairs, and when she started talking I opened my door to listen. But she was on the phone to Paul the carer. I heard her asking what Mandy'd had for her dinner, and had they been for a walk? Her voice turned fake and cheery when she talked to Mandy; 'Great, well done! I'm ever so pleased.' Then the whole house was quiet again, waiting for the phone to ring, or the sound of the car in the drive.

Mum stayed up till midnight; after she used the bathroom she stood listening outside my door. I didn't move, and eventually she went into her own room and shut the door.

My window was open and I could pick up the sounds of cars all the way to the main road. There weren't many, and none of them were his. There were lots of other sounds, ticks and clicks as the heating cooled down; an owl, the sound of water rushing down next door's drain like someone'd just let out a bath. If he'd had a crash someone would've found him and taken him to hospital; they could look in his wallet, the police would trace him. He hadn't had a crash. He just didn't want anyone to know where he was.

I thought of everyone dressing up and dancing at YOFI, of twirling around in that blue dress. Of the ones who sacrifice themselves. How clear and simple and *good* that was, in comparison to all the stupid mess of being married and telling lies and fighting. Why didn't he text me? I was convinced he knew I knew about Mum. Maybe he never wanted to see either of us again.

I must have fallen asleep some time after five, because I woke up with a jolt when the letters came at half past nine. Mum'd gone, she'd left another note about coming home to cook. My eyes were prickly and my head ached with tiredness, but I couldn't bear to stay in the house. I thought of talking to Sal but I was afraid she'd go 'So what?' She'd be right—so what if they did split up? Her mum and dad split up, it was just one of those things that happened. Stupid adults; their days were numbered.

I caught the bus to college and sat in the front seat upstairs. The sky had clouded over and everything through the window was flat and factual, like a crime scene. Like a place waiting for something bad to happen. Like suspended animation. I thought, a Sleeping Beauty wouldn't know anything. Being dead, the state of being dead, would be OK—just the same as before you were born. A dreamless sleep. I could do that—it wouldn't really matter. No more feeling upset about stupid parents, no more waste of energy and emotion. Just peacefulness and calm. Then I suddenly saw Dad. He was walking along the near-side pavement and the bus was coming up behind him, I recognised his shoulders and his striding walk. As I jumped up and the bus passed him I glimpsed his face. Not Dad. It wasn't Dad at all, it was a man with a moustache.

I fell back into my seat, my heart was making my whole ribcage shake. Might Dad kill himself? The thought flew in before I could block it. Maybe that was why he didn't want to speak to me—he'd lost hope. Because of Mum, because of MDS, because everything had gone wrong. Yet again I rang his mobile. No answer. I remembered him that night he and Mum brought Mandy into our house, half-dragging her between them, and Mum put her to bed in the spare room. He stood by the sink staring at the kettle as if he could see the future in it, as if it paralysed him. Now he thought I'd betrayed him too. He must think we didn't know where he was and we didn't care, we hadn't even tried to find him.

I got off the bus at Guide Bridge and took a train into town. From the station the next bus down to the clinic. Surely he would be at work? I walked through the car park looking for our car but I couldn't spot it. I couldn't get in the lab doors because I didn't know the key code. I had to go round and up the steps to the front doors. The security guard stared at me but when I told him my name he grinned and nodded, 'Haven't seen you for a while!' Just getting inside the building made me feel calmer; the corridor was peaceful, with names on every door—I passed a nurse with a tray and she winked at me. As I ran down the stairs to the labs I smelled that old friendly smell which only belongs to the lab. It's a bit like alcohol, and it clears up the back of your nose. A warm smell, that brings out the dark scent of the wooden work benches. Dad would always be here, I thought.

But he wasn't. The door to his lab was locked—no Dad, no Ali. I tried to peer through the little wired-glass window but it was dark in there and I could only see my own reflection. Even the corridor was still and empty; there was nobody to ask. I had to go back the way I came until I found myself outside again, with the cold grey day glaring down on me, not knowing what to do.

I walked back fast into town and now I was angry. It was idiotic. Idiotic to come all this way, looking for him. Of course he wasn't at work—if he was, Mum would've spoken to him. And there was no way he'd kill himself, the old cynic—he even laughed about the suicides doing the Grim Reaper's job. Why was I wasting my time chasing after him and worrying, when he'd gone off somewhere without a second thought for me—gone off probably to visit some old friend or the British Museum or some amazing library. Was he so upset about Mum he didn't even *remember* me? Why on earth should I care about him? If he could abandon me then I could abandon him.

I was starving and I stopped at The Eighth Day and got a smoked tofu burger and an apricot smoothie to guzzle on the bus. The taste of apricot flooded me, orange mixed with hyacinths, gritty behind my teeth. I wished I had bought two.

I finally got to college with half an hour to spare before History. I did a diversion past the music rooms, and my luck was in: I could see Baz in the practice room on the grand piano. He looked up and grinned, but kept on playing—I walked in to a waterfall of tumbling notes.

I wanted to tell him about my parents. Why shouldn't I? At least his dad couldn't help being mad; mine behaved like idiots without any excuse at all. Why should I cover up for them? Baz finished and jumped up from the piano. 'Nat's found out what's happening at Wettenhall!'

'You what?'

'The animal lab near Chester that they've been investigating. They've managed to infiltrate it.'

It took me a while to grasp what he was on about, but it turned out the ALF had been trying to get into this place for a long time and now they'd managed to take some secret film of the animals, drugged, with tubes and wires attached to them, strapped down and unable to move.

'But why are the researchers doing it? There must be a reason.'

'What could excuse that? I'm going down there as soon as things settle down at home—'

'What's happened?'

'He's in hospital. Mum didn't want me to but I finally rang the doctor, and they came for him in an ambulance. He was so busy raving on he didn't even notice until they'd got him outside.'

'Is he OK?'

Baz shrugged. 'Mum's going to see him twice a day.

She says he seems calmer. I don't know.' He glanced at his watch. 'I've got to go. She'll be getting home soon.' He picked up the metronome from the lid of the piano and put it in his rucksack.

'Baz?'

'Yeah, they know I'm taking it. Mine's broken, and I've got another exam.' He edged towards the door. 'Mum gets upset, it's better if I'm there when she comes home.'

His mum was bonkers too, I realised. I walked to the playing field door with him and said goodbye. Checked my mobile. I hadn't told him about my dad; well, he had enough to think about. And as soon as things got better with his parents, he'd be off to join Nat, saving the lives of animals.

Sal wasn't in college again—she hadn't been in all week but I was pretty sure she'd come back from Birmingham, so I called at her house on my way home. She was there, watching a DVD. She urged me into the front room and insisted on starting it again from the beginning. 'You should see this, Jess, you should just see it. It's horrendous.'

I didn't want to see a DVD, I wanted to talk, but it was hopeless. It was playing before I could get a word in. And the DVD was—well, everybody's seen it now. But back then I hadn't even heard of it. She got it from the FLAME women. It was the most horrible upsetting DVD I've ever seen in my life. It's the film of some women who had MDS. But it isn't one of those 'diary-of-an-illness' type programmes, where you go through the stages of anxiety and fear with the person, trying different kinds of treatment and hoping

127

for the best. Where you feel that even though he or she may die in the end, the person has learned something and taught you something. It's not like that at all. They don't even tell you the names of the women, they just show them being ill. Bumping into things. Swearing. Repeating words over and over. Falling down and having fits. Women in homes, in hospitals, in different countries, even outside, lying on the ground. Women dead. The point about it is they don't show the women like people you could care about, they show them like animals, in disgusting states, naked, puking up. People say its pornography. FLAME say it's a record of what's really happened, that people have been pretending not to see, and covering with flowers.

'This'll show them,' said Sal.

'It's not like that now. They put MDS women to sleep, no one has to have all that awful—'

'Put them to sleep?' she shrieked. 'Put them to sleep? We're not talking about aged pets, we're talking about young women. Women who *die*. If you don't have to watch them going mad first, that makes it OK, does it?'

There wasn't anything I could say.

'We're going to campaign with this—we're going to really make them sit up and notice. Imagine if these were men, dying like this. D'you think there'd still be no cure?'

By the end of the DVD I felt sick and wretched, and Sal was completely hyper. I left her ringing up her FLAME friends. I didn't let myself look at my mobile till I got home but it didn't make any difference; still nothing. The kitchen smelled foul and when I looked in the bin I saw Mum had dumped a load of filthy old fag ends. She'd promised me she'd stopped smoking. As if. Like agreeing not to buy more new clothes, when I knew perfectly well the grey wool jacket on the bannisters had just come from Jigsaw. A supposedly educated, intelligent person. If this was the best she could do after being asked and told, what hope was there?

When Mum came in she tried to entice me out for a meal. She followed me up to my room. 'I know you're worried about Joe, Jessie, but so am I. This atmosphere's making it even worse.'

'Your smoking is making the atmosphere worse,' I told her.

She went into her own room and it was quiet. I wondered if she was crying. I knew I was horrible. I wished none of today had happened, I wished I was someone else. Sal was in FLAME, Baz was leaving, and Dad thought it was alright to never even contact me again.

I turned off the light and opened the curtain and lay looking up at the beech tree. It was a tracery of black against the sky. The lower branches had a bit of an orange shine to them, from the street lamp. Behind the black branches the sky was vaguely dark, no stars or moon—just clouds reflecting light pollution. I felt like a creature in a cage. Whichever direction I paced or turned, my way was blocked. There was nothing I could do—I was powerless. I had to find a way out.

Something began to relieve the pressure in my head before I even knew what it was. A pinhole of light. It was the freedom I felt, the night of the blue dress.

Imagining I could be a volunteer. How pleased Dad would be if I volunteered (thought I). He couldn't go on being angry with me then, he'd have to see my mind had been occupied with much more important things than Mum's stupid affair. He'd be proud of me. I could almost hear him saying, 'My heroic Jesseroon!'

How crazy, how crazy how crazy that seems now. But that's what I thought. I lay still, hardly breathing, and allowed myself to float into the ocean of space that was opening before me. To do something straight-forward, where there would be no tangled argument and no compromise. Something that would make a difference to the world. Something that was within my power to do without having to rely on anyone else. Something that would make Dad proud. I pulled my pillow and duvet off the bed and wrapped myself up on the floor, so I could go on and on staring at the beech, letting that freedom unroll. The freedom to act. The freedom to do something I had decided for myself.

Wednesday night

When we discuss it he harps on about that all the time.
'You volunteered because of me. Because of what I
said. If I'd never mentioned it, it would never even
have entered your head.'

It's dark outside and he has brought two mugs of
cocoa upstairs, and untied my right hand so I can hold
the mug by its handle. 'Dad, undo my other hand.
Please.'

He takes the cocoa off me (I seem to have taught
him not to trust me!), undoes my left, then passes me
back the cocoa and moves smartly out of range.

'It's OK. I won't try anything. I just wanted to warm
my hands.' I flex my left wrist and wiggle my fingers.
Luxury. I wrap both hands around the mug. It is a
solid triangle of comfort. I can lose myself in the
loveliness of its heat and smell; all there is is cocoa.

I have to drag myself back to the argument. It
keeps feeling so nearly within reach, the moment of

convincing him, that I have to keep plugging away at it. It's impossible that he won't understand. 'I didn't volunteer because of you. If you'd never mentioned it, it would have hit me in the face when I heard it on the news. It is the thing I need to do, so one way or another it would have found me.'

'But you lose me here, Jess. I can't buy it—this destiny stuff, this *thing I need to do*. You're a free agent. You can do *anything* with your life.'

'I know. Listen. Let me explain—because it *is* freedom. That's what it is.'

'You never used to be a fatalist. Where's the girl who said Hindu-ism was ridiculous, when I explained it to you?'

'Father of Wisdom. This isn't Hinduism. This is something I *know*.'

He's shaking his head. Outside, far away in the dark night, a dog barks. Yesterday I tried screaming and he gagged me; my throat still feels raw, and my bottom lip is split at the side. Explain. Explain to him; if only he could *see*.

'And then I wasn't even there,' he says. 'I told you about it, and then I buggered off. If I'd been there for you to talk to—'

'It wouldn't have made any difference. I didn't just go, *oh yeah, I'll volunteer*. You know? It *grew*. That's how I knew it was meant to be.'

'Jess—'

'OK. OK. I'll tell you what it was like. It was like getting in and swimming in the sea.'

He wiggles his eyebrows at me in the old way, meaning he thinks I'm a loony, and I laugh.

'It's true. Listen. On a big wide beach, MDS is the waves, and you're trying to get in the water. At first you're on the edge of the beach, playing about. But the tide is coming in. The first waves, they just froth around your feet, they're cold but still quite small, and you can run giggling up the beach.'

'Interpret, oh poetic one.'

'That's hearing the first news about MDS, when I was too young and silly to understand. Then bigger waves start to come, one after another. They break against your legs and you feel the force of the water smashing against you, and the undertow sucking your ankles. Then the water's getting deeper, the waves slam into your body and you stagger from the force of them, they almost knock you over.'

'I get the picture.'

'The heavy weight of the water beats against you. But you stand upright and resist it and keep walking. And then you're in quite deep, your head and shoulders are clear and your feet are still flat on the sand, but the water is deep and smooth all around you, and when the next wave comes it's not breaking, because they break closer in to shore. It's just a swell, a smooth running mound of water rolling towards you. And when it comes it doesn't beat against you, it doesn't smash its strength against yours. It simply lifts you off your feet. It lifts you up and carries you, and you start swimming in the sea.'

'You start swimming in MDS?'

'Don't be thick.'

'Which one equals volunteering, among all these

waves? Or is that the tsunami that's coming to drown you?'

'It's about accepting what's happening and finding a way to deal with it.'

'Your metaphors are as illogical as your thinking, Jess.'

I swirl the last of the cocoa round in my mug, trying to get the chocolaty sludge at the bottom to mix in. I wish he could understand. I wish this would stop. 'Can I talk to Mum?'

'Why?'

'I just want to.'

'OK.' He dials the number on his mobile and passes it to me. How quickly could I dial 999? Before he got it off me? If he left the phone with me for just a *minute*, I could do it.

'Hello?'

'Mum.'

'Jessie! Where are you?'

'Where d'you think?'

'Are you alright? Is Joe there?'

'He's here. He told me I could ring you.'

'You're angry now but honestly Jess, in the long run you will see things differently.'

'I don't think so.' I'm trying to see where the nine is while holding the unfamiliar phone to my ear. Mum is saying something else, I can't follow. 'Sorry? What?' I inch the phone up into my eye line and cover the nine with my thumb. End this call—end this call and then—

Dad leans forward and grabs it. 'That's enough.' He puts it to his ear. 'Cath, sorry. But I can't trust her with the phone. Look, I'll call you later. Yes. We're fine.'

'What did you think I was going to do?' I say angrily.

'The thing you were thinking of doing.'

'You're not a mind reader.'

'No, I wish I was, then maybe this would make some sense to me.'

'*I* wish you were.' The saddest thing about this room is the way there is no curtain. There's something so bleak about light reflecting on a night-time window, when you can't see out. A black shiny dead end. I'd prefer sitting and talking in the dark, so I could see there's a sky outside.

I am not going to think about the dark. What you have to remember is that light changes. Everything changes. Even though the window looks black from here, there *is* light outside. Another kind of light. 'D'you remember the glow worms?'

He looks at me blankly.

'In Cornwall? When we went on holiday.'

'The glow worms! Yes. On the verge at the side of that lane.'

'I thought they were shining green and you said no, it's because they're buried in the grass.'

'Did I?'

'You picked one up for me, on a leaf, but it was still greeny-yellow, so you had to admit—'

He nearly grins. 'You are occasionally right. But not now.' There's a silence. 'They shine to attract a mate,' he says.

'Father of Wisdom.'

We look at each other.
'Please let me go. Please.'
He shakes his head.
We sit in silence, holding our empty mugs.

Fifteen

So I volunteered.

I hurried out of the warm clinic because I didn't want to have to talk to any of the other girls. Coming out of the revolving door was like jumping into ice-water, I felt the skin on my face shrivelling in the cold. Then I was already at the stop before I remembered the bus strike.

I'd walked *to* the clinic from the station, but now I could barely stand up straight. My heart was kicking my ribcage like a footballer; booting me, thwacking me, so I nearly overbalanced. I leant against the bus-shelter and tried to breathe steadily: in, out, in, out, trying to order the *thing* in my chest to stop pummelling me. I cupped my hands around my mouth and captured my warm breath, pretending it was Sal's panic-attack paper bag. Sucked the used air back into my lungs. Once Dad took the bag Sal had finished with, scrunched it around his lips and blew it up then burst it like a balloon, bang. Enough to give you a panic if you didn't have one already. I switched on my mobile and stared at it while the light came on. No messages.

I told myself I could walk. If I walked fast I could merge myself into the rushing noise of the street, the streaming traffic, the sirens blaring up from the distance, drowning me out then dwindling away, being over-lapped by the next one coming up. The faster I walked the more my heart would have to beat in time, it couldn't just leap about like a demented frog; after all, it had a job to do.

A man was making a little moaning noise at the edge of the pavement. I saw his feet as I hurried past; women's suede ankle boots with fur at the cuffs. All those men, I wished they could vanish, take their misery and simply vanish. I hated walking past empty houses. Windows smashed, doors kicked in, someone'd made a bonfire in one front garden and there was a half burnt sofa with its springs uncoiling. I pulled my hat down over my eyebrows, turned my collar up and walked faster. I was practically running. From the next corner the houses were inhabited, with pruned hedges and security shutters, so I could slow down.

That's when the thought of it finally registered, warming me inside like a hot little secret that I'd swallowed; a glowing roasted chestnut. I'd done it! I'd really truly done it!

Too late I spotted the road block ahead. Once they've seen you they're suspicious if you turn back. I waited behind a woman with a Co-op bag, she was impatient and kept trying to attract the policewoman's attention. But the policewoman was searching a weirdo and concentrating quite hard because he was trying to touch her. 'Hold your hands out straight please sir. Straight.' And, 'Keep your hands to yourself sir, thank you.'

She was skimming over the surface of his clothes, he could have had a bomb belt and she'd never even have noticed. She just wanted to get rid of him. The lady before me said, 'It's just shopping, Officer. I need to get back, my grand-daughter will be waking up—' The policewoman nodded her through. And then of course felt she had to justify herself so she took all the stuff out of my bag and flicked through the pages of every book and folder before telling me to put them back. All the warmth I'd generated was draining away, and I felt like crying. Or asking her, could I stay in her little cabin for the afternoon, hide myself away there until I knew what I felt?

It started drizzling again, icy little needles against my skin. At the station I checked the board for the Ashton train, and walked across the grimy forecourt to the stairs for platform four. A strange feeling crept into my head, of how many hundred times I must have been there, smelling that dry bitter station smell, with the loop of stupid announcements about unattended personal belongings being destroyed and the roaring clatter of trains and beeps of opening doors and the cracked slippery-when-wet floor with its yellow warning triangles, and of how I always hurried through it trying not to hear or see or smell its ugliness. What would it be like to never see it again? You wouldn't want to see it, it's horrible. But if you thought you were never going to see it again, you might not want to block it out.

I pulled myself together. Checked the mobile.

Climbed the steps to the bridge and then down to my platform. But I was staring at each person I passed; I was thinking, I don't know you and I'll probably never see you again in my life. It was weird to imagine there being no possibility, ever, of getting to know even one of those strangers.

The train came in with its heating blasting away. I flopped into a seat and conjured up the clinic. It was a strong bright core inside me, that no one else could see, like the glowing centre of the earth. It was made up of Mr Golding's clever kindly face and the clarity of what we were going to do and the polished table and the sweet blue scent of hyacinths. It was real. It was in the centre of me, Jessie Lamb. The train clacked along effortfully, I could practically feel the weight it was pulling.

In the clinic we had stared at each other in fascination before Mr Golding came in. It was like we were looking at ourselves; looking at other girls who were going to do it and thinking, now these are my sisters. There were five of us. I liked the girl opposite, she had little black plaits all over her head and she looked up and smiled when I tried to drag my heavy chair across the carpet to the table. The girl at the end was pretending to read.

I recognised Karen from Dad's lab and thought, surely she's too old for this? There was a bowl of blue hyacinths in the middle of the table, reflected in its polished surface like a mirror. Everything in there was so warm and bright I had to rub my eyes. And then Mr Golding and two nurses came in and he was plump and bald and smiley like Humpty Dumpty. He started talking in his foreign accent calmly and kindly telling us everything we need to know. The clinic would safeguard our privacy and we in turn were asked not to tell anyone about our interest in the programme. The nurse switched on a tape recorder, 'for legal reasons', he told us.

He outlined what happens at implantation. He said in the current situation 'there are few scenarios which allow hope,' and that this was one of them. And he said we are each making this sacrifice not just for one child, but for all that child's descendants—for the children of the future. The girl near the door started to cry and a nurse took her out.

I spread my hands out on the shining table, and I thought, this is real. This is a place where there is the power to make something real happen. Mr Golding gave us a timetable. If we were still interested we should sign up for a medical. If the medical was OK, our Implanon would be removed. After the medical we'd have a counselling session, to help us think about our reasons and feel confident about our decision, whichever way that went. Finally, there'd be an interview, and we'd be accepted or rejected.

He asked if we had any questions but no one did. He smiled a twinkly smile and I noticed his bow tie was patterned with blue and green overlapping fish. On anyone else it would be ridiculous, but it was exactly right on him. He has a quick, searching way of looking into each person's face and making you feel as if you have known him for ages. 'One thing must be crystal clear from the start, ladies. No one has to do this. You understand? All are free to walk away at

any time; today, next week, the day before implantation—' he spread his arms wide '—is not a problem.
You change your mind, I am happy. You are young.
The immune system is stronger in the young. So we
are looking to the 16 year olds. In some countries,
they are going younger still.' He looked at us, then
took off his bright round glasses and rubbed his eyes.
'You are young ladies of great courage. The law says
you are old enough to have a child. But do not forget
that in your parents' eyes *you* are still the child. I ask
you to discuss this with the parents, listen to their
advice. And now I hand you over to my kind Nurse
Garner.' He gave another of his quick, grave little bows
and went to the door. Nurse Garner smiled at him and
brought her pad to the front of the room; we could
sign for the medical if we still thought we might want
to volunteer. So I did.

The train whirred madly as if its wheels couldn't
engage, then began to pick up proper speed at last. I
checked my phone. Nothing. I wondered if Mum would
ask where I'd been, and what I would tell her. I had
the idea of sending Dad an email telling him I'd got
important news, and asking him to come home to hear
it. I'd tell the pair of them together. How proud he
would be!

Oh yes, I remember that, I remember feeling happy
at the thought of his coming home. How stupid can a
person be?

Sixteen

At home Mum was lying in wait for me and asked if I'd heard from him, so she obviously hadn't. Her face was grey and her eyes were red and I suddenly felt terribly sorry for her. She wanted to know if I'd tried to contact him and when I said yes, her eyes filled with tears. 'I thought it was just me. If he's not replying to you either—maybe I should call the police.' I was positive he would reply to my email. I was full of hope but of course I couldn't tell her why. I suggested waiting one more day before calling the police. As I heard myself calmly saying it and watched Mum twist her face into a pale attempt at a smile, I realised the balance had changed. Like a see saw, when you are the heavier person, and normally go down, down, down, bumping your bum on the ground. Now I was rising up, up, up. *I* was reassuring *her*. A breathless kind of happiness swooped into me, lifting me like a bird. I *knew* I was doing the right thing.

I emailed him 'Hi Dad, I know you and Mum have fallen out but I have some really important news. I need to tell you NOW! Please e me straight back, when and where we can meet. Miss you! Xoxo Jess.' I put 'life and death, honestly' after 'news', then deleted it again. I wouldn't tell him how sad and angry and worried I'd felt, and in return he wouldn't be mad at me for not telling him what Mum had been up to. The deal was perfectly clear in my head.

After tea Mum went to visit Mand. I wasn't going to check my email till the morning. He would reply, I knew he would. I turned on the TV. There was a supposedly healthy pregnant woman in Ethiopia who people had started worshipping. They showed the crowd in the lane outside her hut, with the oranges and sweet potatoes they were bringing her. A little boy answered and gravely accepted the gifts, then the door was firmly shut behind him. The people in the lane knelt down and prayed. They announced that eleven UK volunteers out of thirty who'd been in an MDS research drugs trial had died after an unforeseen complication. Police had stopped a public screening of the FLAME MDS film after fighting broke out between the audience and *Mothers for Life* who were demonstrating against it. I switched the TV off. I could feel the ghost of that angry powerlessness boiling up, then I remembered and laughed with relief. I was doing something, and there was no need to concern myself with all this—idiocy. The pressure in my head whooshed out like steam jetting out the spout of a boiling kettle.

I sat there, staring at the blank screen, hugging the beautiful sharp knife of my secret to me. I was glad I would die because it was the only perfect solution to all this mess and suffering. To imagine it was a soft green garden in the desert; a place of cool and shade.

My phone jangled into the silence—Sal. She had an announcement to make. She wanted to tell me she and her mum had been discussing something and they had finally decided. They were moving house.

'Why? Where are you going?'

'We're moving to Glossop, there's two spare rooms in the FLAME house.'

'But Sal—how will I see you? Glossop's miles away!'

'We can get buses. We can meet in Ashton.'

How long would it take them to sell up and move? I realised maybe it wouldn't matter, maybe I'd be gone before they went. 'Shall I come round?'

'Yup.'

I was longing to tell her. Mr Golding said not to tell anyone about our interest in the programme, but this was Sal. It felt almost like a present I could give her—a sweet slice of calm, a promise of peace. For a crazy moment I imagined that when I told her, she'd say 'Fantastic! I'll volunteer too, we'll do it together!' I knew it would make her feel better from the fury that was eating her.

When I saw her it wasn't so easy. She was tight and sharp, thin as a stick and dressed in black. Her house felt cold and I was shocked when we went up to her room, to see empty shelves, and boxes stacked against the wall. 'When are you going?'

'Soon. This week. When Mum can borrow a van.' She cleared stuff off her bed so we could sit. 'Mum says it'll be cheaper sharing bills with other people.'

'Right.' I hated the idea of not being able to just trot down the road to hers. I started idly picking up some of the things in the box by her bed. There were toys she'd had when she was little. She gave me her clockwork nun to remember her room by. 'You moving everything? Is your mum selling the house?'

'The building society'll take it back.'

'Why can't she sell it?'

'Doh, have you seen how many houses there are for sale?'

I knew, of course I knew. There were boarded-up houses everywhere. But I asked, 'Why are so many for sale?'

'All the dead women.'

'But their husbands and kids still need houses.'

'You don't think any single mothers died? You think young kids can stay home alone?'

Sal's mum was a single mother, but Sal never used to be so spiky about it. 'Sorry.' Dead single mothers wouldn't account for that many empty houses anyway. Perhaps people moving were like Sal and her mum, moving in with other people to save money and to band together. Fearing the worst. Once they knew there was hope again, it would be different. I couldn't stop myself. 'Sal, have you heard of the frozen embryos?'

'The old ones? From before?"

'Yeah. They might be able to vaccinate them against MDS.'

'They can vaccinate till they're blue in the face, they're still going to have to find a new way to incubate them.'

'What d'you mean?'

'They're not going to be using those poor little Sleeping Beauties any more.'

'Why?'

She glared at me as if I was an idiot. 'Because FLAME are going to stop them.'

'They are?'

'They're going to make sure no more girls get brainwashed into accepting torture and death. There's going to be a campaign targeting teenage girls, telling them how they get turned into zombies like the waking dead.'

I dug into the box and brought out some lego. A random clump of blue and red pieces were snapped onto a green base. I pulled them apart and started making them into steps, one on top of the other, overlapping. 'Don't you think some of them are actually doing it because they want to?'

'No,' she said. 'Sleeping Beauties are like any other suicide. It's a cry for help.'

'I think someone could be quite sane and decide it was worth doing.'

'Why should women go on and on making sacrifices? The only way this will ever be sorted is when women refuse point blank to be victims.'

'You really think that?' The steps weren't going anywhere. I dropped them back in the box.

'If someone says, Oh my life isn't very important, I'll sacrifice it so you can have a child, what's a man going to say? *No thanks*? Each girl who agrees to be a Sleeping Beauty is making it that much worse for the rest of us.'

'What will FLAME do when they've stopped them, all the Sleeping Beauty volunteers?'

'*We* won't do anything. We'll sit back and tell the men it's their turn to do something. Let them volunteer for something dangerous.' I thought of the drugs trial volunteers, they were nearly all men. But it was becoming a pointless conversation.

'Will you still come to college when you live in Glossop?'

'My mum wants me to. She knows someone who can give me a lift. But I'll see.' Everything Sal said felt like needles. I asked her about her little cousin but he still hadn't been traced. I said I had to go. 'You should come to Glossop. Come to FLAME. You could help with getting the message across to girls at college, the crazies who might try and volunteer.'

I told her I'd think about it. As we went downstairs she said, 'It's not the same here any more.' The sitting room door was wide open and we both glanced in. It was clean and tidy, but I could remember how it had been that night, the take-away trays and cans and bottles, the smell. 'I have nightmares,' she said. 'Maybe they'll stop in a different house.'

'Oh Sal—' At the bottom of the stairs we hugged each other and my eyes filled with tears. I wanted to say something to make her feel better and the one thing I could think of was the thing she despised. I was useless. All there was in my brain was 'please let it end, please let it end soon.' Like a calf crammed into a cattletruck, on its way to the abattoir.

I crept down to check my email at six before Mum got up. Dad hadn't replied but I knew he would. I was giving him till tea time. I had breakfast with Mum and she told me Mand was loads better, that the carer Paul seemed to have worked a miracle. After she'd left for work I got ready for college. I was feeling as if I would burst if I didn't tell someone, but I wasn't going to tell Mum without Dad. Sal was impossible; Baz was wrapped up in his parents' troubles and Nat's stupid plans; and Dad—why didn't he reply? What if he never came back? What if we actually did have to call the police this evening? I reminded myself what I was going to do. Panic and relief, panic and relief, the two switched through me like an electric current being turned on and off.

Outside there was freezing fog, tasting of stale ice cubes in my mouth. Everything was dulled and quiet. I didn't feel like going to college. There had to be someone I could talk to, even if I didn't tell them my secret, there had to be someone I could just burble at.

I thought of Mandy. At least she was always happy to see me. And she knew about Mum's affair; I could ask her advice about Dad. I walked past the bus stop and on down to the main road, where one after another blue flashing ambulances loomed out of the fog, their sirens suddenly loud then gone. What if Dad was in one of them? I caught the bus to Mandy's.

When I got close enough to see, her curtains were still drawn although it was after nine. If she was so much better, surely she wouldn't be lounging about in bed? For a moment I thought I shouldn't have come. But I told myself not to be silly, and marched up and rang her bell. She must have been waiting in the hall with her hand on the doorknob, because she opened the door in an instant. Her hair was glossy black and she was wearing the heavy eye make-up I used to love on her when I was little—smoky kohl circles around her eyes and loads of mascara. She seemed pretty surprised to see me, though, and peered into the thick whiteness behind me. 'I've come on my own,' I told her, 'Mum's at work.'

She stood on the doorstep holding the door open for me so I went up the stairs. I could smell incense sticks burning. The place was lovely and tidy. There were candles lit in the sitting room, and soft tinkly sitar music playing. The turquoise walls seemed to glow. I wondered if she'd been meditating. Yoga was one of her few fads Mum never complained about. She followed me up into the flat.

'Are you going out?' I asked. 'You look fantastic!'

'What's the time?'

'Half nine.'

'Well, I've got a little while. D'you want a drink?'

We went into the kitchen and she made tea. 'So what brings you here at this time of a Thursday morning? Shouldn't you be at college?'

'Hasn't Mum told you?'

'Told me what?'

'About Dad.'

She shook her head. Mum had been to see her the previous evening! I explained about the row and Dad storming out.

'Oh Jess, I'm sorry—' She came and put her arms around me and I couldn't help it; suddenly I burst into tears. She was so kind, that was what made me cry. 'It'll be alright,' she said. 'It'll all come out in the wash.'

I told her Dad hadn't come back and neither of us had heard from him.

'He'll be back. Give him time to lick his wounds. He's responsible, Jess, he's not going anywhere.'

'But I don't know what's going to happen!'

She laughed at me, but kindly. 'Look, Cath and Joe have been here before. I remember when she found out *he'd* been seeing someone—No Jess, don't look like that—a long time ago. They have these great traumas then they kiss and make up. Everything'll be back to normal within a month.'

'Why do they stay married if they're going to be like this?'

'They've been together for seventeen years, d'you think they're going to leave each other now?'

'I wish they *would* split up. It would be more honest.'

'No you don't. If they split up you'd have to start living in two places, it would be terribly inconvenient. You need to get them into proportion. They're only your parents!'

It was hard not to take them seriously with my silent phone burning a hole in my pocket. 'It feels like Dad's mad at me. I think he thinks I knew—' I looked at her but she didn't say anything. 'You knew, didn't you?'

'Jess, this is about Cath and Joe. It's no one else's responsibility, and no one else needs to feel guilty.'

I blew my nose and unpeeled the apricot chewy bar she'd given me. She always remembered my favourite. Time to stop being childish; she was right. They were only my parents, and just because they'd made a hash of everything it didn't mean I had to be part of the mix.

'You think I should just ignore them?'

'Of course. Think of them as squabbling kids—they'll get over it. And haven't you got something much more important to think about?'

I bit my tongue mid-chew. How did she know? I tasted blood. When I could, I nodded.

'Well there you are. Focus on *you*. When you're a teenager your parents should be the chorus—around, in support, but not centre stage—not hogging the limelight. That's for you!'

She knew. It must be because of wanting so much to have a baby herself. We sat and grinned at each other, then Mand glanced at her watch. 'Jess, you'll have to go, I've got to get ready.'

'Who's the big date?' I asked.

'Oh it's not a person—what gave you that idea? It's a meeting, I have to go to a meeting.' She led the way out of the kitchen. It was always horrid leaving the bright colours of her flat and going down into the dinginess of the hall. The downstairs tenants had brown doors, painted in streaky paint to look like wood.

'What's it about?'

'Look Jess I'll tell you later, OK?' She was already opening the door. 'You'll be the first to know. But don't tell Cath you've seen me today, please.'

'I won't. And don't you tell her—you know.'

Mand nodded. She pecked me on both cheeks and quickly closed the door after me as if she was afraid something in the street might try to dash in.

As I walked away an approaching shape became a man who said 'hello' and I realised it was Paul, the nurse Mum had organised to look after Mandy. His hair was wet and combed back, he must've just washed it, he looked a bit like a friendly seal. She's going to be cross, I thought. Another interruption! I turned round to see if she would answer the door. He went towards the entrance then the building seemed to swallow him; in the fog, everything merged. I heard Mandy's door shut with a muffled bang. Maybe he was taking her to the meeting.

As I walked along I couldn't stop smiling to myself. I felt as if she'd given me her blessing. She understood. She must know I was doing it for her as well. She recognised that that was more important than any of Mum and Dad's nonsense. She was happy for me! I could see the white disc of the sun now, peering through the foggy air. Mand was the first person and the best to know my secret.

Seventeen

On the slowly crawling bus I checked my mobile. Not just one text but two! But the first was O2 telling me about my rewards and the second was Baz. I reminded myself that Dad would certainly reply by email. Baz wanted to know where I was, and when I told him, asked me to get off near his road and he'd meet me. So I did, and soon enough his blurry outline became visible, and he materialised in front of me.

'They're OK! No one's hurt!'

'What are you on about?'

'Nat and the others. They were all out.'

Apparently it had been on the news; two houses in Chester had exploded, and been reduced to rubble. They were where Nat and his ALF mates were staying. We headed for Baz's as he explained it all to me. They'd been working with explosives.

'Why?' I asked, and Baz looked at me pityingly.

'Why d'you think?'

'Bombs?'

'How else are they going to get anyone to pay attention?'

I knew they were serious, but—bombs! Baz told me something was unstable because it went off unexpectedly and it was pure luck no one was in. He had been petrified when he heard the news.

'I wouldn't even have known it was their house,' I pointed out. 'Do the police know it was them?'

'The house was rented under false names. So provided everything was destroyed in the blast—' He let us into his house, it smelled of bleach.

'Is your dad still at hospital?'

'That's the good news. They've moved him to some sort of residential place for nutters, and they're going to keep him there long-term.'

'Is your mum OK with that?'

'Ish. She knows it'd be awful if he came home. She's doing a lot of cleaning. But she's going back to work next week, thank God.'

We went downstairs to Baz's room and he sat at the piano and played a happy triumphant little series of trills. I took off my coat and sat on the bed. 'So what will you do now?' I asked.

'What I planned. Go down and help Nat. He rang to say they were OK, but they need help more than ever now. They've got to move fast in case the police trace them. They're posting their film up on the net.'

'Film of the animals?'

'Yup. He reckons there'll be a big fuss. They're planning simultaneous demonstrations, and they need help with the internet stuff. I said I'd go tomorrow.'

'Wow. Tomorrow.'

'Yup.'

'So—goodbye.'

'Only for a bit. Jessie?' He was staring intently at the piano keys.

I waited, then I said, 'What?'

The silence was long. My heart turned into a feather and floated up though my hollow chest, almost to my throat. 'D'you think . . . ?' His eye-beams were practically boring a hole in the keys.

'Yes?'

'D'you think—you know?'

I couldn't help it, I started to laugh, and after a moment he laughed too. 'I thought you didn't like me,' I said.

'You liked everybody *but* me.'

'What d'you mean?'

'Snogging Danny. Then you kept walking home with Nat, everyone could see how much you fancied him. Then *Iain*—'

'I *don't* like Iain. Not like that. He did kiss me once but it was horrible, I didn't want him to.'

Baz looked at me like he was gathering a reply, but I couldn't wait.

'I never liked Danny either, I just snogged him when I was drunk that night. I *wanted*—'

'Yes?'

'I came down to your room. But you just played the piano and ignored me.'

'What did you expect me to do? I'd just seen you with Danny.'

'I liked Nat but not—nothing ever happened with Nat.'

'All the girls like Nat.'

'You act as if *I'm* the one who's been difficult, but what about you?'

'Me? What about me?'

'You invited Rosa Davis to that party.'

'Why not?'

'And she was helping you clear up, in the morning.'

'So?'

'Where did she go to, after that?'

'How should I know? She has her own reasons for what she does.'

I knew he didn't really like her. She went with loads of lads. There was a rumour she was on drugs. 'Well . . .' I could feel a red hot blush spreading over my face like a spilt pot of paint. 'Do you . . . ?'

'Yes,' he said. We sat there looking at each other in the most paralysing awkwardness.

'OK,' I said eventually. 'Glad we've got that sorted.' It was pure nervousness, I began to laugh again, and we sat laughing at each other like a pair of loons. Then he got up from the piano and came over to me. He sat beside me on the bed, not very close, and picked up my left hand with his right. We both stared at our hands as the fingers slowly folded and intertwined, like creatures that didn't belong to us. Then awkwardly, bumping noses, we kissed. Gradually there was a change of speed. We fell back on the bed and our hands started going everywhere. We were both so hot and firm and close and smooth under our clothes that I could hardly bear it, I wanted to do everything at once, my whole body felt alight and alive. Suddenly Baz froze.

'What is it?' I whispered.

'My mum's just come in. I heard the door.' We rolled apart and pulled our things straight.

'Will she come down?' I asked.

'No, but—'

I knew what he meant. We made ourselves decent and slowly climbed the stairs. Baz went into the kitchen to find her. I waited in the living room, and after a minute he reappeared shaking his head. 'She's been to see Dad and she's upset.'

'Should I go?'

He pulled a face but nodded. 'I'll call for you later on.'

I let myself out. The fog had cleared, the sun was bright. I floated home as light and happy as a bird. And as soon as I got in I checked my email. There it was: a message from Dad. 'Hi Jessie I'll be back tomorrow to hear all the news. Lots of love, your runaway Dad. Xxx' *Yes*! I did a couple of twirls then texted Mum to let her know. He was OK, he was coming back, he wasn't mad at me. Everything was working out perfectly.

Baz called for me after tea and we walked down to the old rec. It was clear and our breath puffed out of our mouths like smoke in the dark air. We sat side by side on the swings. Even with gloves on it was too cold to hold onto the chains, and I swung gently with my hands in my pockets. We talked about our parents and I told him what had happened with Dad. We tried to imagine what our lives could have been like if there was no MDS. Baz would have gone to Austria on his piano scholarship, he would have become a concert pianist, travelling round the world to all the great concert halls. Maybe he still will. But I—I didn't know what I would have done, I couldn't imagine it at all. And that brought back to me what I was going to do. My warm dark secret, my destiny. I thought about telling him, though I knew I shouldn't. But there would be nothing wrong in talking about it in theory. I asked if he knew about the plan to vaccinate stored embryos, but he didn't, so I started to explain it to him.

'Sounds like a science fiction nightmare,' he said.

'It's not. Well, it is for one generation, but once the first set of children are born, women can go back to having babies naturally.'

'Freezers full of embryos, like frozen peas? Then they're going to vaccinate them—how do they know what effect that will have, on tiny unborn children? Then they're going to put them inside women who'll get diseased and die, and grow them there like—like parasites. Then they'll cut them out? Can you imagine how many things could go wrong! Why can't they just stop mucking about with life?'

'Baz, listen, real children will come out of it. They'll be normal, like us—like we used to be. And they can forget about all this horrible stuff, they can just lead normal lives and fall in love and have babies together.'

'The usual scientists' lie. *Just let us do whatever mad thing we think of next, because it's progress.* Is this better than in our grandparents' day?'

'This is science which can rescue us from extinction.'

'Right. I can guess who told you that.'

'People will change the way they live if they can see there's hope. It's like everyone's being given a second chance.'

He laughed and jumped off his swing. 'You are such an optimist! Come on. She'll have gone out to the hospital again by now.' He stood in front of me and caught my swing as I came towards him. We kissed, and his lips and mouth were hot as cocoa. It didn't surprise me then that he was against the idea; after all, I had been against it myself, to begin with. I knew I'd be able to talk him round.

We hurried to his house and went straight down to his room. As soon as we were there we fell onto the bed. There were so many clothes to pull off! And the more we took off the hotter we got. 'Have you done it before?' he whispered, and I said, 'No, have you?'

'Sort of.'

For a moment I wanted to ask him who, then it passed and we were just two hot slippery sweaty creatures intertwining until it was almost unbearably sweet and then he whispered 'Can I come in?' He pushed against me and suddenly I was afraid. It was pushing against me, hurting, and I wondered if he was doing the right thing. I froze, and asked him to stop. He pressed his face into my shoulder and we lay still as fallen logs. I could feel his heart pounding against my chest. 'Baz?' I said. 'Baz?'

After a moment he said, 'It's OK. It's because you're a virgin. Do you want me to use my fingers?'

I wanted it to be like it was before. Now it felt like an operation or something, all the lovely feelings had gone. I wanted it to be proper, like what Sal had told me, with both of us moaning in ecstasy. 'No,' I whispered, 'no.'

'I'm going to try again. I'll stop if it hurts you. Oh,

Jessie—' and he kissed me and stroked me, his breath coming in quick panting gasps which somehow transferred themselves to me so that my breaths started racing too and rays of heat were darting up from my vagina, then he was butting his head against my shoulder like a baby lamb trying to get at its mother's teat. His head was butting and he was pushing into me and it was sore and hot and fiery as if we were going into meltdown and then he gave a sudden sharper jab and I could feel him sliding properly in like a fish slipping into water and he cried 'Aah!' and his head came to stillness on my shoulder. It was as if I'd been stabbed with a knife, I wanted him to take it out of me. But at the same time I was desperately wanting him to carry on; the deep swimmy wetness almost made me swoon. He lifted his head.

'Are you alright?'

'Yes. Yes.'

He reached down with his fingers and then brought them up to show me. Blood.

'I didn't hurt you?'

'Not much. I feel—I feel . . .' We lay quietly for a while.

He began to kiss me again. And to move as slowly and gently as a little pink earthworm when you pick it up from the garden in the palm of your hand. And the sweetness came back, sore and sweet, sweet and sore, climbing and climbing till I could hardly get my breath and we were rocking together in the most perfect fit, and then clutched in a spasm of pleasure.

Afterwards we lay sprawled on the bed with just our fingertips touching—too hot for anything else. I was glad but I think I was in shock. Every part of me was tender. Then I remembered that Baz was going away, to help Nat and the ALFs, and I thought I couldn't bear it. I couldn't bear to be left on my own, I was so sensitised I needed him to keep his arms around me at all times. It was like I had been peeled. When he asked, 'What is it?' I told him, and he hugged me and said he'd be back soon. But I couldn't help it, and I cried. 'Stop it,' Baz whispered, 'stop it, stop it,' and he licked the tears off my face like a dog until I couldn't help laughing, and he called me an idiot. We talked about him going to help Nat and he promised not to do anything dangerous. 'But don't try and phone or text me—we'll have to stay out of contact for a few days, Jess; so the police can't trace us.' It was fine, everything was fine. Part of me wanted him to stop talking and just start kissing me again, my blood was fizzy and it made my whole body tingle. But another part of me wanted to have my clothes on and be outside in the cold night walking home, breathing the dark air and letting the thinking bits of me catch up with the feeling bits. We heard noises upstairs so it was definitely time for me to go; Baz said he'd walk me.

We went upstairs to find his mother vacuuming the curtains. She turned the vacuum off for a minute to hear where he was going and to say goodnight to me, then carried on with her task. As we walked back to my house with our arms wrapped round each other I felt terribly sorry for her. The sky was full of stars. We stood for a while in the shadow of a fir which blocked the streetlamp, and looked for the constellations either of us could name. Then we walked back to my house holding hands and not talking, feeling as if we owned the night and everything in it: moon, stars, the dark shapes of trees, the crouching quiet houses. We knew we would never be stupid in the ways our parents were stupid.

Eighteen

It was the sound of the car in the drive that woke me. Dad was back! I pulled on my dressing gown and ran downstairs to meet him. His big grey coat, his purple scarf, his monkey face and grey floppy hair all seemed brighter than usual, larger than life, more vivid than I had remembered. He gave me a big big hug.

'Where were you? Didn't you get my texts? What's happened to your phone?' I heard Mum come downstairs behind me.

'Hello Joe,' she said.

'We need to talk,' he replied quietly.

Mum nodded. 'I'll make some tea.'

'I wanted time to think,' he said to me. 'That's all. I just needed some time on my own, to think things through.'

'But you could have texted!'

'No, it was better to keep it switched off.'

'But Dad we were worried, we didn't know where you were—'

'Well I'm home now. Listen Jess, your mother and I need to talk. Give us some peace, alright? There are things we need to sort out.' He followed Mum into the kitchen and shut the door.

I went slowly backup to my room. I had news to tell him, had he forgotten? I sat on my floor and listened to the ups and downs of their voices, they were both keeping them low, a running murmur. What were they sorting out? How to get divorced? How to divide up the house and the car and the furniture and knives and forks, how to divide me?

Mandy was right. I should ignore them. They caused all this distress and disruption because of their argument, so that I had to lie awake night after night worrying, and now they didn't even apologise! For all they cared, I was perfectly irrelevant. I imagined marching downstairs and telling them, 'OK, put your big splitting-up drama on hold and listen to me for one moment. I've been to see Mr Golding, and this is what I've decided to do . . .' I would tell them, and they would both stand staring at me, then I'd say, 'OK. Now you can go back to your self-obsessing.'

But really, there was no point in telling them. If they hadn't got time for me, then I hadn't got time for them. It was none of their business anyway.

I remembered Baz, and heat crept into me. I could feel my nipples tight against my T-shirt. I squeezed my hands against them. The feeling was so—so—oh, I don't know, I can't describe it, for a moment I was petrified. I thought, if I could do that every day of my life I wouldn't even care about anything else. Not the planet, not the future, nothing. I'd be like Sal was with Damien at the start—just a one-track mind. If Baz really liked me surely he wouldn't go away, how could he? Even for a week? Nobody had told me. Nobody had warned me I would feel so—so—like this. Like a sex maniac.

I wedged my chair against the door and rolled back on my bed and touched myself. But it wasn't the same. I wanted him. Then the soreness reminded me and gave me that shocked feeling inside again. I was dripping wet. I couldn't stop, I made myself come. After, I felt disgusted. Sex wasn't important. Relationships weren't important. What was important was what I had decided to do.

I went into the bathroom and had a long wasteful shower. When I looked at myself in the steamy mirror afterwards, I looked just the same. Nobody would have known what I had done. I was going to stick to my plan, I wasn't going to let the thing with Baz distract me from it. Any more than he was letting the thing with me distract *him* from his plans. He'd gone to Chester hadn't he. Who knew when I'd see him again? I wondered again who else he had done it with. I didn't care as long as it wasn't Rosa.

I was drying my hair when I realised my phone was ringing—I switched off the dryer and grabbed it. Unknown caller. It was Nurse Garner from the clinic. 'Jessie Lamb?' she said. 'You came to the meeting for volunteers.'

'Yes.'

'Sorry it's such short notice, but if you're free Dr Nichol can do medicals today.'

'Today? What time?'

'Twelve o'clock?'

'Fine.' Good. I didn't have to sit there waiting for Dad to have time to talk to me. I dressed and got myself out of the house so quietly the murmuring voices in the kitchen never even paused. Let *them* wonder where *I* was, if they ever had time to notice!

All the way on the bus to the clinic I could feel a pulse beating inside me, deep between my legs. I hoped the medical wouldn't examine me down there. That would be truly embarrassing.

Dr Nichol is a small woman with silvery hair and a dark, quiet face. Dark eyes, black eyebrows, something watchful and far back in the way she looks at you. She has a low clear voice. 'Well Jessie,' she said, 'how're you feeling?' She's the kind of person you want to speak honestly to, because you know she's listening with every scrap of her attention. After she'd taken some samples and done my blood pressure and listened to my heart, she asked about my periods and warned me that she'd need to remove my Implanon next time she saw me, if everything went according to plan. She didn't make me undress or examine me there at all, thank goodness. Soon I wouldn't have to think about it.

At the end she shook my hand and said 'Well done, you're fighting fit.' She smiled at me kindly. 'But remember, no one will think any the less of you if you don't go through with this.' I wondered how it had been with the other girls, if they were all 'fighting fit'; I wondered if she believed any of us would really do it. I wanted her to believe in me. I didn't want to disappoint her.

When I came out of the medical room there were two other girls waiting. Theresa, the quiet one from the volunteering meeting—and Rosa Davis! She was dressed in goth-type black and skinny as a whippet, but there was no mistaking her sly smiling face. I was gobsmacked. She hadn't been at school since before GCSEs. Obviously she couldn't have been pregnant, because here she was. We said hello in amazement, and Theresa went in for her medical. Rosa seemed really happy I was volunteering. 'How did you hear about it?' I asked her.

'My Mum's a nurse.'

I realised that of course all of us must have some connection to the clinic—how else could we even have heard about the pre-MDS embryos? 'Are you back at your mum's?'

'I'm living with my boyfriend. He's got a really big flat on Deansgate.'

I asked her where she'd been since she left school, and she said loads of places, London, Paris, California. She said she'd been to so many places she'd lost track. As she spoke she kept glancing at me with her eye that meets yours, and the other one that seems to be staring over your head, as if to dare me to say I didn't believe her. Of all the people in the world, she was just about the last one I ever wanted to meet again. She insisted on swapping phone numbers so we could stay in touch through the different stages of volunteering. I told myself it didn't matter, she'd be bound to drop out. As soon as I decently could I told her I had to meet someone, and hurried to the exit.

I had no desire to go home so I decided to visit Lisa. When I got off the bus it had started snowing—big polka dot flakes that were silently pattering a layer of white over everything. It was cold enough for it to lie; the first proper snow of the winter, and it had waited till the beginning of March to fall. By the time I got to the Kids' House my face was wet and numb. No one answered the door but I could hear noise from inside so I let myself in. There was a bunch of lads playing pool in the big room, and rap blasting out of the speakers. It looked better now it was painted white, but there was still something scruffy and echoey about it. I went up and knocked on Lisa's door and she called, 'come in'. Her room was completely different. There was a row of feathery ferns and plants with dark glossy leaves all along the windowsill. In the middle of the room were two old-fashioned armchairs covered with faded Indian bedspreads. Her bed was a mattress on the floor, with a pile of velvety red and purple cushions, and she had a little wooden table and chair in the corner, with her laptop and a glowing lamp. There was a double pile of books against the side of the desk. She'd painted the bare floorboards a dark gloss red. 'Nice skirting boards!' I said, and she laughed.

'Yes, very well painted.'

'You've made it lovely.'

'It's good to have somewhere that no one messes up.' She went to get us a drink and I looked at the titles of the books around her desk, *21st Century Smallholder, How to Grow More Vegetables, The Complete Book of Self-Sufficiency*. I didn't know there was a garden at the Kids' House. She brought us mugs of orange and we sat in the snug armchairs and admired the room. 'My Dad gave me some stuff from home.'

'Was he alright about it?'

'He says we're better off without him. But then he cries so I'll feel guilty.'

I hadn't planned to, but I found myself telling her about wanting to volunteer, and about the medical I'd just been to. There was something lovely about being in that room and talking to her, nestled in those chairs with the lamp reflecting darkly off the shiny floor. It felt almost like we were floating, it reminded me of the feeling I had when I wore that blue dress, of being above the rest of the world, in a calm place where things seemed possible.

But when I finished she said, 'It would be a bit mad, wouldn't it?'

'You think?'

'I think staying alive's a good plan.' She laughed. 'Either they'll find a cure—which seems pretty likely, I mean already they've got a vaccine. Or, if they don't, everyone'll get old and die and everything will fall to bits. If that happens—frankly—who's going to cry about it? I mean, the human race has to end some time.'

'But how will people bear it?'

'Everyone who's alive now will have had as much life as they can. Anyone who's not born doesn't know what they're missing. Maybe something better'll evolve.'

It had been getting darker as we spoke, and the sky behind the plants on the windowsill was nearly black now. 'Our lives won't be worth living if we know there's no future.'

'Why? There's no future for anyone beyond 80 years or so. Everyone dies.'

'But we always know there'll be more people. We know it'll all carry on.'

She shrugged. 'You wouldn't be there to see it either way. So why should you care?'

'But *you* care what happens, you wouldn't have come to YOFI and done all this work on the house if you didn't. Even if Iain hadn't been there—'

'Iain,' she said disgustedly. 'That perv.'

A shiver went through me. 'Why d'you say that?'

'He asked Gabe—who is nine years old—to go to his flat.'

'Why?'

'Some crap about planning and talking in peace. Haven't you noticed? Iain's thing has always been for younger and younger kids to join.'

'D'you really think he is?'

'A paedo? Yes. The whole thing—YOFI—it's a joke.'

'You've got this house because of it!'

'I want to move. We're going to get somewhere in the countryside, where we can grow our own food and be self sufficient and not have anything to do with the outside world.'

'You and Gabe?'

'There are five of us so far.'

'But the whole thing of Kids' Houses—'

She shrugged. 'The idea always was to live separately, and that's what we'll be doing. Getting on with our own lives without expecting anything from *them*.'

'If you opt out, you don't change anything.'

'Why should I run round helping to get power for

a group of idiots who'll end up just as dangerous as
the ones already in power?'

'You really don't think anyone can make things
better?'

'No. What's going to happen will happen.'

'What about people like Nat and the ALF? They're
not trying to get power.'

She laughed. 'No, they're trying to set fire to scientists' cars.'

'Who told you?'

'Nat was here last weekend.'

After the explosion. Nat and Lisa. A few things fell
into place. It was quite interesting, considering how
opposed to each other they'd been.

'At least they're trying to do something.'

'Trying to close an animal research lab. Frankly Jess,
on the grand scale—'

'You can't think on the grand scale. You have to
think on the small scale. Otherwise no one'd ever do
anything.'

'That's what I'm doing. Thinking on the small scale.
Planning the life *we* want to live, instead of joining in
with this whole fucked-up mess.'

I left soon after that. She came downstairs through
the pool room with me and out into the snow. 'Jess—
don't volunteer. Seriously, I wish you wouldn't.' She
gave me a quick strong hug. It made me think of Sal
and I felt sad. I got a bus home, it was too cold and
dark to walk. I was the only passenger. We rode through
empty streets where the snow on the pavements glowed
with a bluish light.

I was relieved when my phone rang, happy that

someone wanted to talk to me. Until I saw that it was Rosa Davis. 'Hiya Jess! Isn't it exciting? Are your mum and dad really proud of you?'

'Well, I haven't told them yet.'

'My mum's thrilled. She's told all her friends and they keep sending me presents, flowers and chocolate and stuff. They think I'm so brave—it's embarrassing!' She giggled her fake giggle.

'Does your boyfriend know?'

'Yes, he's heartbroken. He says he's going to put a red rose on my grave every day for as long as he lives. Are you still friends with Baz?'

I told her someone was calling me and I had to go. I did not want to discuss Baz with her. Baz was none of her business. I couldn't believe they would let her volunteer; as soon as she talked to a counsellor they would realise she was a nutter.

I should have told Mum and Dad that evening. They were both there—Dad cooked tea—and although it felt pretty strained, they were speaking to each other. There was no great announcement about splitting up so all I could assume was Mandy was right and they would get over themselves. But when Dad said, 'So Jessie, what's this great piece of news you have for us? YOFI ready to assume world command?' I simply couldn't bear to speak. I mumbled something about telling them tomorrow, and slipped off to my room.

Nineteen

I should have taken the opportunity when it was offered. Because it certainly didn't get any easier. I promised myself I'd do in on Monday evening. Then Mum came in quite late (she'd been to visit Mand) and started pouring something out to Dad, I could hear them from my room. I was half afraid the whole thing was flaring up again. When their voices finally quietened I went down to the kitchen. Dad was loading the dishwasher and Mum sat at the table stabbing out a fag as I walked in. I pretended not to notice. 'I've come to tell you my news,' I said. 'I've decided to volunteer.'

'Hi Jess,' said Dad. 'Can you finish up this fruit salad?'

'To be one of those surrogate mothers.'

Mum stared at me blankly.

'You know, the ones who'll have MDS-free babies.'

Dad grinned at me. 'You still thinking about your seahorses?'

'No. I'm thinking about me.'

'I should go back,' Mum said to Dad, and he glanced at his watch.

'D'you want me to take you?'

'I'll get my stuff together.' But she didn't move.

'Listen,' I said, 'I'm trying to tell you something. I've been to the clinic to volunteer.'

'Which clinic?' said Dad.

'Yours. To Mr Golding.'

'What are you on about?'

'To be a Sleeping Beauty, for one of the frozen embryos.'

'Joe? What is this?' asked Mum.

'I've no idea. Jessie?'

'I keep telling you. I'm volunteering to be a surrogate mother.'

'Oh Jess. Look sweetheart, it's a noble idea, but now isn't the moment.'

'I've done it. I've put my name down.'

'Jessie,' he put on his warning voice. 'Enough. Look—your mum's had some bad news, this isn't the time for this kind of discussion.'

'I thought we agreed—' Mum said to him.

'It's not fair,' he said. 'She ought to know. Listen Jess, Mandy—Mandy's been trying to get pregnant.'

I started to ask but he gestured to my mum. 'Tell her, Cath.'

'It's Paul,' she said. 'The carer. Mandy decided it was a good idea to take out her Implanon and get herself pregnant. She thought—she thought they'd let her have a baby. At her age.'

I had a sudden vision of Paul with his sleek smiling

face in the fog. Of him disappearing into Mandy's building. 'She had sex with him?' I asked, and Mum burst into a laugh that was more like a sob.

'Yes love. It's how babies used to be conceived.'

'*Is* she pregnant?'

'We don't know,' said Dad. 'We can get a pregnancy test done tomorrow.'

'But it won't necessarily show yet,' my mother pointed out. 'Even if it's negative, we'll have to test again in a couple of weeks to be sure.'

'Will she get MDS?'

They looked at each other. 'Well Jess,' my dad said gently, 'what do you think?'

'Yes.'

'With any luck she won't be pregnant. But if she is, then yes.' He came over and hugged me, and kissed the top of my head.

Mum reached in her pocket and pulled out another fag. Dad and I watched as she concentrated on lighting it. I thought about Mandy—happy, pretty, together, with her smoky eyes and glossy hair, waiting for Paul to come and see her. She was doing what she wanted, why was it wrong? But it was so contradictory. If she died, for no reason—then everything would be wrong.

From then on, everything *was* wrong.

Mum did a pregnancy test for Mand, which turned out to be negative, and took her to have a new Implanon. Mand had cut the old one out with a razor, Dad told me. He said Mand was very angry with Mum for getting rid of Paul. They were trying to make sure someone was with her 24/7 because they didn't trust her. As he said to me, it was hardly a long-term solution.

I realised neither of them had remotely taken in what I'd told them. At night I heard Mum sobbing in their bedroom, and I knew it would be impossible to talk about it now. Even though what I was doing was volunteering to produce a child, and what Mandy was doing was simply suicide, I could see it might be difficult for Mum to grasp the difference. She'd never liked the idea of girls volunteering anyway—she wasn't like Dad.

I got a text from the clinic with my counselling appointment, and went along to it as if I was going to an exam, afraid I might give the wrong answer. The counsellor's room was on the top floor of the clinic; a quiet, carpeted, secret-feeling place with corridors of closed doors. I had never been up there before. Below was the hospital part, with the wards—and on the basement floor below that were the labs where Dad worked.

The counsellor was about 30, I guess. She was very grave, with a flat unemphatic way of talking, as if everything was of equal, measured importance. It began easily, because she was asking if anyone had influenced or pressurised me in any way and of course the answer was no. But then she started on Why? *Why* did I want to do this? And when I gave my reasons she kept on asking, 'but why?' Why did I want to help humanity survive? Why did I want people to be able to breed naturally again? I felt embarrassed, repeating the obvious things, and she still kept patiently repeating, 'Yes but why?' I wondered if I was supposed to boast about how heroic and self-sacrificing I was, but I knew that couldn't be what she wanted. 'Tell me about your friends,' she said patiently. 'What's different in your life, that makes you the one to volunteer?' So I told her about Sal and how she came to join FLAME; about Lisa, whose mother had died, telling me it was a good idea to stay alive.

'You're saying they've both had difficult things to reckon with in their lives,' said the counsellor. 'D'you think you haven't?'

'Not really.'

'And d'you think that's part of it? That volunteering makes you more like them, evens things up?'

'No. It's like a pressure that builds—men crying in the street, my aunt Mandy cracking up, the way there are always sirens and bad things on the news . . . I can feel it all—filling me up.' I stopped myself. If you said the wrong thing, they might reject you.

But she gestured for me to continue. 'Look—what you say to me is confidential. My job is to help you think it through.'

'Sometimes I feel like my brain will explode and I want to bash a nail into my head to let some of it out—'

'To get relief,' she said quietly.

'Yes. Because my heart's pounding like mad. And when I remember I'm volunteering and imagine the injection, and everything draining away from me—it makes me feel peaceful.'

'Isn't there anything else you can do?'

'Like what?'

'Well you could work with some of the distressed

people you mention—you could train to be a therapist, for example, and work with childless women like your aunt—'

'But how can anyone help them? No one can give them what they want.'

'Help can be as small as taking someone to the park to look at the flowers. Distracting them.'

'But I can't bear it! I can't bear it to be *small*, and *slow*, and pointless. I have to do something that will make a *real* difference—'

'Have you ever hurt yourself deliberately? Have you ever self-harmed?'

'No, of course not.'

'But you understand why people do?'

This wasn't like that. Not remotely.

'It's all right,' she said gently. 'I'm not here to judge you.'

'Look I'm not trying to make myself feel better,' I explained. 'I just—I want it to stop being like this.'

She nodded.

'I want it to stop.'

There was a longish silence then she asked about my parents. Which was a relief; rattling off their sorry story was easy and I hope made me sound more sensible and objective. At the end she gave me a card with her number and told me we could talk again any time I wanted. I felt awkward leaving; I couldn't see that we'd got anywhere. I'd said some stupid things.

'You don't think I'm mad do you?'

She smiled. 'I don't believe in madness.' We shook hands and said goodbye.

*

179

Walking down the corridor I wished I'd told her that *everything* people do is pointless—none of it fixes anything, and their lives just go on more and more disastrously. The only solution is a new beginning. And the only relief is in doing something to make that happen. That's not mad. It is completely sane. It's everyone else who's just pottering along in the same old way, who's mad.

I needed the toilet so I automatically headed down to the basement. I didn't even think—but there, as I was coming out of the *Ladies*, was Dad, making for his lab.

'Jessie, what're you doing here?'

'I've been to my counselling.'

He stared at me. 'You'd better come down to the lab.' I told myself it was for the best, because he had to know I meant it sooner or later. There was no one else in the lab and he boiled the kettle and made us both a coffee, while I peered down the big microscope.

'Can I switch it on?' He turned it on for me and the light came on, and I pulled out a hair and put it under the lens. I tried to adjust the focus, like he's shown me to before, but it was way too high and I couldn't even see the edge of the hair, just great big blobby shapes that could've been anything. He didn't offer to help me. 'Here,' he said, and put the coffee on the bench. 'Who did you see?'

'She was young, dark brown hair. Serious.'

'Susie Kenyon. Have you really volunteered?'

'Why else do you think I've been for my medical and for counselling?'

'But—'

'But what?'

'I don't understand. What happened while I was away?'

'What d'you mean?'

'Did something happen? To make you think of this? Has somebody been talking to you?'

'No.'

'But I don't understand *why*?'

Again! Over and over again! 'To help end MDS.'

'Look,' he said. 'There's plenty of other people in the world taking care of that. Scientists. People whose job it is.'

'But nobody's got an answer, have they?'

'It's only a matter of time.'

'Dad *you* said girls need to volunteer, and be honoured for that.'

'Jesseroon, I didn't mean you! Look chicken, if you want to make things better why not use your brain? Why not pass your exams and train to do MDS research? Why not work to help *solve* this wretched thing, instead of—'

'Lots of people are doing research. You said so yourself.'

'There are ways and ways of helping people. Think about something you can actually *do* to help someone else, instead of these great heroic gestures.'

'It's not a *gesture*.'

Before Dad could say anything else, Ali bumped the swing doors open and came into the lab backwards, dragging a trolley after him. 'All sweet,' he said to Dad, and smiled hello at me.

'Tell Jess what you've just been doing, Ali,' said Dad. 'She's very interested.'

Ali pulled a wry face. 'Wouldn't call it interesting myself. It's the Sleeping Beauties, you know. We have to take blood for tests.'

'Any of their mothers in?' asked Dad.

'The chipmunk woman. Wanting to know if she can play Mozart to baby.'

'What did you say?'

Ali shrugged. 'Told her to ask a nurse. I don't see why they can't tape an Ipod to the belly.'

'That's all these girls are, you see,' Dad said to me. 'A belly.'

I wasn't about to be brainwashed by him. I told him I had to get back to college. He followed me out into the corridor and down to the service doors. 'There's a lot you don't understand about all this, Jessie. This isn't the time or place, but—'

'OK. Bye, Dad.'

'Let's go for a walk together on Saturday.'

'Fine.' I walked across the slushy little road and when I turned along the path between the parked cars, I gave him a wave. He was still standing there in his white coat, holding the double doors open. He looked a bit pathetic. I supposed I should be glad he wanted to talk. At least now he was taking me seriously.

Twenty

On Saturday morning Dad packed a rucksack with snacks and a flask of cocoa, like he always did when we went for a walk. 'I'm not going in the car,' I told him.

'Well how are we going to get to Dovestones?'

'Bus to Greenfield then walk.'

Dad rolled his eyes. 'We'll die of hypothermia before we even get there.'

'You don't listen to anything I say, do you? People have to stop guzzling oil.'

'Yeah yeah yeah,' he said. 'They have to squat in their hovels gnawing root vegetables by the light of a smoky fire. And never go further than they can walk.'

'Ha ha.'

'That's what you lot are advocating, isn't it? A return to the dark ages. Have you got a bus timetable?'

'Online.'

'Tssk tssk. Electricity!' he grinned.

I was putting on two pairs of thick socks when he called me into the spare room. 'Regard, wise child.' The next bus was at 12.15, in two and a half hours. 'Come in the car with me and I promise you faithfully that I will get the bus to work one day next week to offset.'

'It's cheating.'

'Two days. I promise. I need to go over to Mandy's this afternoon to give your mum a break.'

'Have you and Mum made up?'

'Yes.'

'You're not going away again?'

'No, Sweetie. We've had enough stupidity to last us a while.'

Thanks for telling me, I thought. But I let it go. It was a sunny day and he was in a good mood. I didn't want an argument. As we drove up past the Pike the sun was shining and sparkling across fields of new snow, the light was dazzling. And up at Dovestones reservoir all the moors were blanketed, rounded and softened, and the fir trees' branches weighted down in great white blobs, on the side the wind had blown from. 'I've never seen so much snow up here,' said my dad. He'd started to turn into the top car park but then backed out and parked on the road, for fear of getting stuck. When we got out the air was as sharp and bright in our lungs as the dazzle in our eyes.

'Maybe we'll see the kingfisher?' I joked.

Dad laughed. 'Bluest bird in all the land.'

'Better than a peacock?'

'Better than a peacock.' We pulled on hats and gloves and set off down the steps into the little forest. The steps lead you from being level with the tree tops to being down amongst the roots and trunks, as if you've changed scale. The lower side is bounded by a big stone wall, and the only way out is over the stile. So when you're in it you feel safe and cut off from all the rest of the world. When I was little Dad and I used to play hide and seek there. He'd shut his eyes and count to a hundred and I'd hide, scrambling over fallen branches to find a good thick trunk to stand behind, peeping round to watch him crashing off in the wrong direction. I could just smell the resin and faint fungussy mouldiness of the trunk against my cheek, and feel the scratchy little pine needles that used to get inside my trainers and poke through my socks.

'Remember playing hide and seek?' I said.

'I used to panic that you were really lost.'

'It can't be much bigger than a football pitch!'

'I know,' he said, 'it's ridiculous.'

I remembered trying to stand still as a statue, my heart hammering nineteen to the dozen. Listening to the snapping twigs and soft crunch of needles, his footsteps coming nearer then moving away. Judging when to make my dash for home. When I beat him he used to groan and pretend to tear his hair, and I laughed so much I always got the hiccups. We went over the stile and down the lane and then straight on along the track by the top reservoir.

'Well Jess,' he said. 'Shall we talk about all this?'

'I'm not going to change my mind.'

'What do your friends say?'

'They don't know. I'm not supposed to tell anyone.'

'So what started you off thinking about it?'

'You.'

'I was afraid you'd say that.'

'You said it was necessary. You can't be so hypocritical—'

'I said it was necessary. That didn't mean I thought it was necessary for *you* to do it.'

'Every girl who does it is someone's daughter.'

'Right.' We went on crunching through the snow in silence. I knew he would miss me—of course. 'I'm not doing it because you made me think I should. I'm doing it because I want to.'

'Tell me your other reasons.'

'Lots of things.'

'Like what, Jessie?'

'How else can the world get back to normal?' He just walked in silence. 'Women having to die when they have babies,' I said. 'The gangs. People wanting to kill themselves. Stuff we discussed at YOFI.'

'Ah, YOFI. Your friend Iain. What did they say?'

'Nothing. Anyway, I've left.'

'Look Jess, just because you've arrived somewhere in your thoughts it doesn't mean I can automatically leap there after you.'

'If you want things to get better, it's no good just *telling* people what to do. Like you said, someone has to fire the first shot.'

'Have they asked other people to set an example?'

'No one's asked anyone.'

'But are some of the other girls going to volunteer?'

'Not as far as I know. None of them went to the clinic. It hasn't been on the news, has it?'

'You only heard of it because of me,' he repeated.

'I would have heard later, is all.'

'Isn't it one thing to try and live differently, and quite another to volunteer to die?'

'It's the same cause.' I stopped to look back the way we'd come. No one else had walked in that snow along the track, and we'd made two brilliant sets of footprints. I pointed them out to Dad. 'Look. Great for anyone following us.'

'Yes,' he said vaguely.

'Perfect crime,' I said. 'Walk with the other person to the top end of the reservoir. Kill them and take off their shoes, dump the body in the res. Then go back with their shoes on your hands making a set of tracks next to yours, as if they've gone all the way back with you. Perfect alibi.'

He looked a bit surprised. 'You're not really serious, are you?'

'About the alibi?'

'About volunteering.'

'Yes.' Just because I didn't want to drone on about it all the time. Sometimes grown ups are so pathetic, you lose all patience with them. You can be serious and then your mood can flip, and there's something funny, you can lighten up. Adults plod along as if they're weighted down with stones.

'OK, let's talk about the science.'

'You're not going to put me off.'

'Fine. But since I do know about the science I think you deserve to go into this with your eyes open.'

'Dad, you won't lie to me, will you?'

'Jesseroon.' He put his arms around me and gave me a big hug, and quite suddenly, I was smashed by a cold wave of anxiety about the whole thing. I didn't want to cry. I didn't want him to see me cry. Dad kissed me on the forehead. 'My poor wee nut brown maid. No lies. Just the facts, OK?'

'OK.'

'Let's start with artificial wombs. They were developing them before MDS, but now it's a priority. You put an embryo in an artificial uterus, and it can be monitored and looked after in a stable environment. There's no risk of receiving any infection from a human mother—and no woman has to sacrifice her life.'

'Have they tried it?'

'They're close to a breakthrough.'

'Then why is Mr Golding asking for volunteers?'

'I told you, it's in development.'

'So they still might not be able to make it work.'

'There are a number of strands to this, Jessie. Not only are there the artificial wombs, there are genetically modified sheep. Which is where I personally think the breakthrough will come. The sheep uterus is similar in size to the human, and there's been some very plausible research to suggest that it might be possible to develop implanted embryos in modified sheep.'

'Transgenic sheep?' I asked him. 'The ones that are half human?'

He laughed. 'Who told you they're half human?' According to Baz, they had these monsters at Wettenhall.

'I read it somewhere.'

'They're just sheep with slightly altered genes. They're indistinguishable from any other sheep. Just as woolly and just as dim. I know which I'd rather sacrifice, between a sheep and a girl.'

'Wouldn't it be embarrassing to have to explain that your mother couldn't come to parents' evening because she was a sheep.'

Dad laughed. After a bit he said, 'Another angle, although no one in this country really wants to acknowledge it, is that brain-damaged or seriously disabled young women might be used.'

'Why should someone who can't *choose*—'

'I agree, not nice.' There was a silence. 'The other thing you need to think about, though, is that they're developing better ways of helping ordinary women tolerate MDS. They're testing cocktails of drugs which might help to delay the onset of symptoms. One day they may be able to sustain women through pregnancy without having to put them to sleep.'

He was like a devil, tempting me.

'All I'm saying is wait. Wait a year, give the boffins a chance to come up with a few answers.'

But I know the younger I am, the better it is for a baby. Everyone knows that. I'd be trading a year of my life against a child's whole existence. We came to the dam at the top and we had to scramble down that steep slope, to get to the path on the opposite side. The snow was really deep. I tried to step sideways for a bit then I ran in giant strides, and when I got to the path I stopped and waited for Dad to catch up. I could feel the lumps of snow in my boots, starting to melt and soak through my socks. The reservoir was black down at this end, deep and dark and peaty.

'Why doesn't it freeze?' I asked him.

'It's moving, there's water flowing in.'

'It would be good if you could skate on it.'

'Would you like to skate?'

'Yes.'

'You could have lessons. We can go to an ice rink.'

'They must waste tons of energy keeping an ice rink cold.'

'You are a bit arbitrary, Jess. Don't you think they use energy in SeaLife, heating and lighting all those tanks?'

I hadn't thought of that.

'Another thing,' he said. 'You need to consider the likelihood of a successful outcome. The survival of a baby.'

'What d'you mean?' My feet were freezing now.

'Lots of the Sleeping Beauties' pregnancies fail. Either the foetus spontaneously aborts, or the woman develops MDS symptoms more aggressively than predicted, and the baby's damaged—there are all sorts of things that can go wrong. But the survival rate for babies is creeping up, it's about one in two now. Give them another year and it may have increased to two in three. Wouldn't it be better to wait, for that reason alone? For that increase in your chances of a live birth? There's nothing sadder than seeing these girls lose their lives for nothing.'

'But sixteen year olds have the best rates of all. Mr Golding told us.'

'This will be a new procedure. It's not the same as Sleeping Beauties.'

I glanced at Dad. He was looking very carefully where to put each foot. 'You think if I waited, I'd change my mind.'

'That's not why I'm saying it.' He did look at me

then, screwing up his eyes against the glare of the snow.

'Alright,' I said. 'What?'

'There are a lot of frozen embryos, but not an inexhaustible supply. And they are our only stock of potentially MDS-free children. So I think everyone will want to move slowly. There'll be the initial programmes where they'll implant a limited number of girls. But they'll decide what to do next on the basis of the results.'

'Results?'

'How many children survive. If the vaccine is one hundred per cent effective. My guess is that most clinics will do one experimental batch and in nine months, when the first trials have produced results, doctors will compare and analyse those, and then embark on a second programme. Which, by definition, is likely to have higher success rates. These first volunteers, they really are the guinea pigs.'

We both stopped walking. I was wriggling the toes on my left foot to try and get some life back into them.

'Look,' he said. 'I'll promise not to try and dissuade you, if you agree to dip out of this round and wait nine months for the next one.'

'I'm cold,' I said. 'Let's go back to the car.'

'D'you want some cocoa?'

'No.' I set off fast in front of him, crunching through the snow, my eyes aching now from all the glare. I thought, when I get home I'll sit in a hot deep bath and unpick everything he's said. I'll work out what to do, sensibly, on my own. I'll make a list of questions to ask Mr Golding. I am not a child. But walking through the secret forest and trudging up all those steps, I was feeling sick and empty inside, as if all my hopes had been crushed.

When we got into the car Dad didn't follow the Ashton road, he turned off towards Oldham. 'Where are we going?'

'I'm taking you out for lunch. We won't talk about it any more, OK? Let's just have a nice lunch and enjoy ourselves, Jess. All I wanted was for you to know the facts.' He turned down the lane to the White Hart, which was a lovely surprise. We hardly ever go there because it's wildly expensive. Their home-made veggie bangers and mash are one of my favourite lunches of all time, and also they have a fire so I'd be able to thaw my frozen toes. Then I began to have a little, trickling feeling of excitement, at the thought of all the things I could do if I had nine more months. Going on with college, and getting back to proper friends with Sal; making a vegetable garden with Dad in the spring; and—and Baz!

There were only a few other people in the pub, an elderly couple and a group of businessmen having lunch. The old couple didn't say a word to each other, and when the old man got up and shuffled off to the toilet, his wife carefully poured the clear drink from her glass into his tumbler of what looked like orange juice. She was wrinkled as a prune, with mad white fluffy hair, and when she noticed me watching her she nodded and smiled. 'Perfect alibi,' whispered Dad.

'Go on.'

'The pills he takes for his heart disagree with vodka. He's on orange juice. She pours her vodka into his glass and he drinks it. She tells everyone he must have drunk hers by mistake.'

'Half a glass of vodka wouldn't be enough to kill him.'

'You don't know how many times she's done it before.' As if to prove him right, the shrivelled lady went off to the bar and ordered more drinks. The old man drained his glass in her absence. Dad and I giggled.

When we got back to the house there was a nice smell of fried onions. Mum came out of the kitchen. 'You must be frozen. I've made soup.'

'It's OK thanks, we had lunch at the White Hart.'

'Oh.' She stood watching us in the hall as we took off our stuff.

'How's she doing?' Dad asked kindly.

'Mandy? She's still angry. It's really hard, Joe.' We went into the kitchen, and she ladled some soup into one bowl and sat at the table.

'Is Caroline with her?' Dad asked.

'Yes. I had to have a breather. She spends the whole time ranting at me, because I sent that little shit packing. I'm ruining her life—'

'Look,' said Dad. 'Every day you get her through is a plus.'

Mum shook her head. 'She's driving *me* mad.'

'I'll come back with you,' he said.

'Why did you go to the White Hart?'

'It seemed like a nice thing to do,' said Dad. 'I didn't know you were coming home.'

Mum looked at me as if she hadn't seen me for a while. 'So has he managed to talk some sense into you?'

'It's OK, Cath,' said my Dad. 'We've had a discussion.'

'And?'

'Just leave it,' said Dad.

I didn't want them to start. 'I'll think about waiting a year, like Dad said.'

'Right.' Mum stared at Dad then bent her face to her soup. I hung up my coat and went upstairs. I needed to know there'd be a baby who was OK. I sat on my bed and looked up at the tree. I felt like a traitor.

Twenty-one

There was a blizzard of news about the Sleeping Beauty programmes, over the next few days—including stuff about the pre-MDS embryos. There were allegations that clinics were tricking girls into volunteering; that money was changing hands; even that girls were being kidnapped and drugged to take part in the programmes. There was a lot of publicity about the natural parents of the frozen embryos—how their rights were paramount, and how they might choose not to have their embryos used experimentally. I was watching TV to keep up with it all, and so I knew as soon as the Wettenhall film was posted.

I checked it on the internet. It was gruesome—dark shadowy footage of a concrete building like a multi-storey car park, with hundreds of wire cages and the most pitiful creatures inside them. Terrified monkeys that clung to the bars and chattered at the camera; sick dull-eyed monkeys that rested propped in the corners of their cages, scratching feebly at scabs or at tubes that ran into their arms and legs; comatose monkeys that lay strapped down with wires and monitors wriggling out of them, their fur shaved back to reveal the raw pink skin. There were naked sheep wired up and strapped in place like astronauts in a space shuttle; cage after cage after cage, stacked high with misery. In some the animals lay sprawled in vomit, dead.

I could see why Nat was angry. You couldn't look at this and not be angry. You couldn't believe human beings were responsible for this. I remembered Dad cheerfully talking about transgenic sheep, as if it was just science. Clean, tidy, painless science. Either he didn't know what was going on, or, if he thought this was OK—well, I simply couldn't trust him. I switched off the computer and went into the kitchen.

I think at that point I was almost equally balanced between going ahead, and backing out. The nastiness of science, the drugs and tubes and machines, appalled me. If I gave myself up to it, I'd be no more than one of those sheep. And if, as Dad said, I might die and produce no baby—die for no reason . . . ugh.

What would it be like, to die? I told myself it would be like the time before I was born, when I knew nothing, a dreamless sleep. But imagine not seeing sunlight. Not getting up in the morning and wondering what would happen today. Not feeling the soft cotton of my clean T-shirt as I pull it over my head. Not getting that ache in my fingers from the cold water when I clean my teeth. Not swinging open the door of the kitchen cupboard with one hand while I press down the lever on the toaster with the other and my feet are jigging to some tune on the radio. Not seeing something bright—oh good, a flower!—in the back garden then realising a fox has raided the bin and rubbish is spilled across the lawn and going out in my slippers to pick it up and feeling the cold damp of the grass soaking through at the edges of the soles and picking up the soggy mess and realising that Mum or Dad has not only thrown away potato peelings which should go in the compost but also tins which should be recycled, and standing in the cold garden feeling irritated but also enjoying the fresh air on my face and the creeping chill at my feet and my head crowded with everything that's going to happen today . . .

Dying just didn't seem *possible*.

From the moment the ALF film was posted up, the news was jumping with it. The ALF claimed these animals were all part of the transgenic breeding programme. They had been doctored to make them capable of incubating human embryos. Large numbers of them had already been implanted with embryos, without the donors' consent. People were flocking to demonstrations at the research lab—crazy numbers of people, enough to cause havoc on the motorway. There was something up at the airport as well, traffic was at a standstill all the way from Chester to Birmingham. I was staring at the helicopter views of the miles of cars when the doorbell rang.

I wasn't expecting anyone, I assumed it was post. But when I opened the door I had a nasty shock. Iain.

I didn't know he even knew where I lived. He'd locked his bike to the gate, and he was busy taking off his waterproofs. His face was pink and wet. 'Hi Jess, can I talk to you for a minute?'

I let him in with a sinking feeling. 'What's wrong?'

'Nothing. Nothing's wrong. How are you doing?' He dumped his cycle helmet and his wet things on the hall chair. 'Can I borrow a towel?'

I fetched the kitchen towel and he rubbed his face vigorously. The thought of kitcheny stuff together with his sweaty skin was disgusting. I wanted to grab the towel off him and put it in the wash. I turned quickly away into the living room, but he followed me. I muted the TV. 'You know this is Nat's lot?'

'Yes. A happy conjunction of protests—that one and the airport. The police will be stretched.'

'The YOFI airport protest?'

He nodded. 'Finally got off the ground.'

I could tell he'd said it before. 'Haha.'

'Yes,' he said, sitting down. 'It's been hard maintaining momentum. YOFI's very much reduced. People dipped in and then dipped out.'

'I—I got fed up of all the arguing.'

'I know. I always knew you really believed in the group Jess. I was sorry you left.' He stared at me evenly with his calm hypnotic Iain-stare, until I felt really bad at letting him down.

'The thing is,' he said, 'you need a critical mass to keep a group like YOFI going. I still believe it can achieve a lot, but not as a single group. I want YOFI to affiliate to London *New World*, and recruit a northern membership for them.'

'That sounds good,' I said. 'A good idea.'

'I knew you'd be pleased, because you're a really committed person. I've heard what you're doing, Jess.'

'What d'you mean?'

'Volunteering. The MDS-free babies.'

'I'm not! It's a secret.'

'It is a truly heroic action. I wanted to tell you how proud of you I am.'

Who had he got it off? Lisa? 'Nobody's supposed to know.'

'Don't worry, no one else in YOFI does. I've got a proposal to make.'

On the TV scores of police vans were arriving, and riot police jumping out with their massive shields. 'What?'

'I want you to let YOFI handle the publicity surrounding your volunteering.'

'YOFI? But I'm not even a member any more.'

'That doesn't matter. Listen. The way the press are treating this is rubbish—patronising the volunteers, insulting girls who're being incredibly brave. If we handle your publicity, I guarantee people will understand exactly why you're doing it; that you've made a politically aware and responsible decision.'

'But I don't need publicity.'

'Jessie, you'll get it whether you need it or not. D'you want them putting words into your mouth, and pretending you're some giddy young fool who doesn't know what she's doing? Or do you want everyone to know precisely that you care enough about the future to consciously decide on this selfless act?'

'But why d'you want YOFI—'

'This could multiply the effect of your action tenfold, a hundredfold—can't you see? Not only will you be rightly understood and respected for what you've done, you'll be an inspiration to thousands of other young people, to work for world change. With you as our figurehead we can join *New World* from a position of strength. Members need to feel they have the power to change things. Other girls will volunteer. You'll be their role model!'

Would it help other girls to volunteer? I thought about Ursula Johnson. I suppose in a way she had inspired me. 'The thing is, it's confidential.'

'Of course. All I want to do is be able to tell the London *New World* people that it's coming, so we can plan in advance. And so that they realise YOFI is bringing something pretty amazing to the merger.'

I lost track of what he was saying because something had happened at Wettenhall and clouds of smoke filled the screen. An explosion? Iain followed my glance.

'I hope that's not a bomb,' he said. 'They're going to get themselves arrested, and then how effective will they be?' We stared at the TV, I could see flames leaping from the buildings now, the place was on fire. 'Protest is about effectiveness,' he went on; 'rallying people to your cause, creating weight of numbers. That's why what you represent is so amazing.' He was staring at me unblinkingly. His light eyes made me think of an owl.

I knew he was right—it was like the old days again. He could see the whole picture, cause and effect, not just the thing under your nose. He was right, what good would it do if Nat and Baz were arrested? I might not even be able to *see* Baz again. My stomach felt like it was shrivelling up.

Iain stood up. 'OK, thanks Jess. This is the best thing for everyone—politically, what you're doing is pure gold. And I can make sure hundreds of girls will want to follow in your footsteps. You'll be making it a choice they can respect.' He stepped towards me and I was afraid he might try to kiss me, but then he held out his hand to shake. It felt hot and damp and meaty. He went out to put on his bike gear. I turned up the telly again, and waved through the window when I saw him unlocking his bike. When I knew he'd gone I went and double locked the door. I didn't like the feeling in my stomach. I didn't know if I'd done the right thing.

Twenty-two

Then Dad came home that evening and told me Mand was pregnant. Mum had done another test, and the doctor had confirmed it.

When it actually happens, the bad thing, you can't feel anything. Feeling seems to drop right through you like a stone, and you're just this empty hollow tube. Even though I knew it was a possibility, hearing Dad say it was a complete shock. Mum was staying with her, and after Dad told me and I'd tried to take it in, he set about gathering his and Mum's things together. He asked me if I could sleep over at Sal's. They didn't even know she'd moved.

'Aren't you bringing Mand back here? Or can't I go there with you?'

Dad sighed and put down his bag. 'No. I'm sorry Jess, but no. Is there someone else you can stay with?'

'*Why?*'

'Because it's horrible.'

I knew about MDS. I knew what happened. But a flicker of terror licked at my heart, as if there was something more, something unknown, that I hardly dared to ask him.

'I have to go and be with your mum. Look, Jess, this is very hard on you love, but it won't help you or Mandy or Cath if you go over there now. You need to remember Mandy the way she was.'

'Why? What's happened? Has something happened already?' Just asking made me break out in a sweat.

'She thought she'd be allowed to have it. That's what she believed—that we would take her into the clinic and have her for a Sleeping Beauty.'

'Can't you pretend?'

He gave a little hopeless laugh. 'That's what Cath said. No, of course we can't. The clinic has serious work to do—you can't start taking people in and lying to them about their treatment. It's not a game.'

'So what's going to happen?'

'She'll start to get ill—and, and then—the doctor'll sedate her—and, she'll die.'

'But right now, right *now*—'

'Sweetie, Mand didn't understand. She didn't understand why we weren't taking her to the clinic. When she finally started to understand, she broke her heart. She wants us to save the baby. She thinks everyone's betrayed her. It's not . . . it's just too miserable. It's not going to help you to see her like this, and it makes it harder for your mum to handle. D'you understand?' He hugged me and I started crying and he was crying too. I told him I didn't want to stay anywhere else and that I'd be OK at home on my own. I went out to the car with him and watched the rear lights to the end of the street. When I went back in the house I didn't know what to do with myself. I didn't know what to do.

For a while I sat in the dark trying to think about Mand—trying telepathy, trying to will her into some sort of peace, so that at least she and Mum could kiss and make up before she died. It was useless, I couldn't focus. I couldn't stop my racing mind. I went in the kitchen and started cleaning. I sorted the recycling and emptied the dishwasher and scrubbed the sink and the oven, then I cleared out the fridge. No one seemed to have eaten anything proper for days, loads of things were going off. Finally I washed the kitchen floor. At least it would be nice for them when they came home. Not that that would make any difference to anything.

Nothing could make any difference to anything.

Only what I was going to do.

I went upstairs and sat on my bed. It came clear in my mind like a great tangle of string that suddenly unravels when you pull in the right place. I was Mandy's mirror image. Her opposite. Because it didn't work for her, it was going to work for me. She was the minus and I was the plus, what I was going to do could cancel her out. Not *her*, but the badness, the sadness, the hopelessness. I could cancel all that. No baby for her = baby for me. Negative/positive.

And I wasn't going to be scared. Because I had already been scared about her. Mr Golding wouldn't let anything bad happen. It would just be the same as going to sleep.

By the time I'd gone downstairs and made myself

poached eggs on toast, it had all got in tangle again. The awfulness for Mum and Dad—Mum especially. The awfulness for Mand—how could this have happened? My fault. If I had been the least bit observant or thoughtful, the day I visited her, when she was waiting for Paul, I'd have asked what was going on. Instead of obsessing away about Mum and Dad and thinking the only problems that were important were my own. Why didn't I ask her? Why didn't I *think*? Maybe it even happened that very day—maybe that was the day Paul made her pregnant, after he passed me in the street, looking so sleek and cheerful.

I wanted to cry but I couldn't. I went backup to my room and looked at all the things I owned, the clothes and shoes and books and makeup and earrings and soft toys, my hand-embroidered shawl and mirror cushions from India, the pearl necklace Nanna Bessie gave me. My CDs, my DVDs, my iPod. I fetched a box from the garage and filled it with teddies and books and DVDs; and packed up all the rest in bags. The box was too heavy for me but I could take the bags on the bus into town, to one of the charity shops for motherless kids.

When I dragged the last bag out onto the landing and went back to inspect my room, it was cleared of all the knick-knacks and clutter of someone who only thought about herself. You could see the lighter patches on my shelves where books, jewellery box, lava lamp, etc, stood. I liked that, the ghostly outlines where they were. I told myself, each time I walk into this room, each time I miss something, and see its empty space, I will remember her. I felt as if I wanted to put my hand under my ribcage and squeeze my own heart, squeeze it till it hurt so much I couldn't feel it any more.

It was nearly midnight but I knew I wouldn't sleep. I took my duvet downstairs and turned on the TV again, low. That reminded me of weekends when I was little, creeping down in the morning while they were still asleep, switching the telly on low and curling up on the sofa with cushions pulled around me to keep me warm. When Dad got up to make their tea he'd peer in at me and say 'It's the lesser spotted nut brown maid! Got a cosy nest there, have you?' That's what let me cry at last. Thinking of Mum and Dad.

I must have fallen asleep in the end, because when I opened my eyes the phone was ringing and it was morning. Dad was calling to check I was OK, and to let me know they'd given Mand a sleeping tablet and both she and Mum were asleep. We agreed that if she was calmer when she woke, maybe I could go over and see her. Dad's voice was flat and tired but he said he had to go straight into work, there was something going on.

I went looking for breakfast. There wasn't any bread so I had to eat soggy weetabix. On the news, the airport had re-opened. They were showing footage of the evacuation, and focussing on heaps of luggage. They said there had been explosives in some cases, and that it was a terrorist plot. Experts were sifting other unclaimed items. Two people were supposedly helping police with their enquiries; I wondered if they were YOFI members. We'd never planned to use explosives, so what was going on? Then there was a report on Wettenhall, about how yesterday's confrontation started. The number of casualties hadn't yet been confirmed. The main clash was between the Animal Liberation Front and FLAME. On screen came footage of a FLAME coach drawing up outside the research labs, where a crowd of ALF with placards stood shouting by the gates. The camera closed in on the first woman off the bus. 'These dickheads want to save furry animals!' she yelled. 'This is what scientists *should* be doing!' 'We're here to make sure they can carry on doing it!' shouted another. 'We're here to fight for every woman who's died!' I stared at the faces as they came off the bus, waiting to see Sal. There was a great crowd of Noahs screaming and yelling '*Abomination!*', angry about human seed being planted in animals. The images flashed past—fighting, smoke, police grappling with protestors, people being bundled into police vans or lifted into ambulances.

Police had got control of the research labs this morning, they claimed, but when they showed it from the air you saw chaos, a war zone—nose-to-tail vehicles, burning, abandoned, or deliberately overturned and made into barricades. People had climbed the embankment and were crawling under fences and stumbling through ploughed land, like refugees. There were *New World*ish kids rampaging up and down. Some gangs had joined in—one lot crashed through the police barriers and came up the other side of the motorway in an old bus. They were targeting empty cars and grabbing anything they could get—food, money, clothes. In London the company that owned the research lab had had their offices firebombed, and there was some kind of siege going on at Charing Cross

Hospital maternity wing, which is one of the biggest centres for Sleeping Beauties. I checked my mobile, no messages.

I was busy scanning all the faces on the screen for Baz or Sal or Nat. They interrupted the news for an appearance by the prime minister, promising extra security for IVF research facilities and hospitals. That's when I realised, *that* was why Dad had to go to work this morning. All maternity clinics and wards were on security alert—anywhere they treated Sleeping Beauties or collected donor eggs.

I wasn't sure who was making the threats, the FLAME women or the gamete donors? The TV said it may be the people who introduced MDS. So the fights were between those who didn't want women to be able to have children again, and those who did; between people who were opposed to using animals to help repopulate the world and people who were opposed to using women.

The Noahs and the ALF and the Donors were all fighting the animal research labs and the FLAME women. But if MDS terrorists were really still about, why would they be exposing themselves to danger on the streets when they probably had the scientific know-how to turn on the dormant virus in the whole of the rest of the population? Dad had been saying that for ages, they can hold us to ransom whenever they like. If it really is a *they*, and if *they* were in control of what they did. But he said they're probably not, it's probably just a lone nutter who never realised what the consequences would be.

My mobile went. Rosa. I really didn't need it. She'd

had her counselling, she was feeling great. 'My mum's having a special video made, to remember me by and to show the baby. I'm going to be filmed in all my favourite places like this really lovely restaurant where we usually go, and sitting in my boyfriend's sports car, and in a big armchair on the patio with roses and apple blossom all around me.'

'That's nice,' I said. I didn't say roses and apple blossom aren't in flower yet. Well, I suppose she could get them from a florist. If it was true.

'I'm just choosing the music,' she said. 'I'm going to have all my favourite songs.'

'Good,' I said. 'Lovely.' I went back to watching TV. If I turned it off Mandy would come into my head, like a massive noise that was too big for my head to hold.

Twenty-three

At some point in the afternoon there was a soft knocking at the door. I crept into the hall and stood there paralysed staring at the door. Another little knock with a special rhythm to it, and I knew then it wasn't Iain. I ran to the door and yanked it open. Baz stood there grinning down at me. He was wearing so many clothes he looked almost fat. There was a thick red fleece bulging out of the collar of his coat, and a woolly green hat pulled down over his ears, with tufts of black hair sticking out, and his trousers tucked into big padded boots like a Cossack. 'Hello,' he said, grinning like mad, as if we both knew it was a joke. I stood back for him to come in but somehow we bumped into each other. He put his hands on my shoulders to steady me, and we managed to get the door shut. Then we put our arms round each other and hugged tight. His coat was rough against my face, I snuffled up the layers of cold and smoke and wool, and the close secret heat of his body underneath.

When we stumbled apart he said, 'I'm starving,' and I took him into the kitchen and started to make scrambled eggs. There was still no bread so I put ryvita on the plate. He pulled off the coat and the fleece and the boots and sat drumming his fingers at the kitchen table.

'Have you just got back?'

He nodded.

'Did you go into the lab at Wettenhall?'

'No. Josh—who did the filming—and Nat were in a student house together and I joined them, all they were interested in doing was getting the film sorted and up on the web. They knew the media would jump on it. But there was another cell with some kids from London, who wanted to break in and liberate the animals. And we didn't even know about that till the morning.'

'So the fire at the labs—'

'Nothing to do with us. We literally didn't plan any violence. The idea was, go public on what's happening inside the place, and let everyone else slug it out.'

'They're having to barricade clinics,' I told him. 'People like my Dad are under attack.'

'Nobody thought this would happen. I mean, a few reporters and ALF hardcore, maybe some grumpy donors—Nobody imagined this . . .'

'What did you do?'

'After we posted it up, we made placards and stuff, and went out there in a couple of taxis early morning for a demo. We arrived just after the explosion. Security were going mental, then we heard there were ALF kids already inside the building trying to get animals out. They thought we were part of that—they wouldn't let us anywhere near—then FLAME coaches started arriving—and the Noahs—'

'I saw on telly.' I dolloped the eggs onto his plate and cut up a tomato.

'They were like locusts, everything you could move or throw, sticks, stones, bushes, the fence, they just ripped it up.' He'd been with Nat and they got separated when the police broke through their line, and someone lobbed a burning thing. Black smoke belched out so that everyone was coughing and he lost sight of Nat. 'Then the police were attacking us from behind as well. They must have come through the buildings from inside. There was more and more smoke blowing over from the main gates, someone said it was tear gas.'

'How did you get away? They closed the roads—'

'I managed to get to the wall and I followed it round to the back of the site where the incinerator is. I climbed over and ran across to the lane. Then I just followed the little lanes, looking out for any signs to Chester. I could see helicopters in the distance, they must've been over the motorway. After it got dark I found a church that was unlocked and slept in there. And this morning I walked into Chester and caught a train.'

'So what happened to Nathan?' I asked.

'I think he must have been arrested. Jessie?'

'Yes?'

'Have you seen Iain?'

'Why?'

'He's put a weird thing about you on the YOFI website.'

'What kind of weird?'

'That you're volunteering for something.'

'He can't have done—' I ran into the spare room to turn on the computer.

Baz brought his food in and sat on the bed eating while I waited impatiently for the computer to chunter through its waking up. I went onto the YOFI homepage and typed in my password. The members' page came up and the first thing I saw was a photo of me. *New Volunteer Jessie Leads the Way.*

'It must have been posted early this morning. I went on the internet at Chester to check the ALF site.'

'It shouldn't be here! He's got no right!'

'Want me to close it down?'

'It's secret!'

I watched as Baz typed in his own password and went into the message section. He typed intently—a string of characters, some other password, I guessed. A warning message came up and he overrode it and kept on typing. The image on the screen froze, then half of it disappeared. He hit the keys repeatedly. Nothing. He switched it all off then turned it on again. Went on to Google and typed in YOFI's address. *The webpage you have requested is not available.* He laughed. 'You try.' I tried and then I pressed *refresh*, and still nothing happened. 'Pretty good, eh!' laughed Baz. 'Thank you Iain. He suggested that, when we set up the site. In case it ever got infiltrated.' He turned his laughing face to me and leant forward and kissed me. It turned into a proper, long kiss. When we stopped for a moment to breathe, Baz whispered, 'So, do you still like me?' and I whispered back,

'Yes. D'you like me?'

'Idiot,' he laughed. He sat beside me on the bed and we started kissing again. Suddenly he broke off. 'What d'you mean, it's secret?'

'My volunteering.'

'Your volunteering?'

I was in a lift up at the top of a skyscraper and then the cable snapped. I was suddenly plummeting towards the ground. 'Yes. I wanted to explain to you . . .'

'Explain what?'

'Well, d'you remember, I started to tell you about it that night on the swings—'

'What are you talking about?'

'You remember, the MDS-free babies?'

'Injecting them with vaccine and sticking them inside girls who're going to die?'

'I—yes—I've volunteered.'

'For that?'

'Yes.'

'Are you mad?'

'No.' Stupid really, there was no point in replying.

Baz got up from the bed and leant against the opposite wall, facing me. 'Has he put you up to this?'

'Who?'

'Iain. Is this his master plan?'

'No, of course not. It's my idea.'

'He's brainwashed you.'

'No! *I* thought of it, *I* decided to volunteer.'

'Why does he know about it?'

'He came round yesterday and asked—look, that bit's not important.'

'But you—you—' He was staring at me and his voice

had stopped being angry. 'Jessie, what's going to happen?'

My heart was hammering. I knew he wouldn't understand. The more he asked questions, the more I panicked. I started to tell him about Mandy, then I tried to explain about Mr Golding, then about the sea-horses I'd seen with Dad.

Eventually he said, 'Is it true?'

'Yes.'

'You really want to volunteer, and go in hospital, and be killed?'

'Baz, it's not like that.'

'Then I can't understand why you're saying this shit.'

'OK, listen.' I made myself go through it again slowly, from start to finish. Then I explained about Iain coming round and how random it was. Everything I said sounded flimsy. When I had finished Baz turned and went out of the room. I heard him going into the kitchen, and it was quiet. I got up and followed him. 'Baz? Baz?'

'What?' He was putting on his fleece.

'Where are you going?'

'Home.' He slid his feet into his boots and bent to lace them.

'But—'

'But what?'

'I—I don't want you to.'

No reply.

'Look you can't just—go.'

'Why not?'

'Why are you so angry?'

He straightened up. 'You want me to stand here and clap and say *Aren't you brave?*'

'No, but—'

'Iain'll do that. Ask him.'

'It's nothing to do with Iain. I hate Iain. Stop it!'

'What d'you want me for? If you're going to do all this?'

'I thought you liked me.'

'I thought *you* liked *me.*'

'I do! I do!'

'Right.' He grabbed up his coat and pushed past me, he yanked the front door open and then it slammed shut behind him.

I froze. Surely he would come back. I couldn't make head or tail of it. I tried to reason it out but every time I was blocked by how hateful he'd been. He didn't care about me, he didn't even like me, he just thought I was stupid. He thought what I was doing was shit. The injustice of it took my breath away. How I would feel if I was him? He tells me he's volunteering for a drugs trial, to help solve MDS. The trial will cost his life. Wouldn't I think he was brave? Wouldn't I admire and love him even more? Wouldn't I want to try and make the best of the short time we had together? Wouldn't I *support* him? I wanted to get up and bang about the room and shout and throw things.

But I made myself stay sitting there, hunched at the table. I didn't allow myself to stir. I forced myself into how I would really feel, like squeezing myself through a tiny crack under a door, into a different room. If he volunteered he'd be saying 'I care about this more than I care about you.' For a start. OK. He'd be saying

216

'I haven't trusted you enough to discuss this with you and actually I don't care what you think, because I'm going to please myself anyway.' He'd be saying, 'I'm superior to you because I'm doing save-the-world, while you just go on muddling through, doing stupid little actions like demonstrations.'

I thought so hard my eyeballs felt like they were being pushed out of my head. He couldn't love me. No one could love me. What I was going to do was the most selfish thing in the world. I sat there so long I couldn't tell which was hard wooden chair and which was stiff bony Jessie-bum. I had no right to ask anyone to help me, because I was deliberately putting myself outside their reach.

You can't go round to his house, I told myself. You can't go and ask him to be nice; you can't kiss him and hug him, because he's right, it's a lie. You love what you're going to do more than you love him. It was like I'd stopped being human. If I went on with this I'd be alone. Upsetting Mum and Dad; making my friends angry; leaving them all behind.

Whereas if I stopped—Baz and I could be happy together. I could see Sal, and gradually she would get back to her old self. I could look after Mum and Dad and help them to feel better after all the awfulness of Mandy's illness. I could love and be loved. But I already knew I was thinking about all that with the sentimentality you feel for something lost. The shock of understanding was cold, like being parachuted into the North Pole. Being alone and knowing it was real, and everything else was playacting. Everything else was a *picture* of my life, a story. Going ahead to that needle point at the clinic—that was real. I was an arrow fired straight at that, and I couldn't expect any sympathy or kindness from anyone.

When I finally hobbled off the chair and round the kitchen to turn on the kettle, I had aged a hundred years. Like Rip van Winkle. There was ice in my heart.

Twenty-four

I didn't see Mandy again. She had what Dad called 'a bad episode' in the afternoon and they called the doctor, who sedated her there and then. From that point really, it was as if she'd already gone.

Dad came home the night after she was sedated, and we talked about her and Mum, and then we got out the photo-box and went through the old pictures from when I was little. Pictures of Mand on holiday with us; of Mand teaching me to ride my bike; of Mand laughing and splashing; of her making my seahorse puppet dance. We picked the best ones for the wall at her funeral. I knew that soon enough, Mum and Dad would have to do this for me. I couldn't afford to think about it. For the first time, looking at those pictures of me toddling along the beach grinning, or shoving fistfuls of sand into my mouth, I imagined the baby. The baby; my child. I imagined her with Mum and Dad. I imagined the three of them together, and I was jealous and glad and terrified all at the same moment.

Dad told me that a group of women from FLAME were picketing the clinic—as they were picketing clinics up and down the country, wherever there was a Sleeping Beauty programme. Security guards had been placed on the doors, but there was also a rota for the lab staff, to patrol inside the lab, in case of any threat to the embryos. He was having to stay overnight once every five days.

In the morning when he'd gone I took three of the bags of stuff from my room, to the children's charity shop in Ashton. Inside was a depressing sight: heaps of bags still waiting to be unpacked, dumped on the counter, on tables, and on the floor. I asked the woman where to put mine and she shrugged. She told me nobody bought anything any more. People just brought more and more stuff in. Women's clothes and household goods; they had more than they could handle, they were sending unsorted lorry-loads of it as rags to paper manufacturers. I had a pang at leaving my beloved possessions where no one would even get any use out of them. Then I remembered it was Mum and Dad who'd have to clear my room, and I was glad I'd done it.

As I left the shop my mobile went. Lisa. She was ringing about her latest plan; she still wanted to move away from the Kids' House to somewhere in the country-side where they could be self-sufficient. Through someone who knew someone who'd told someone else, there seemed to be an offer of a small-holding for motherless kids. It was in Wales and she was asking me to go with her to see it. 'I know you think it's a cop-out,' she said, 'but you can still come and look, can't you.' She didn't mention dissuading me from volunteering, but I heard her thought behind the words. It didn't matter. I was glad she asked me, I was sick of being on my own. We agreed to meet at nine on Friday at Piccadilly, to get the train to Wales. She said to bring my bike because they'd told her it was quite far from the station.

I had one more thing to get through before Friday—my clinic interview. Dr Nichol had texted me to ask how I was getting on and whether I wanted another counselling session. I had texted back, *No*. Now this was the interview, where—as far as I knew—the final decision would be made about me.

I tried not to think about it, I tried to hold my mind entirely away from the subject. I would just go there and they would say 'Yes'. In the very edges of my brain, in the peripheral vision you have when someone's holding their hands over your eyes, I allowed the flickering possibility of them saying 'No'; of having a life to live again. It seemed remote and frightening.

I fiddled about for ages getting ready for the clinic interview, putting Sal's clockwork nun in my bag for luck; changing into three different sets of clothes, feeling more and more peculiar. Then I realised I was going to be late and had to run to the bus stop. The weather had changed, it was mild and muggy, and I was sweating when I got onto the bus. I rode staring straight ahead with my bag balanced on my knees, feeling like a statue. When the nurse showed me into a waiting room I'd never seen before, there was a new girl sitting there. We glanced at each other and nodded, I don't think either of us could remember how to smile. At least it wasn't Rosa. She was called in straight away. I got my book out of my bag and stared at the page so I wouldn't have to look at her when she came out. I didn't want to see her crying or smiling or whatever the interview had done to her. Time passed slowly. When they called me in at last, Doctor Nichol was sitting behind her desk writing. She got up and came round to pat me on the shoulder and lead me to a comfy chair. Then she pulled up a chair opposite. 'Well Jessie,' she said, 'how're you feeling?'

'I don't know.'

'That's not surprising,' she said. 'It's a very big decision. What do your parents say?'

'Well actually, they think they've convinced me to wait a year.'

'Ah.'

'I'd be too old, wouldn't I?'

She nodded. 'Mr Golding's not taking anyone over 16 and a half. The Sleeping Beauty statistics are showing that every month of maternal age makes a difference, in terms of live births.'

'Mum and Dad know that.'

'Maybe you should take your mother to a *Mothers for Life* meeting,' she said. 'The women there are a good support network. They understand the process, they help each other through it.'

I had no desire to raise the topic with Mum again, ever.

'What about you yourself? How have you been feeling?'

'Well, I've felt a bit confused.' I suddenly thought,

she can see I don't know what on earth I'm doing. All I have to do is be honest and I can save myself. Until that moment, I didn't know I wanted to save myself, I didn't know I had a treacherous bone in my body.

'Have you been sleeping?'

'I've had some wakeful nights.' I laughed, so she wouldn't think I was being pathetic.

'I'm glad,' she said. 'It would be very strange if you were calm, faced with such a decision. You know we don't want girls to come into this with any delusions. You're choosing a difficult and terrible path, one that people in the future will certainly thank you for, but one in which the only end for you must be death. You need to think about it realistically. After a certain point, there'll be no turning back, and all the strength of your character will be needed.'

I tried to think but my head was swirling.

'I want you to take as much time as it takes,' she said. 'This is your decision. I don't want you to say anything now, I don't want you to decide anything today. I want you to just go away and get on with your life for as long as it takes, until you are completely and utterly certain. If you're not certain for six months, that's fine, it means you won't do it. OK? There's no harm and no shame in not doing it. You're not certain at the moment, I know, and there's no one in the world who'd want to put you under pressure. Just live with it, see how you feel, see if it comes any clearer. OK?'

I laughed, partly out of relief and partly out of annoyance at myself for stringing it out. 'What happens when I *am* certain?' I asked.

'You can ring me.' She passed me a card with her

number. 'Here at the clinic, or on my mobile. You can ring me any time.'

'But will you select me then?'

'If and when you know you really want to do it, then we will be glad to have you on the programme.' I sat there like a lump. I couldn't understand what the resistance was. I had decided. Surely to goodness, I had decided long ago?

'Tell me exactly what happens, when I come to you and say yes.'

'Well, we remove your Implanon. And we give you a temperature graph so we can tell when you're ovulating— so we know the best time for your implantation.'

'Can I do that now?'

She hesitated. 'Have you got a boyfriend?'

'No. No. I don't need the Implanon. I'd like you to take it out today.'

'But why?'

'Because—because I know I *want* to do it, and I'm driving myself mad. At least if you take the Implanon out I'll know I've taken one step forward. And if—in the end—I can't . . .'

'We can always put it back,' she finished. 'Alright Jessie, if you want.' She made me sit on the hard chair by her desk, and used a little whirring implement on my arm. I felt it for a moment vibrating like a dentist's drill, then there was a sensation of soreness. She swabbed with something cool and put a neat plaster over it. I had a vision of Mandy hacking out her Implanon with a razor. She knew what she wanted.

Dr Nichol gave me a temperature graph and explained how I should use it. We inserted the date of my last period and she counted to where I should begin. When we shook hands and said goodbye there was at least a crumb of comfort in my sore stinging arm, and the graph folded neatly in my bag.

The first person I saw after I left Dr Nichol's office was Rosa. She was sitting outside on the steps. 'Are you still doing it?' Her face looked a bit funny and I guessed they must have turned her down.

'Yes. Of course. Are you?'

'Yes. Within the month,' she said.

'Oh!' I glanced at her again, and noticed that she was wearing really thick makeup. Something had happened to her face. She got up and walked beside me towards the bus stop. 'Did you go away and think it over?' I asked her, 'before you finally decided?'

'I didn't need to! I've always been one hundred per cent sure.'

'So next time you come in—'

'It'll be to stay!'

'Is your mum really OK with it?'

'Yeah, I told you. She's making a video.' There was a silence then she said, 'When she wants to make me mad she says I won't have the guts to go through with it. But I will. I'll show her.'

'And your boyfriend?'

'Oh, I've dumped him. Loser.' She laughed. 'You should see my page on Facebook. I've got hundreds of fans, hundreds of fit men who'd go out with me if they could. All sending me messages about how brave I am and everything. I don't need him. I could pick anyone.'

'You put it on Facebook? That you're volunteering?'

'Yeah.'

'But we're supposed to keep it secret.'

'Not for much longer. Soon our faces'll be known around the world.'

Surely Dr Nichol could have seen through her? I wished she wasn't volunteering; it tarnished it, as if it was a thing someone flaky might do. Maybe she was lying.

Dad called in at home late that night, he'd been to Mand's and all was peaceful there. He said if I didn't mind, he'd go back and stay with Mum, because he thought Mand might not last the night. I told him I was going to Wales with Lisa. There was no point in telling him anything else. The uncertainty now seemed like a puzzle you have to solve before crossing a threshold. I would do it, I knew I would do it; but something had to unlock my tongue so it could say 'yes.'

In the morning I took my temperature and put a little x in the right place on the graph. Then I went out to the shed. It was quite a novelty, seeing my bike again. There were lumps of ancient mud deep in the tread of the tyres. It must have been there since I did the towpath marathon with Sal, a lifetime ago, before MDS. The dried mud spattered to the ground as I wheeled my bike to the gate. I cycled to Ashton station on it, wobbling like crazy as I tried to get the gear lever to shift down. It was stuck on high.

I was half-expecting to see Gabe with Lisa at Piccadilly. But she was on her own; he'd told her he didn't want to live some dirty hippy life with no one but sheep for company. 'He'll probably change his mind,' she said, but I could see she wasn't happy about it. It crossed my mind that that was why she'd asked me. We swapped news about Wettenhall. Nat had called her from a safe phone saying he was in hiding but nothing more. And I asked what she knew about the airport protest. 'Well it made it blatantly obvious that airports are prime targets for terrorism. So, a success.' She hadn't heard of anyone from YOFI being arrested.

At Shrewsbury we got onto a smaller, slower, emptier train, where we kept our bikes with us in the compartment. Lisa had a map and showed me where we were going—the farm was eight miles from the nearest station. Through the windows the countryside was empty and rolling, with fields of sheep and the odd huddled farm. In the distance it rose to higher hills. The day had started off misty grey but now the clouds were breaking up. We watched a patch of blue appear.

The place we had to get off was just a platform with a name board, there wasn't even a ticket office. We wheeled our bikes off and we were the only people there. Away to the right was a dark terraced row of houses, with empty gardens running down to the tracks. 'It's over the level crossing and left.' Lisa swung up onto her bike, and I followed her up the hill at a pace that was slower than walking and twice as much effort. But I managed to stay on till I got to the crest, and then magically, once I was whizzing down, the gears clicked and became usable again.

The air was bright and fresh in my lungs, after the stuffy train, and the pumping of my legs sent oxygen fizzing round my body. Sunshine was rolling across the countryside, between clouds, like a spotlight singling out a stone wall here, a green splash of field there, a silvery copse. The next hill was steeper and Lisa hunched over her handlebars and pedalled furiously to get to the top. When I'd reached halfway I got off and pushed. There was no sound but my own panting and the slight rubbing of my back brake block, and the distant cawing of rooks. The landscape around me felt huge and empty, with just me at the centre of it. Lisa waited for me at the top and we went spinning down together, shrieking at the speed and breathlessness of it. The fields unrolled before us like a carpet.

Eventually there was a smaller lane turning off to the right, and then Lisa stopped by a gate. 'It's up there.' A track wound away uphill and into bare trees. The gate wasn't locked but the hinges were knackered. We managed to squeeze the bikes through, and pushed them up into the woods. From the top we could see down to a stream in the valley bottom, and a farmhouse with a cluster of outbuildings. The sun came out again, a wash of light flooding the valley. We looked at each other and laughed. Then we parked our bikes against trees and set off down to the house.

There was a stone flagged yard in front, with buildings to three sides—the house, a dilapidated barn, and some wooden sheds that looked like animal pens. A couple of mouldy straw bales lay in front of the barn. Lisa lifted a stone from the farmhouse doorstep and uncovered a big old-fashioned key. She unlocked the door and we went in to the dim kitchen. 'God,' she said, 'it's perfect!' There was an old cooking range along one wall, and a big black dresser, cluttered with cups and plates and yellowing papers—bills, junk mail, newspapers. The table was piled with jars and bottles, seed catalogues, a computer and printer, a washing basket full of clothes. There was a pair of cracked boots by the range, and waterproofs dangling from a hook on the door. The place smelt of damp and decay, with a sweetish sickly tinge which I realised was probably a dead mouse or bird.

'What happened to the people?' I asked. There was a rusty frying pan in the washing up bowl, in a sludge of stagnant water.

'It's a sad story,' said Lisa. 'But look! A solid fuel stove, how good is that? We can have heat and cooking and hot water, just by chopping up some wood.' She tried the tap, it spattered briefly then the pipes clanged and it stopped. 'They've turned it off,' she said. 'We'll get plastic barrels and catch the rainfall off the roof.'

We went through into the sitting room, where a flowery sofa was pushed up close to the fireplace. Soft white ashes lay in the grate. There was a telly in the corner, and a calculator and pen and handwritten lists of figures lying by the sofa. Through the lounge was a junk room piled high with boxes and broken furniture. 'What happened, Lisa?'

She told me as we went upstairs and explored the bedrooms. The farm belonged to a young couple who were going to do it up. The woman was pregnant, then came MDS. The husband stayed there on his own until October and then he killed himself. The farm reverted to his parents. Now they were the ones donating it to motherless kids.

'Did they both die here, in this house?'

'How should I know? Is that all you're interested in? Can't you see the fantastic potential this place has?'

'Sorry. Yes.' In the main bedroom the bedclothes lay in a tangled pushed-back heap, as if someone had got out of them that very morning. In the other room a stepladder leant against the wall, and there was a tin of paint with a brush balanced on it. One powder blue wall. There was an attic above the bedrooms. You could see the sky through the roof in a couple of places, and there were leaves and feathers on the floor. 'I bet there's a nest up there,' I said, but we couldn't see it.

Outside we checked out the other buildings, which were all pretty decrepit, and she launched into her plans. There was donated money in the Kids' House bank account. She was going to buy tools and seed. She'd plant vegetables: potatoes, onions, beans, cabbage, beetroot, sweetcorn, sunflowers. They would have to put proper fencing round the garden to keep out deer and rabbits. She was going to buy a polytunnel and grow tomatoes and strawberries and lettuce in there, and also get chickens and goats. She had read about keeping livestock and reckoned she would be able to milk a goat and make yoghurt and cheese. She was going to buy apple and plum and hazelnut trees and raspberry and blackcurrant canes, and get someone who knew about bees to come and set up a hive and teach her how to look after it. Household waste would be composted with urine and used to fertilise the gardens. They would mend the gates and repair the roof and make the house weatherproof. And if they could get all that done this year, then next year they would plant bigger crops, some grain, maybe an orchard, and start to keep cows.

'We can convert the barn into more sleeping places,' she said, 'and we can use the sheds for storage. We can sun-dry things like tomatoes, we can make jam and preserve fruit, and make an underground storage place for root vegetables so they don't get frosted in winter. The stream can supplement our rain water, and there's no reason why we shouldn't fix up our own wind turbine on top of that hill.' She laughed. 'I'm going to call it Eden!'

I sat on an old bench in the back garden while she went into the house again to make an inventory of tools that were already there. The spring sun was almost warm, and there was bright yellow coltsfoot growing between the paving stones of the path. I imagined Lisa coming here with a bunch of the others, unloading supplies and deciding who'd sleep where, clearing up the kitchen, dragging rubbish out to make a bonfire. They'd stand around the flames as it got dark, laughing and making plans.

The coltsfoot was the first flower of spring. Everything was renewing itself, soon the valley would be full of new green leaves. Lisa came out and called that she was ready. When I went into the yard she was wrestling with the key which wouldn't turn in the lock. She laughed and said it didn't want her to leave. I did it for her and put the key under the stone, and we walked backup to our bikes. Lisa rattled on about how the place could be improved. I wasn't thinking but there was something hissing in my head like static. It went on all the time we were cycling to the station. As we wheeled our bikes onto the platform my head cleared, and I realised I didn't want to go home.

If I could just be on my own for a bit—really on my own, not where other people could get at me—and have some time to think, then I'd be able to get it straight. Eden was the perfect place to stay. This wasn't to do with anyone else any more; not Baz or Iain or Mum or Dad or Lisa or Sal; only me. My life. I needed to let myself expand to fill a space—a room, the house, the valley—to be really, one hundred per cent certain.

I thought for a moment Lisa might decide to stay too, but she wanted to get back to Gabe. I asked her to phone Mum and Dad for me when she got back to somewhere with a signal. When the train came I stood on the platform with my bike and waved her off. I told myself this was the right thing to do if I could cycle all the way back without getting off once, and I managed it, even though I had to stand on the pedals near the top of the second hill, and wobbled all over the road because I was going so slow. I hid my bike in bushes near the gate and everything sounded louder as I walked up the track—the cawing rooks and little chirruping woodland birds, the rustle of my footsteps, the soft wind in the tree tops. Bright green garlicky-smelling leaves were poking through the dead leaves. A startled bird went off in a bomb of song. If the key turns without sticking, I told myself, if I can get the stove to light, then it proves I should be here. The key turned easily at the first try. I explored the house again, seeing different things now I was on my own; the basket of twigs and logs beside the living room fire; the airing cupboard in the bathroom, with neatly folded sheets and pillowcases inside. There was a sack of wizened sprouting potatoes in the pantry, and some tins—tomatoes, tuna, sweetcorn. I could make myself a meal.

I decided to light the fire in the sitting room, and to sleep on the sofa there where it was cosy. I brought down clean sheets and a duvet. They were damp but I could warm them by the fire. I spent some time looking through the kitchen drawers for candles. I couldn't find any except half a packet of birthday-cake candles. It didn't matter. I could keep the fire going until I was ready to sleep.

I cleared the ashes out of the grate then went on a hunt for water to wash my hands. I remembered the airing cupboard with its big round hot water tank. Lisa had tried the cold tap but not the hot, and when I turned the hot tap in the bathroom, the pipe gurgled and water came. A tankful would be more than enough to last me.

The afternoon was gone and I scrumpled up the papers lying on the floor, and laid and lit the fire with the last of the matches in a box on the mantelpiece. I made it up with a couple of logs then put the guard in front. I drew the thick curtains and went out into the yard. The sun had already set and the sky was a clear dark blue. I could see the first, brightest stars. The rooks were cawing in the woods but apart from that it was quiet—open and peaceful to the sky. I peed in the garden and hoped I wouldn't need to come out again that night.

When I went indoors I couldn't see in the kitchen and had to feel my way past the table and chairs. My fire was blazing, filling the sitting room with the lovely smell of woodsmoke, making long black shadows behind the sofa and armchairs. I'd already gathered everything I needed—tins and tin opener, saucepan, spoon, mug of water. I held the saucepan over the flames for as long as I could, and ate my tea lukewarm, with my face glowing from the fire. Then I sat staring into the flames, letting my mind empty of everything but those red and yellow dancing shapes. As they died down I wrapped myself in the duvet and snuggled down to sleep, with the warmth of the firelight flickering across my eyelids.

I don't know how long I slept but I woke up with a jerk. When I opened my eyes it was black. I lay still remembering where I was. I turned towards where the fire should be but it had gone. I sat up and put my feet on the gritty carpet. The blackness was like a smothering cloak. There weren't even darker outlines of things, it was all just pitch black. The best thing to do would be to open the curtain.

I made myself creep-shuffle towards the window. My fingers found the heavy velvet of the curtain and pulled, then I put my hand out and touched the cold pane. But it wasn't any lighter. I pulled both the curtains back with a great tearing noise, but my eyes couldn't make any sense of it, there was nothing there but blackness. Was there a wall out there, facing the window, blocking the sky? I was shivering now, I felt my way back to the sofa and pulled the duvet around me. It was like the world had filled up with soot. I imagined being buried alive. No matter how wide you think you're opening your eyes, still dark. Darkness pressing against your face and no way out of it. What if you knew that, even though they thought they'd put you to sleep?

I tried to be sensible. There was no light outside because there weren't any streetlamps or other houses. Good, no light pollution. But my heart was thumping so hard it was making my chest ache. I thought of the young couple who had died here. Being dead is the darkness pressing itself into your eyes and ears and mouth, shutting you into your aloneness. If only there was just the faintest glimmer to show the shape of the window. But everything had vanished. I remembered my mobile which lights up when you press it. I'd switched it off to save the battery because there was no signal. I felt around the floor but it wasn't anywhere near. I was afraid to move, I needed to keep quiet and listen. As each minute passed it was more impossible for me to bear the next. If I can get through this, I told myself . . . if only I can get through this night . . .

When morning came at last my eyes ached from straining for it. They were playing tricks, seeing black shapes in blackness, moving layers of black. Eventually I could make out greyness at the window. Once I was sure the light was there I curled up and dozed.

I went outside an hour or two later, and it was a low misty morning with new puddles. Soft rain must have fallen in the night. The whole valley was muffled in cloud, I couldn't even hear any birds. I felt bleached and thin with sleeplessness. I knew I had been pathetic. But it would be better to back out now than fail at the last minute, and run away. Dr Nichol wanted me to be certain and I was too scared even to close my eyes. I was too scared of the dark.

Thursday night

When he's emptied the bucket he says, 'You're smelly, Jess. You need a bath.'

'I can't smell me.'

'You'd be more comfortable if you had a bath. I don't understand you.'

'Clearly.'

'Oh for God's sake. D'you want to make yourself ill?'

'Why not? I think I'll go on hunger strike.'

'I doubt it.'

'You doubt it. You still think I'm a greedy little kid. You still think you *know*, don't you? You still think you know everything about me.'

'I know you better than anyone alive. That's why I know you're making a mistake. And that you'll come out the other side of this and thank me.'

'You don't know. There are millions of things about me you *don't know*!'

'I'm going to run you a bath.'

'I'm not getting into it.'

He goes out and I hear the clank of the plug, the faint squeak of the tap, the water gushing out in spurts through the old unused pipes. I hear him swirling it about, adding cold, turning off the hot. Eventually both taps go silent and he comes back in. 'It's ready.'

I don't move. The tap drips.

'I'll undo your locks in the bathroom then shut you in and leave you in privacy to undress and sort yourself out. I'll bring your clean clothes up.'

How kind of him. I don't move.

'Come on Jess.'

'I'm sorry but I can't help you.'

'Look, just come and look at the bath—you'll see how much you want to get in.'

I don't move.

'Have I got to carry you?'

I shrug.

'For God's sake Jess, what game are you playing now?'

'Passive resistance.' You taught me about that, remember? Remember telling me about Mahatma Ghandi?

'Stop being silly.'

I guess he doesn't remember.

'I'm going downstairs. Your bath's getting cold. Call me when you change your mind.'

When you change your mind. He thinks he can make whatever he wants happen—not *if*, but *when*. 'I'm not your puppet!' I yell.

His footsteps on the stairs pause, then continue down.

I don't owe him anything. This is enough now. He has plotted and planned against me, bullied me, hurt me. He has kept me here since Saturday! And he still thinks he knows best, he's completely undented. I shouldn't hold anything in reserve. I should do whatever it takes to get my way—lying, fighting, damaging—using whatever means I can find.

He hasn't hesitated to use force. And what about that box? This is on day one, when he's got me tied up on the floor. He goes out to the car and brings in a cardboard box. With *tools*. There's a hammer and drill and screwdriver, and he goes upstairs and I hear him drilling into the doorframe, fitting the thing that he slips the lock through when he locks me in. He *planned* that. At our house, in our garage, he went through the tool box and put stuff in the cardboard box, with new bikelocks and rope and the scarf for a gag, thinking 'I'm going to use these on Jessie.' How *dare* he?

I'll show him. I'll show him whether he can control me. I am so angry I start shaking with hunger. 'I want FOOD!' I shout.

He runs up the stairs.

'Food! Food!'

'I'll make you something when you've had your bath.'

'FOOD!'

He goes downstairs and shuts the door.

I have to fight back tears. I'm not going to cry again here. He's wrong and I'm right, and now it's time to do anything I have to do, to prove it.

But I'm so hungry I can't think. When did he last

feed me? Lunchtime, scrambled eggs and veggie sausages. I shouldn't be this hungry. I try telling my stomach that but it's not interested. I see my little pimple of a brain sitting on top of a big greedy body trying to order it about. When they put your brain to sleep that's all you'll be: a big greedy body.

No. No. Calm down. Inhale. Exhale. Calm. I think of the swishing machines.

My body is clever. With rhythms and secrets and powers that are nothing to do with my mind. My body will take over, growing the perfect life inside me. And my silly jabbering mind will be still.

I make myself focus on the fragment of grey sky I can see through the window. It's not completely dark. It's going to be alright. I am in control. I can feel myself getting stronger. I haven't gone through all this, just for him to foil me now.

I'm going to beat you, Dad.

Twenty-five

In the Eden pantry I found a tin of peaches and had them for breakfast. By the time I'd had a wash and packed up and made it look as if I hadn't been there, the mist was lifting. I was ashamed. I walked out through the back garden. There was a raw new latch gate at the far end, swollen with damp. It let out onto a path which ran alongside the stream. On the other side there was a hedge of bare black prickly twigs sprinkled with star-white flowers. *Blackthorn* popped into my head and I remembered walks with my Father of Wisdom when he was trying to teach me plants' names. I used to tease him by deliberately getting them wrong and calling everything 'hydrangea', but now I thought to know about plants would be one of the most useful kinds of knowledge, if I was going to live here.

As I picked my way through the puddles I started to hear all the layers of distance around me; close by the rushing of the stream, and a robin singing in the hedge; further away the bleating of sheep and cawing of rooks building their nests in the high bare trees near the top of the wood.

The path was becoming boggy and I climbed up away from the streamside to drier ground. It smelled bad, and as I pulled myself over the wall and jumped down into the field, two crows flapped up in my face nearly making me overbalance. A dead ewe was lying there. And a raw mess of blood and slime beside her. It must have been her lamb. I steadied myself against the wall. There were a load of sheep by the opposite hedge. Their matted wool was trailing off them in clumps.

They watched me as I went on slowly to the next gate and then back down to the stream. For an instant I thought I saw a searing flash of blue. Was it a kingfisher? It was gone before I could tell. 'Better than a peacock,' I whispered to myself. I crossed a footbridge and took the path up the opposite side of the valley, climbing till I could look down on the whole thing as if it was a model. The sun had finally broken through the mist, in soft white light. I imagined Lisa's pear and apple trees in a haze of blossom, neat green rows of vegetables growing, smoke spiralling up from the farmhouse chimney. The goat and her kid gambolling in the field, hens clucking and crowing, Lisa with a basket collecting eggs. It would be an idyll.

But I could still taste the smell of the dead sheep. As we grew old and stiff, weeds would start to choke the fields. Foxes would take the chickens, the goats would run wild through the decaying fence, cabbages and onions would go to seed. Then unpruned trees would grow into a tangled thicket, the bees would swarm, and winter gales would lift slates from the roof again. I imagined an old crone hunched over a fire gnawing a wizened apple. The last human being.

To live in this Eden, you would need fruit of the tree of No-Knowledge. How else could you dig the ground, repair the buildings, rebuild stone walls? You could only do it if you blanked out MDS. You could only do it in ignorance—like the poor young couple who had lived here last year. I sat on a tumble-down wall and stared at the view as the mist burned off. It came to me like a leap beyond my own fear. Like taking off and flying. I could see there was only one thing to do. And this time I really really knew.

I knew it was real because I was frightened. I would do it.

I phoned Dr Nichol from the train as soon as I got a signal, and told her I was ready.

'Sure?'

'Sure.'

'So soon?'

'Yes, I promise you.'

'Take one more week, Jessie. Come and see me a week on Monday: 11.15.'

There was a message on my phone from Mum, sounding upset, asking me to call her. I knew what that was. When I rang she told me the funeral would be next Sunday. I said I was on my way home.

*

Over that week I helped Mum clear Mandy's flat. She had started on the kitchen while Mandy lay sedated in her room; she told me she couldn't sit and do nothing. She wanted me to have the puppets and masks. I filled a suitcase with them because I didn't know what else to do. How could I ever tell her? I imagined ringing her up from hospital on the day of my implantation. Or even asking Mr Golding to do it, afterwards. Maybe that would be kindest. At least she wouldn't have the anguish of waiting for it to happen. It would be clean and sudden, as if I'd been knocked down by a bus.

Dad and I wrote the speech about Mandy's life, and I agreed to read it at the funeral. It was the least I could do. There were only twelve people there; her old friends had drifted away, over the months she'd been ill. Clive came, looking wretched, and her neighbour Caroline, and Christine and the others from her theatre group; with us and the celebrant, that was about it. It was just another MDS funeral. None of us cried, the crying had all been done. There was comfort in the routine of it, the singing, the account of Mandy's life, the happy pictures on the wall. In my head I kept transposing it to my own funeral. Maybe Sal and Baz and Lisa would be there. There would be less of a story to tell, since my life was so much shorter than hers. But there would be one new person there. A brand new life, cuddled in Dad's arms. She would make it up to them. Somehow we got through the weekend. And then it was Monday morning, when I could go and see Dr Nichol.

I told her what had happened to make me certain. I *was* certain, I was clear; she called in a witness and I signed the papers. I wanted it to be soon, because every day that passes makes me older. The younger the mother, the better chance the baby has.

'You have to tell your parents.'

'But how can I? How can I when all this has happened?'

'You have to tell them.'

'If I'd left home—or if I ran away—they wouldn't know then.'

'Don't be silly Jess. Looking at your cycle, you could be ready for implantation in ten days. Or, of course, we could wait another month. Either way, they need to know. And if you want early implantation they need to know today. Think how it would reflect on the clinic, if we were seen to be taking on girls without their parents' knowledge.'

Publicity. Iain. Baz had taken it off the website for me, but what else might Iain be planning? Well, in ten days I wouldn't have to worry about any of this—in ten days I would be free.

I went home with dragging feet.

I told them as soon as they were both in from work, and I felt like a monster. Mum kept repeating, 'You can't do this, Jess.' Dad didn't believe me; and after he'd asked about every stage of the process, he got angry with the clinic, and took the phone into the spare room to ring Mr Golding. We could hear his raised voice through two closed doors. Mum was pelting me with questions. Was it because of Mand? Was it because of those boys who attacked me? Was it because of her and Dad fighting? Or YOFI? Or being left on my own so much recently? Had they pressured me or ignored me or somehow made me think . . . ?

'You don't pull my strings, Mum. I've thought this out for myself. It's not because of *any*one.'

I was upset, she said. What had happened to Mandy was enough to upset anyone. I was depressed, there had been too much bad news. What I needed was to see a counsellor, to get some treatment for depression, to be helped and loved and protected until I could feel good about my life again.

'I feel good. I'm happy. I know what I'm doing.'

Pointless talk, I couldn't make her see anything but what she already saw. Dad came back white-faced and furious and told Mum he'd go and see Golding first thing in the morning. 'We'll get this stopped.'

I told them I was sorry, really really sorry, but that it was up to me. When we got into the same round of questions and objections for the third time, I told them I was going to bed. I washed my face and cleaned my teeth then lay on the floor listening to the rise and fall of their voices down below. I knew they were telling each other it was impossible. They would find a way to bring me to my senses. I stared at the beech tree through the open curtain; at the way the street light made the branches shine with a dull blackish-orange. I wanted this time to be over because none of it would be any good now. It would all be tears and anger. Ten days had seemed short but now it was too long.

After a while Dad came up and knocked. He apologised for being angry and said we needed to talk.

'I don't know what to say, Dad. I can't make it better.'

'Come in to work with me tomorrow. I want to show you something.'

'D'you promise not to fight with Mr Golding?'

'I promise, if you come in with me.'

'OK.'

He went back down and the voices ran on and on, until Mum's broke down in sobs. I peeled myself off the floor and pulled off my clothes and got in bed. I felt as flat and heavy as if a steam roller was on top of me. I just wanted it to end.

Twenty-six

I woke up feeling happy; everything was clear for me.
Then I remembered Mum and Dad. It was pitiful to
see them in the morning, crashing around the house,
ugly and clumsy, stiff with unhappiness. I tried to cheer
them up with a story I read in the Sunday paper, under
the title *Monkey Business*. There was an animal rights
protestor who set off by car from Chester, trying to
get to the research lab demo with his friend and his
friend's pet monkey. They took the monkey to show
solidarity with the victims incarcerated in the research
lab. They got stuck in the traffic jam, and then their
car was singled out by a gang who'd come down to the
motorway from a footbridge. The gang dragged the two
friends out and stole their iPods, phones, and the
monkey, tying a scarf to its collar and dragging it away.
But then a carful of FLAME women spotted them
trying to get the monkey over the crash barrier, and
rushed over and attacked them. They rescued the

monkey which they thought had been stolen from the labs. They flagged down a passing police car and handed it over to them. The police got a few miles down the road and had to stop at a barricade of burning cars, and while they were sorting that out, a bunch of Noahs liberated the monkey to take back to their congregation as evidence of the devil's work being committed in the research labs. The monkey's owner walked ten miles up and down the motorway to find it. The Noahs had to give it back because the monkey started hurling itself around their van with joy when he came to the driver's window.

They both looked at me as if I'd fallen from another planet. Then I got Mum on her own in the bedroom and asked her to come to the *Mothers For Life* meeting with me.

'Jess, I'll do anything you want—anything in the world, but you must listen to what Joe and I are saying.'

'I'm listening. I've listened. Will you come tonight?'

'You're *not* listening. You're not taking any of it in.'

'I've already thought about it, Mum, I've been thinking for weeks. Tonight?'

She sighed and pulled a face but she didn't refuse.

By the time we got into the car they had both lapsed back into grim silence. When there's that kind of silence between them it's like a force field, you simply can't break through it. I didn't say anything about travelling by car. It wouldn't have been fair to make a fuss.

Even after we'd dropped Mum off, Dad still didn't talk until we were walking across the car parks to the lab. Then he said, 'There's something I want you to see.' I hadn't been down to my dad's lab since the day of my medical. When he tapped in the code and pushed open the door for me there was that lovely smell it always has, that hits a funny-bone in my head.

I remembered all the times I'd been to Dad's lab; hanging about waiting for him to finish work, chatting to Ali, looking down the microscope. But today the lab was different. It was so full you could hardly move. One wall was crammed with stacked-up freezers. They were all wrapped round with that yellow and black police tape, the sort they put around the scene of a crime. I asked him why.

'The FLAME women were still on the front steps yesterday,' he said. 'But they haven't come round the side, or tried to get in, since last Thursday. We've moved all the freezers down here, security's been tightened up.' I hung my coat on the back of the door and sat on one of the high stools at the bench. 'I've got to take stuff up for the morning clinic,' he said, 'then we'll visit the Sleeping Beauties.' He's never taken me on to the ward before—I've only ever seen the labs. In the little washroom he scrubbed up and changed his clothes and put on his white coat. 'You too,' he said. 'You can wear Ali's.' He started taking racks of test tubes out of the sterilising unit and putting them on a trolley; bottles of clear liquid, vacuum-packed instruments.

I wanted to ask about the police tape but something held me back. I thought there must be bodies in the freezers. I scrubbed under my fingernails with the tingly soap and switched my mind to the subject of the morning clinic. What on earth were they doing in the clinic? 'I thought there wasn't any more IVF?'

'There isn't. These are egg donors. How do you

think we're supplying the research labs with embryos to work on? We're fertilising as many eggs as we possibly can, we're an embryo production line.'

'For experiments like at Wettenhall?'

He put down the box he was holding. 'Yes Jess. Weren't you listening when we talked at the reservoir? Don't you understand how much research is going on all the time, to find a way of ending this?' He covered the trolley and pushed out through the swing door, and I buttoned up my white coat. It was the first time I'd really thought about the donors—apart from the ones on TV fighting at the animal labs and making a fuss. But women were coming here every day to donate their eggs. They were taking drugs to make themselves super-ovulate, then going through the whole business of egg extraction. They came here quietly, day after day, giving up their eggs to help solve MDS.

By the time Dad came back I had plucked up the courage to ask him about the freezers.

'They're the pre-MDS embryos.'

'Why have the police put tape around them?'

'They're Government property.'

'Government?'

'I thought you were supposed to know what you're getting yourself into?'

'I do.'

'Alright then,' he said. 'Now I want you to come with me onto the ward.'

I realised then that one of the embryos in those chests would be given to me. She was like those people on star-ships who get frozen so they won't grow old while they travel through light years. She'd been frozen

since her first spark of life, and lain hidden and innocent, waiting for the moment when they'd take her out
and gently warm her, and put her inside me to grow.

My dad turned round and adjusted my mask, then
he hurried down the corridor, pushing open the swing
doors with his elbow, turning right and up the stairs,
and at last stopping to glance through the window in
a door, before elbowing it open and leading me in to
the ward. It was a long dark half-empty room. I could
hear a rhythmic swishing sound, a bit like waves
crashing on a beach. I remembered the ALF film of the
monkeys and sheep in the research lab. What if I saw
something terrible?

That was why he'd brought me. He wanted me to be
frightened. Something cold and sharp seemed to stick in
my throat. Dad walked between empty beds to the first
one surrounded by a bank of machines. In the strange
glow of the monitors I could see the still figure lying
there. Dad stopped a little short of the bed and
motioned for me to go ahead. His eyes above his mask
looked glittery.

I walked closer to the bed. There was a chair at one
side for visitors. I made myself look. She was lying
very neatly, with her arms outside the covers and a
tube going into white bandaging on her throat. Another
tube snaked down under the sheet to her chest. There
was a peg on one thin finger, attached to a wire that
led to a monitor. She looked as if she was asleep. I
wasn't sure what Dad was wanting me to do, but he
just stood there staring at a screen. So I sat in the visitor's chair. The loud swishing sound made my heart
race. After a while I realised that it was actually

breathing, it was the thing that was pumping air into and out of her lungs. I forced my own breathing to slow until I was inhaling and exhaling in time with it. In, out, in, out, this is how we breathe. Calm. In the dimness she had a sweet face. Her nose was turned up just a tiny bit at the end, and her fair hair was spread out on the pillow. She looked about 17. I watched green lights winking on the monitors, and liquid moving through a transparent tube. It was alright. I could see why they called them Sleeping Beauties. She had a wide wedding ring and she had tiny studs in her ears, gold with a blue stone in the middle. I thought about her choosing the earrings—or maybe being given them as a present from her husband. I thought of her opening the box and smiling; 'I'll wear these for luck.'

Dad motioned me over to the next bed. This girl was Asian and she looked even younger. She had a tiny frown on her face, a little crease between her eyes, as if she was having to concentrate on something in her dream. I wanted to kiss her and smooth it away. My dad flicked some switches and a greenish picture came up on the screen. 'That's her baby,' he said. 'There's the head, see?' It was hard to make out, the image was moving and flickering a bit, it seemed terribly remote. I could believe it was hidden deep deep inside her, and was shy maybe of being seen. I nodded at Dad and he switched it off. I didn't know if I was allowed but I just wanted to touch the girl, and I brushed my fingers along her arm. Her skin was warm and soft, it wasn't frightening—she was alive. I thought, the whole of her is turned inward. Turned inward to that fragile creature we just saw glimmering on the screen, all her stillness is focussed on that. She was suspending her whole being for the baby.

Dad set off back towards the door. When we got to the lab he ripped off his mask and asked me what I thought of the Sleeping Beauties.

'They look peaceful.'

He stared at me. 'Peaceful? They're in a coma. Their brains are rotting with MDS.'

'They're doing what they've chosen to do.'

He sat on one of the stools and put his elbows on the workbench. He rested his head in his hands, staring down at the dark wood.

'Dad?'

'It makes me feel sick.'

'Why?'

'They're living dead. Zombies. Machines are pumping their lungs. And then their mothers come and sit by them and hold their hands and comb their hair—'

'It must help their mothers to bear it.'

'You really don't find it disgusting?'

'You said yourself, for there to be new life—'

'You know what happens to them afterwards? After the baby's taken out?'

'They get switched off.'

'Some families want to believe a person's still there. They keep this—this piece of meat alive, pretending to themselves that one day it might magically be restored.' He carefully moved his stool under the bench. He lifted the next one and put it under the bench too, not scraping it. He began to walk up and down in the little space he had made. 'I don't know how to get through to you.'

'I understand you, Dad. I just don't agree.'

'You think you've got some sort of mission.'

'I know what I want to do.'

'No you don't. You're in a fantasy world, playing the role of heroine.'

'I'm doing what I've chosen.'

'You want to save the world.'

'What's wrong with that?'

He sighed in exasperation. 'You are too young to understand. People get by.'

'I don't want to get by. I want to know my life's been useful.'

'You'll be a lump of meat that people have to wash and turn!'

We stood staring at each other hopelessly then I went and put my arms around him. After a moment he hugged me back. 'This is so silly,' he said softly. 'All this talk about death. Please, Jess, this has to stop.'

'It can't stop now. You said yourself—it's helping the survival of the whole race.'

'I am going to have to lock you up till you come to your senses.'

He said this very calmly and regretfully, as if it was not a new thought. And if I'd had a grain of sense I would have believed him. 'That would be kidnapping.'

'Not always. When youngsters are indoctrinated by dangerous cults their parents employ experts to de-programme them.'

'You know I'm not indoctrinated. You couldn't hold me against my will.'

'If I can't persuade you rationally, what choice have

I got?' A timer bell rang and he glanced towards the heat cabinets. 'We'll have to finish this conversation tonight.' He began to shift things around.

'There isn't anything else to say,' I told him, pulling on my coat. He came and let me out into the car park. It was drizzling and I had no umbrella. I strode to the bus stop, feeling the rain sticking my hair to my head and making chilly runnels down my neck. Feeling the gritty pavement through the soles of my shoes, and the specks of water in the air as they hit my face. Imagining lying there in the dimness with the big swishing machine pumping my lungs. I wouldn't be dead, because something in me, a little green shape, would be alive and growing. I would be lying there dreaming her into existence.

I'd been home about half an hour when the phone rang. Sal. She launched off before I could get a word in. 'Jess, don't do it. Baz has told me. You mustn't do it.'

Baz—well, I guess I shouldn't have been surprised.

'Jess, you have to listen to me. It's not just because I don't approve. Listen, you'd be in danger—'

It was hard to see how I could be in any more danger than I was already putting myself into. Sal'd been anti-everything ever since the rape, and I couldn't help it. I couldn't fix it. I told her I was expecting a phone call from Dad.

'You know FLAME are targeting Sleeping Beauty clinics?'

'Well there's been a picket at my dad's work. But people still go in and out.'

'For now. But the tactics will be changing. The plan is to be much more aggressive.'

'Look Sal, I'm sure I can get into the clinic, and once I'm in there's not much FLAME can do.'

'They don't know about this embryo implant programme.'

'So?'

'So. Imagine what a coup it would be for them to stop it.'

'Well if they don't know about it they can't, can they.'

'I could tell them.'

I thought of the peaceful face of the first Sleeping Beauty whose bed I'd sat by. Sal was my friend. 'I trust you,' I said. 'Sal, I trust you to keep my secret.' I put the phone down. Then I tried Dad's direct line at the lab but there was no reply.

I paced about for a bit and made myself a cheese sandwich, and checked the news. The Wettenhall lab area was still sealed off but they'd finally cleared the motorway. One commentator said the animal experiments were terminated, another said that no decisions had been taken and there would be a government announcement shortly. The police had made eighty-seven arrests and taken them to that special terrorist detention centre in the Lake District. Arguments raged about the legality of the Wettenhall research, and could donors sue, and would the company be prosecuted? Since their office in London had been firebombed, prosecution sounded like the least of their worries.

I decided to go and see Baz.

There would never be a good time; he had every

reason to be furious with me. But I imagined him putting his arms around me, even if it was only for a minute. I just wanted him to hold me. I persuaded myself that it would be easier for him, once I'd gone, if he could remember one last moment of kindness between us.

At Baz's house his mum answered the door. I smiled to myself because I could hear his piano playing from the doorstep. She said she'd call him but I told her it was fine, I'd go and tell him myself. As I was going down the stairs to his room she said, 'I think he's got a visitor.' I knocked but I knew he wouldn't hear me while he was playing, so I opened the door. Baz was hunched over his piano keyboard, oblivious. The person who was sitting wrapped in a duvet on his bed looked up and met my eyes. Rosa.

For a moment I couldn't move. Then I ran up the stairs and out of the house as fast as I could. I ran all the way home. I sat on my bed and gasped for breath, with my heart pounding under my ribs as if it was trying to escape.

I sat there all afternoon. Quite simply I couldn't think of anything else to do. Every thought I tried to think curled up and died before I got to the end of it. How long had Baz and Rosa—? Why had she asked me if I was still friends with him? Had the pair of them talked about me? I couldn't move, not even to wrap the duvet around me, although I was cold. The light faded and it began to get dark. My phone rang. For a moment I thought I wouldn't answer it but then I did.

'You came to see me,' he said.

'Yes.'

'*She* came to see me.'

'Why?'

'She was upset.'

'But why *you*?'

'Why should you care?'

'Because I do.'

'There's no reason why I shouldn't see her.'

'Why aren't you angry with *her*?'

Baz sighed.

'Her reasons for volunteering are mad. She's mad. Do you really—' I'd started crying. I didn't want to, but I couldn't stop. 'D'you really like her?'

'Her reasons aren't any more mad than yours.'

'Baz? Baz?' I couldn't believe it. I needed him to understand it was *me*, Jessie, talking to him.

'Her boyfriend hit her. She hasn't got anybody.'

'Didn't you ever love me?'

'What has that got to do with it?' he asked angrily. 'What's the point in loving anyone?'

Twenty-seven

I couldn't make Mum go to *Mothers for Life*. She said it was unendurable, and I felt about the same. Nothing was endurable. My heart was dead and I was clockwork. But I was wound up and I would run. She called me from work because we'd agreed to meet in town. So I told her I'd make tea ready for when she came home.

I opened the freezer and started rooting through. The icy ache in my fingers was a relief. I was still doing it when Dad came in—in the middle of the afternoon. He was carrying a box of files and papers. 'What's up?'

He dumped the papers in the spare room and came back into the kitchen.

'Dad? What's happened?'

'I've left work.'

'Left?'

'A disagreement with Golding.'

'About me?'

He ran a glass of water.

'Can't you go back?'

'Jess, why would I want to work for a man who is trying to murder my daughter?'

'But you can't give up your job!'

'Don't you think this is more important than my job?'

'No. No. I want you to carry on with your life. I don't want everything to change.'

'Well tough. Maybe you need to think about how what you do affects other people.'

'I know it does—I know it does—I keep telling you I'm sorry.'

'Right. Well, sorry, but I've left work.'

He would go back once I was gone, surely he would. 'What did Mr Golding say?'

'He told me to clear my desk and said he was getting the key code changed this afternoon.'

'What did you do? Did you hit him?'

He shrugged, refilled his glass and went into the spare room. He closed the door behind him.

All the time I was cooking (I found frozen spinach, and there was cottage cheese in the fridge, so hey presto—spinach lasagne) I was conscious of him in the spare room giving off rays of bad temper like a piece of radioactive waste. The more I chopped and fried my onions and garlic, the more I thought, this is simply about misunderstanding. Mum and Dad don't understand. They think it's something awful. If I could make them see that actually it's making me happy; that deciding what I'm going to do, and setting that in motion, is giving me power; that for the first time in my life I feel safe and in control—if I could make them understand that, then surely they wouldn't be upset? Because they must *want* me to be happy, surely? I tried to think of a way of describing it that would make it easy for them. I was on one of those moving walkways at the airport—a travellator; all my preparations had been made, all the fussing and checking and dithering and heartbreak, and now I was simply riding to the check-in desk, where I would be processed and allowed to board the plane. And then—then—I'd fly away. There was nothing to be sad about.

It was emotional blackmail, what Dad was doing— trying to show how unhappy and disrupted I was making his life, so I'd feel guilty enough to stop doing what I wanted to do. He was unhappy—true enough. I wished he wasn't. But I could see his tantrum and his sulking were ways to try and get what he wanted, and I could see he never would.

I can still feel like that now—superior, and almost pitying of him; sad that he can't see the bigger picture. Then suddenly it all wavers and morphs back into me being the child and him the parent, and I'm scared of his anger and of whatever it is he knows that I don't understand. I'm scared of my own mistakes, I can't bear not to have his approval. I chop and change, like Alice in Wonderland when she's taken her *Drink Me* medicine and she grows or shrinks but is always the wrong size. The more I think now, the worse it gets. All I can do is cling on to my decision, for better or worse, there's no steady footing anywhere else.

On that afternoon, as I made my tomato sauce, it seemed simpler. I think that was the first time I felt that kind of condescending pity for him, like a parent who's sent a naughty child to his room. 'That's right, stay there and sulk till you're ready to come out and behave sensibly.'

When Mum came in she already knew; he must have phoned her. She went into the spare room and shut the door and I heard them talking then arguing. I don't know if I imagined it but it seemed to me they were blaming each other for what I was doing. The lasagne was in the oven and I put on my coat and went out into the darkness of the garden. It was damp and cloudy, not very cold: the bare bushes and stalks in the garden all cast black spiky shadows, from the street lamp. Baz crept into my thoughts and I squeezed him out. No. No. Mum and Dad argued before they had this to argue about, I told myself. I can't live my life to please them. Their voices filled the house but out here the darkness was huge, all this space and silence. Would she stand out here one day, my surrogate daughter? Would she stand in the darkness of the garden, looking at the lit windows of houses and thinking, my life is bigger than theirs? She would, I felt sure she would. But I couldn't stop seeing Rosa, huddled in the duvet on Baz's bed, glaring at me like a cat.

Somehow the evening was got through, and at the end of it Dad was in the spare room again, and Mum was sitting at the table staring at her hands. I unloaded the dishwasher. Between the crushing ache of Baz, and Mum and Dad's misery, I felt squeezed almost flat. It was only when I concentrated on what I was going to do that I could draw a deep breath and fill myself up again. I wasn't trapped. I could escape. 'Mum, there's no point in him leaving work, it's not going to make any difference—'

'Maybe it makes a difference to him.'

The only difference I could see would be he'd have to get another job that didn't suit him so well. I sat opposite her and took hold of her hand.

'What do you want?' she said.

'I want you and Dad to accept what I'm doing, and not be horrible to each other.'

'You can't legislate for how horrible we are.'

'No, but—'

'And you can't honestly imagine that we'll ever accept what you want to do.'

'You gave me life. So you have to allow me to choose what to do with it.'

'Not to throw it away—'

'I'm not throwing it away. I'm using it for the future.'

'The future is an abstract concept, Jess.'

'No, it's my child and my child's child.'

'I'm not listening to this.'

'You have to. It makes me happy, you know?'

'No,' she said, 'I don't. I don't know how that feels.'

'Mum. Something must make you happy? Your friends, work—'

'Nothing.'

'Going on holiday.'

She gave a little laugh and shook her head.

'I can make you happy.'

'This is nonsense Jess.'

'Mum, I've found the one thing I want to do with

my life. And you'll be able to look after my baby and love her.'

'I don't want *your* daughter. I want *my* daughter.'

'I don't belong to you any more than you belonged to Nanna.'

She pushed her chair back abruptly and went to the kitchen door. There she stopped, and came round to where I was sitting at the table. She put her hands on my shoulders and kissed me on the cheek, and told me she loved me. Then she went upstairs.

After a bit I went and listened at the spare room door. I could hear Dad moving things about. He was probably going to sleep down there, he usually did when they were fighting. I was their captive. Like in *Gulliver's Travels* when the little people tie him down while he's sleeping, with thousands of tiny ropes which are no thicker than hairs, but which taken all together hold him prisoner. Something had to snap.

I went to bed and lay with my curtains open staring up at the beech tree and the sky. I had to keep slamming the door on thoughts of Baz, just slamming and slamming and closing it away because there was no word from him and there never would be and there was nothing for me to do but shut it out. I had to find a way of getting through to Mum and Dad. One thing. One step at a time.

The cloud was clearing, I could see a couple of the brightest stars, twinkling away through the branches. Those stars had witnessed all this a thousand times; a girl whose boyfriend likes someone else; parents upset because their child is going away. When I closed my eyes the tracery of the dark branches against the sky stayed on the inside of my eyelids like the mesh I was going to escape through. The open skies were waiting for me. When I slept my dreams were as big and wide as space, and in amongst them floated an idea, a solution, about how to talk to Mum.

I love the way your brain can do that—solve things while you sleep. I remember talking to Dad about it, years ago. He said it's true and it goes to show how much of your brain you don't consciously use, like the elves and the shoemaker. The shoemaker went to bed every night leaving unfinished shoes, he was always too tired to finish them off. And every night while he slept, the elves came and hammered and trimmed and sewed, and every morning he woke up to find a perfectly completed pair of shoes.

That's what my elves did that night. I woke up understanding that Mum was shifting. She was coming round. What I needed to do was get her away from Dad for long enough for her to acknowledge it. I needed to take her somewhere where she could look up into the distance and see light and space. Where she could see what I saw. I'd thought of the perfect place: the seaside!

I would take her back to Scarborough. Nanna Bessie's caravan there was one of my most favourite places in the world. I remember kneeling up on my narrow bed, pushing the stiff little curtain to one side so I could see out. I remember the morning sun shining in, making a huge dazzle in the sea behind the other caravans that stood silhouetted like cardboard cutouts, parked up to the field edge. On the other side of the hedge runs the coast path, along the top of the crumbling cliffs. Frilly waves rush at the pebbles and fill the air with their jostling sounds. And you can look out over the sea and see the path of sheer light the sun makes across it, leading directly to where you stand, up on the windy cliff.

We used to go in the car with two suitcases and a cardboard box of groceries and Mum's beach bag with bucket and spade and Frisbee in it, singing daft songs and playing *I spy*. But she and I could go on the train, without telling Dad. I'd tell her I wanted to go there and it was absolutely true. I only had a short time, I didn't want to waste a minute. I crept into Mum's room and snuggled up to her in bed like I used to when I was little. I told her I wanted to go to the seaside. I persuaded her to take the day off work.

Twenty-eight

There was hardly anyone on the train, only three other people in the whole carriage. We sat opposite each other with fields and moors rushing by our window. You could feel the wind buffeting the train. Some of the trees we passed were bent almost sideways with it. 'It's always windy at Scarborough,' Mum said, 'I used to think the caravan would take off, at night.'

'I remember it in the day,' I said. 'Not at night.'

'Oh at night it was like being inside a plane,' she said. 'The roaring noise it made, and that scratched plastic window. I used to imagine we'd wake up somewhere altogether different, miles inland.'

We remembered how Dad used to build these huge fortifications on the beach. Not just a castle and a moat, but earthworks like the Great Wall of China. And wide channels to divert the tide and hold it back. We used to spend the whole day digging and other kids and their dads would come and help us, and Mum

267

found me shells to use for windows and doors. 'Remember the jewellery boxes?' she said. That was what we did when it rained. We sat either side of the red fold-down Formica table in the caravan, with the rain drumming on the roof, and we glued baby pink clam shells and yellow snail shells onto Maltesers boxes, which I took home as souvenirs for my friends.

'And the crabs,' I said, and we laughed. I used to see how many I could catch in a day. All the ones we found when we were digging, or along the tide-line as we looked for shells, I scooped up on my spade and plopped into a bucket. At the end of the day I'd tip them out on the sand and count them to see if I'd beaten my record, and it would be a crab race, as they scuttled back down to the sea. But one day, I don't know why, I took the bucketful back to the caravan and left them by the steps. And Dad got up in the night to pee and knocked the bucket over. I remember hearing him swearing and Mum calling 'What is it Joe?' and both of us got up and went out onto the step. Dad was hopping about trying to catch crabs in the dark, swooshing them onto the spade with a furled up news-paper. We flashed the torch around and they were under the caravan and everywhere, crawling up and down the spiky tufts of grass.

'He could have let them be,' said Mum. 'They would've headed for the sea eventually.'

'But what about the road?' I reminded her. 'Imagine if someone's driving along and suddenly their head-lamps light up a crowd of crabs scuttling across—and then you hear this awful crackle as the car runs over them!'

'A crustacean catastrophe,' she said and smiled, leaning back against her seat. It was alright to be happy.

When we got to Scarborough we zipped up our coats and pulled our hats down over our ears and headed straight from the station to the beach. Massive pale clouds came charging across the sky, with spokes of white sunlight wheeling out between them. At the end of the beach we walked past the empty shops and arcades and closed cafés, and climbed up over the bridge to the castle. The ruins made pockets of stillness in the streaming air. We plunged out again across the bleached meadow to the edge of the castle-island and stood there gulping at the air as it blasted into our faces. Mum pointed to a big rock jutting up further along the path and started to battle her way towards it. There was a log rolled against its base, facing inland. Other people must have used it as a shelter, and we sat there huddled out of the rushing wind. Now we could hear each other speak again.

'You wouldn't want to be out in a boat in this!' she said.

I imagined the icy spray splashing up at you as each wave slammed into the side, and the fantastic lurch and slide of the boat and the excitement of the danger. 'I'd love it!'

'I used to feel like that,' Mum said.

'How d'you mean?'

'As if nothing could hurt me.'

'I don't think that.'

'You think you'll come out of this unscathed. That you're different from all the other girls.'

'No Mum, I don't.'

'You don't think about losing consciousness and never coming back again to places like this.'

'If we don't take MDS seriously—'

'Jessie, they'll fix it. They'll figure something out. They always do.' The twiggy branch of a bush came blowing across the flattened grass, bowling over and over itself.

'This is the way of fixing it.'

'There'll be another way.'

'You mean, let someone else volunteer.'

'The world isn't like that, Jess. One person can't just—'

'One person *can*, Mum. That's the point. That's why it's so fantastic. I *can* make a difference.'

Mum looked at me, then she lumbered to her feet and out into the wind again. I got up and followed her. She was leaning into the wind, going towards the cliff edge 'Mum!' I shouted, but she didn't hear me. I ran after her but she stopped a couple of metres short of the edge. She stood staring across at the rocky inlet to our right. The foam from the boiling waves had been scooped off by the wind, and slathered against the cliffs like meringue. She turned to me, her hair streaming across her face. She was gesturing to the cliff edge but the wind blew her words away. She came and leant right in close to me. Her breath was warm against my ear.

'Why don't you fly?'

I tilted back my head and tried to see her face. But she pulled me close again.

'If you are a superhero? Why don't you just fly?' Her voice cracked.

I put my arms around her. 'Mum, Mum, it's OK.' She let me hold her for a moment then she stumbled back to the shelter. She sat on the log and crouched over, burying her head in her arms. I sat beside her and waited. After a bit she raised her head and wiped her wet face on her gloves.

'I didn't sign up for this,' she said in a flat little voice. 'I didn't ask to be mother of Joan of fucking Arc.'

'Look,' I said, 'this is why I was put on earth.'

'*Not knowing* why you're on earth is the human condition.'

'It's not!' I shouted happily. 'It's not!'

'Jessie, you'll die.'

'This isn't about one individual. The mass of people, the human race—that's more important than any individual.'

'That's a frightening way to think. Once you say individuals can be sacrificed—'

'Mum. Think of the women who've already died. Think of all the women who have died.' We were sitting there with the wind howling past the shadow of our rock. I knew we were both thinking about Mandy. But there were all the women. And their babies. All of them. Mum was staring straight ahead at nothing. Tears rolled down her face. She was like a candle burning brightly. Like wax, melting. I thought, at last, she can see. I knelt down in front of her and clasped her gloved hands. 'You see?' I said. 'You see? It's really really simple.' I put my arms around her. I could feel her gulping for air like a person drowning.

'Now you see, you see, you see,' I murmured into her hair. 'Everything will be alright.' At last she stopped and lifted her head, and I wiped her cheeks with my silky scarf.

'You make me afraid,' she whispered, and I laughed at her. 'No,' she said. 'It's true. You've turned into something else.'

'I don't want you to be sad.'

'What can I do? I love you, Jessie.'

When I went to bed I lay awake for a long time thinking about Mum, hoping she did understand. And wondering how to tackle Dad.

In the morning I made myself get up as soon as I heard him moving about. I went into the kitchen and he looked up from the paper with a huge grin on his face. 'Morning Jesseroon! And how's my nut brown maid?'

I was gobsmacked. I'd forgotten how nice he can be! I looked at his monkey-grin and his standing-on-end hair and had a sudden joyous thought that Mum had told him about going to Scarborough and won him over.

'Got something to show you!' he said, before I had time to speak. And he lifted up the paper to show me the front page. The headline was *EMBRYO EMBARGO!* I stared at it not knowing what it meant. 'An end to all this nonsense,' he said, 'Sanity has prevailed.'

'I don't understand.'

'There will be a halt in all embryo implantation. In response to those shenanigans down in Cheshire last week.'

'But they can't stop Sleeping Beaut—'

'They can't stop women who get pregnant naturally. Obviously. They're stopping implants.'

'But there haven't been any implants into women yet.'

'D'you think Golding's the only one? Now the vaccine's made it possible there'll be clinics poised up and down the country.'

'So why stop them?'

'Consent. The current legislation on consent doesn't begin to cover it.'

'Explain.'

'OK. Before all this, a stored embryo legally belonged to its biological parents, the ones who asked for it to be created. If it came from donated egg or sperm then the donors also had a say in it. And now there'll be the young surrogate who dies to bear the child, whose parents will feel they also have a stake in it. That's six potential parents for each baby. Common sense dictates the biological parents take precedence. But quite a few of them have up to ten stored embryos. What would they do with ten children? So who decides which ones they keep? And why should the surrogates' families come away with nothing? Some people are saying *none* of these should get them—that the babies are so precious they should be assigned to approved foster-parents.' He laughed and rubbed his hands. 'Cath was right, it's a minefield. And the *Mothers For Life* squabbles over Sleeping Beauty babies are *as nothing*.' He pushed the paper across the table to me and got up. 'I'm making a pot of coffee. Want some?'

The whole first three pages was taken up with it.

There were pictures of *Mothers For Life* and Embryo Donors. And a grainy picture of a sheep from the animal rights website. There was an aerial photo of the Wettenhall riot. There was a list of bullet points headed *Draft Proposals*:

- New (post MDS) embryos: individual donor consent must be obtained for animal research usage.
- Pre-MDS embryos: biological parents retain legal ownership of up to three and have one year time-limit to agree surrogates.
- After 12 months all pre-MDS embryos revert to the state for implantation in selected volunteers.

Dad being so happy about it made me fear the worst, but when I read that I realised it wasn't so bad. Why shouldn't my baby's biological parents bring her up? And biological parents would still need a surrogate. Surely they'd be glad to agree to someone a clinic had already vetted? I said that to Dad and he laughed.

'These are people whose embryos are still frozen because they couldn't decide what to do with them three, six, ten years ago. Now they'll get up to a year longer. I don't think they'll be rushing after volunteers tomorrow!' He took a mug of coffee upstairs to Mum. I read a statement from a *Mothers For Life* spokes-woman, which said they would continue to fight for the rights of surrogates and their families. Dad came back.

'They'll wait till the last minute because they *can* but also because they'll be hoping for some scientific breakthrough. The longer they wait the more likely that is.'

'But if there isn't any scientific breakthrough—'

'Then you can do your volunteering next year,' he said smugly.

I turned on the TV. It was the same. FLAME women were greeting the news happily and talking about how they would organise an egg donation programme for animal implantation research. *Mothers for Life* were organising protests. Scientists were worrying about losing a year, and politicians were talking about taking time to get it right.

The phone rang. It was the clinic asking me to come in for a meeting with Mr Golding that afternoon. It was true, then. The phone rang again—Sal. Going on about how pleased she was, that she couldn't bear it if I threw my life away. She said FLAME were going to focus their attacks on Sleeping Beauty clinics, their aim was to take women out of the research entirely. 'I couldn't bear it if you got tangled up in any of that stuff,' she said. 'I want to know you're safe.'

I thanked her and hung up. I checked my lucky nun was in my bag.

Twenty-nine

When I got to the clinic the FLAME pickets were outside the main doors with their banners. *NO MORE SLEEPING BEAUTIES. NO MORE DEGRADATION OF WOMEN.* One of them came towards me as I went up the steps. She looked embarrassed. 'Excuse me—'

'I've only come to see my dad—he works here.'

'On Sleeping Beauties?'

'No. He grows embryos for MDS research. For animals.'

The girl nodded, relieved, and I shoved the revolving door. The security guard grinned and pressed the buzzer. When I was through the double doors I went to the blue outpatients room where we'd had the first meeting for volunteers. Needless to say, Rosa was already there, and the shy girl, Theresa. I nodded at Theresa. I didn't want to look at Rosa and see whatever was on her face. Gloating, I supposed. I could feel I was bright red. Before anyone could speak, Mr Golding and a nurse came in. He was as plump and smiling and dapper as ever, it made me feel happier just to see him. He pulled up a chair and sat next to the three of us. The nurse started her tape recorder.

'They make life very difficult for me!' he said and smiled ruefully.

'Have we got to stop?' asked Rosa. I made myself glance at her. She was pretty, with her pale skin and dark hair. Prettier than me, if you didn't mind the strangeness of her eye. But if Baz liked her, why had he pretended to like me?

'Ah-ha! That's what they like you to think. But we have a secret weapon up the sleeve!' He pulled his chair a bit closer and looked at each of us carefully. 'What do you think about this news?'

'It's no good. We'll be too old in a year,' I said. Rosa nodded.

'And Theresa?' he said kindly. He was wearing a little navy blue bow tie with yellow spots on it, it was comical; underneath his bald head it made him look like an Easter egg.

'I don't know,' she said. 'I don't know what to think.'

He reached out and patted her hand. 'I am not surprised, my dear. Many of us no longer know what to think. Well, I shall tell you what I know and then we decide how to proceed, yes?' He began to talk about the pre MDS embryos. He made it sound like a fairy story. He said the human race is lost in a dangerous forest. And the frozen embryos are one clear path. There may be other paths that twist and turn through the dark trees, that scale ravines and plunge through rivers and lead eventually to a future. But this is the one mapped path. 'We know how to look after Sleeping Beauties, and get live births,' he told us. 'And we know how to vaccinate embryos. You can hear rumours of other cures, miracle drugs, who knows whatnot. But a scientist must look for the answer that adds up in here—' he tapped his shiny head and twinkled at us, 'and my onboard computer tells me this path is the real hope. Every day we delay—' he shrugged—'it will be harder for these children. There will be so many old, so few young.'

'But *why* have they said we must wait?' demanded Rosa.

'What is precious in this world now? Only these embryos. Money cannot help you, land cannot help you, a brilliant mind or the body of an athlete cannot help you. The rich are those who inherit the future. You understand? Survival of the fittest.'

We nodded, although to begin with I barely understood.

'The fittest now are those with frozen embryos. Only their genes survive. Parents of these embryos have power and if we do not yield it to them, they will fight. This is the one instinct without which we *all* die, our race dies—the instinct to safeguard our young.'

I thought of Mum and Dad, and how unhelpful that instinct can be. Dr Humpty Dumpty Golding leaned back in his chair and stretched. Even his shoes were shinier than new. 'So,' he said. 'It grieves me to admit but the politicians get it right. We must proceed by due course of law. We hope so much for these children, they do not need to be the bone every dog is trying to seize in his teeth. Now, tell me. You still wish to volunteer?'

'Yes,' said Rosa and I, together. I glanced at Theresa. She looked as if she was going to cry.

'Thank you,' he said gravely. 'Theresa, you must not be anxious. All the world is rushing but you are one person and you can be still.' He smiled at Theresa and she did begin to cry. He patted her hand gently, and took from his breast pocket a folded pale blue handkerchief, which he shook out and gave to her. He asked her if she wanted to stay while he talked to us, and she nodded. 'I tell you now,' he said. 'It is possible. We have some embryos with no parents.' He looked at us expectantly, pleased with his riddle. 'Sometimes in the old days when we carry out a procedure such as hysterectomy, we have asked the patient permission to take her eggs. Those she has not need of. She already has her children, or has embryos stored. Her surplus eggs can be used for benefit of other women. But—but but but! We cannot freeze an egg!' I remembered about not being able to freeze eggs, I'd heard it from Dad before. 'OK. So we have fine eggs, donated. But how to keep them?'

Neither of us knew.

'We have to fertilise,' he said. 'If we fertilise in vitro, the egg is happy, the egg grows. The ovum, the sperm, the zygote, the embryo. All is well and we can freeze.' He looked at us triumphantly and I was glad it was Rosa who asked,

'How do they get fertilised?'

'In house. The embryo is anonymous.' I noticed the

nurse, who was sitting by the window listening to all this. She had a little smile on her face.

'What does in house mean?' asked Rosa.

'Here, at the clinic,' said Mr Golding simply.

Rosa was still looking blank, so he patiently explained it to her. But I remembered Father of Wisdom telling me about his heroes in the early days of IVF. They didn't know how to freeze anything back then, so they always had to use fresh sperm—their own. Rosa finally got it. 'The egg and sperm donors don't even know they've made an embryo together.'

'The sperm donors know,' he told her. 'But they also know these are embryos only for research.'

'They don't belong to anyone.'

'Correct.' It was like a heavy door being unlocked. First a crack of sunlight had appeared, then it widened into a wedge, and now a whole radiant doorway swung open before us.

'Won't you get in trouble?' said Rosa. 'If everyone's waiting a year? Won't you get in trouble when they find out we're pregnant?'

'Orphan embryos.' He shrugged. 'In clinics this is common practice. At Charing Cross Hospital they already prepare first pre-MDS implantations from anonymous donors. My colleagues in Birmingham are also ready. The only ones we displease are the ladies picketing our doorstep.'

'FLAME doesn't know?' I asked.

He put his finger to his lips and smiled. 'The lack of named biological parents makes our life more simple,' he said. 'If you and your parents wish it, they will receive your child. You must discuss with them.'

'What if I don't wish it?' said Rosa aggressively.

'There is no shortfall of persons wishing to adopt.'

'Can I sign something? Giving the baby up for adoption?'

He said she could, then he turned to me. I said I would discuss it with Mum and Dad. I had already imagined them as the parents. Mr Golding pushed back his chair and stood up. 'So, my dears. Now you have time to digest.' He shook each of our hands very seriously, and then he held the door open. Theresa went out first. I saw that Rosa was hanging back and I waited to see what she had to say. She wasn't going to know more than me.

'Mr Golding, can I stay here?'

'Here?'

'In the clinic.'

'One moment.' He called to the nurse who was already walking away down the corridor, and asked her to come back into the room with us and restart the tape. I could already guess what Rosa meant and it made my heart race. Mr Golding shut the door. 'Rosa?' he said.

'I don't need any time to think. And my date's really soon. If I don't go ahead now then I have to wait another month.'

'I'm the same,' I chipped in.

He looked from Rosa to me and back again. 'Can you both come in on Monday?'

'I'd rather stay now I'm here,' she said. 'Please.'

'Explain to me why,' he said kindly.

'I don't want to do the goodbyes. All that fuss. I just want to get on with it.'

'You must see your mother,' he said.

'She can come and see me here. In the clinic.' Rosa knew how to get what she wanted, and in the end he said yes. Actually, it was a pity I didn't have the sense to do the same as her.

But I didn't. I went home, slipping out through the FLAME pickets and even stopping to tell the embarrassed girl, 'My dad wishes you the best of luck!' I was excited. Excited about Monday morning, excited about the weekend. I thought Mum and Dad were both so near to understanding, that the news about the baby, the baby that would be theirs, would be enough to tip the balance. I was thinking of all the things we might do, how we could go on a walk up to Dovestones and look for the kingfisher; of how I was going to relish every precious last minute of my time.

And when Dad asked me to visit Nanna Bessie's house with him, and said they were going to give it to motherless kids, I was happy. Happy that we were doing something useful together.

Friday morning

When I wake my head is clear. Today's the day. Today
this must end. My feet and legs ache and my ankles are
stiff. As for my clothes, they're disgusting. When he
brings me my breakfast I ask if I can have a bath.

'Of course.' He goes and turns it on. When I've
eaten my brown toast and damson jam and the steam
is beginning to curl into the room, he turns off the taps
and comes to me with the bike key. 'Tell me you're not
going to try anything stupid.'

'I'm not going to try anything stupid.'

He undoes the locks. I massage my ankles, then try
to stand. I'm as bent and rickety as an old woman. He
has to hold my elbow to steady me, I can barely walk.

'The hot water will ease it,' he says. 'You should
have done this last night. I've put your clean clothes in
the bathroom.' He holds me till I get inside the
bathroom then he steps back and shuts the door. I lock
it with the little bolt. I'm alone in here.

Bliss.

Bliss. Peeling off my smelly clothes and trailing my hand in the too-hot water. Watching the cold thundering in and making clouds of steam swirl up into my face. Holding the edge of the bath as I test one wonky foot in the water—too hot but OK—and then the other. Slowly lowering myself like a fussy hen settling down on her nest, and the lovely heat of the water lapping up my body, turning me pink as a shrimp. The dumb ache in my ankles lifting from my bones and floating out into the water.

Gradually, inch by inch, I lie back, until I am completely submerged apart from my face. The water enfolds me, wrapping me round and caressing me like hot silk. This is the best bath of my life. I stare up at the steam and wonder what Dad is doing. I imagine him sitting on the top step of the stairs (in case I dash out and make a run for it), his elbows on knees, head in hands. Staring dumbly at the carpet. Not knowing what he will do. Miserable. I need to save him from this, I need to save him from himself.

I'm hot all over now. Slowly, one at a time I raise my limbs, leg, leg, arm, arm, and luxuriously hold them up in the steamy air to cool. My body is warm and whole and buzzingly alive. I am in command. I am the one with power, because I am the one who knows what to do.

When I've washed myself I step out and wrap myself in the old familiar towel. It's the green stripy one from home—did Mum pack it for him? Imagine them packing, loading the boot, as if they were organising a holiday. Except their faces would be grim and grey, their voices pinched and whispery . . . I'm not going to think about that. The trouble is, there's not enough air in this bathroom, the steam is choking me. The longer all this goes on, the worse it is for them. I need to bring it to an end. I balance on the bath to open the little top window, and have a brainwave. OK, I can do it. I can make it end.

I dry myself quickly and put on the clean clothes. He's given me a blue T-shirt of Mum's but it's not a bad fit. I'm annoyed that my shoes aren't here—but there didn't seem any point in putting them on, when I was only coming to have a bath. When I'm ready I put the toilet lid down and sit on it to consider.

Everything moveable in this room is made of plastic. There's nothing that would be capable of smashing the thick swirly patterned glass in the window. Think. Check. Look again. Above the bath, about a foot below the ceiling, there's a bent metal pole to hold a shower curtain. Not that Nanna ever used her bath as a shower. But there it is, screwed into the wall above the tap end of the bath, then running the length of the tub, turning the corner and fixing into the wall at the opposite end. I climb up on the side of the bath and peer at it, thinking maybe I can unpick the screws. It's old cloudy dirty metal, and the screws are rusted into the tiles. Then I notice a join. The rail isn't continuous, it's in three sections; two straight bits and a curved elbow to join them. I balance on the corner of the bath and try to twist the rail. I tug either side of the join until suddenly there's a tiny give, and then proper movement, and I can pull it apart. Now I can twist it at the other joint, and ease it out. It's the curved corner piece—the long bits are still screwed into the wall. Dad taps on the door. 'Jess? You done?'

'Nearly.'

I jump down with the curved section of rail in my hand. It's hollow so it's still quite light—but if I can put enough force behind it . . . I swing it a couple of times for practice then bash it against the window as hard as I can. There's a dull cracking noise, and the glass fractures.

'What are you doing?'

'I'm just—' I flush the toilet so he can't hear me, and bash again. It shatters. I climb on the bath and peer through to outside; it's a long way to the ground. In a film there'd be a handy waste pipe to balance on, but here it must be around the corner of the house.

'Jessie!' he shouts. 'Jessie, let me in!'

There's one big triangular shard still sticking up out of the bottom of the window frame. Carefully, holding it between my fingers and thumb on either side, I try if it will lift out. Yes. It's heavy. A long sharp triangle, still with old putty stuck to its lower edge.

He's banging on the door. 'You can't get out that way. Don't be ridiculous! Let me in!'

The cold air swirling in through the window has cleared my head. 'I'm not trying to get out,' I tell him. 'Calm down, let me clean my teeth.' I put the glass down and turn on the tap in the sink. I test the pointed end of the glass on my thumb. Sharp. The straight end with putty on is blunt but if the whole piece fractures it could be bad. I try grasping the straight edge through the towel but the towel's too bulky. My dirty T-shirt works better.

'Jessie that's enough. Open the door or I'll break it down.'

'I'm just using the toilet.' I need the element of surprise. I know what I am doing, it is coming to me as I need to know, I can trust it. I will outwit him and escape. Holding my weapon in my right hand I flush the toilet with my left and immediately draw back the bolt on the door. I yank it open fast and he's standing right in front of me. My glass dagger's pointing at his stomach.

'Jess—'

'Listen to me.'

'Put that down before you cut yourself.'

'*Listen!*' I step forward, the point of the glass is practically touching him. He half raises his hands in the air, he's nearly smiling. It is quite comical, he looks like a bad actor in a western. 'If you don't do what I say, I'll stab you.'

'You wouldn't,' he says, and very stupidly he reaches his right hand to the side of the glass to take it off me. I don't let go. He snatches his hand away. He doesn't make a sound, just stands staring at the bright red line that magically appears across his palm.

My tummy does a flip but I have to keep going. 'See. I mean it. Go backwards into the bedroom.'

'Look,' he says, holding out his hand. The blood is running now, it drips onto the floor, drip drip drip, getting faster. Please don't let it be an artery. I have to make this *end*.

'Move,' I say.

'Stop it Jess, you've hurt me.'

'D'you want me to kill you?' I move the glass a

fraction so the point is touching his shirt. I am afraid I might burst into tears. He takes a tiny step back. 'OK. Keep going.'

Slowly he backs into the bedroom, inched along by my dagger. I'm OK. I'm in control. Once we're through the doorway I see what I hoped for—the bike locks are lying where he unlocked me. 'Pick up the locks,' I tell him. 'Slowly.' He bends and grabs both with his left hand. He's holding his right up away from him, and it's dripping steadily, but not as fast as I thought before. 'Now back to the bathroom,' I tell him. Slowly, we retrace our steps. In the bathroom I tell him to wind one lock around his ankle, like he did with me. His legs and trousers are thicker, it only fits round twice.

'OK, now lock it. And now thread the other one through the bottom of the towel rail, and through the lock on your leg, and fasten it.'

He stops and looks at me. 'For goodness sake, Jess.'

'It's only what you did to me.'

He stops short of locking the two together, stands up and faces me. 'Go on then, what're you going to do?'

'I've told you.'

'I'm already bleeding,' he says.

'The quicker you do it the quicker a doctor can come.'

He stands still, staring at me. I make myself stare into his eyes. He has to do what I say. He has to believe me. He glances at his bleeding hand and I make myself inch forward with the glass. Please let him obey me, please—

'Lock it. Lock it. Now!' My voice has turned into a mad squeak. He crouches quickly, closes the lock, then stands again, holding his hand up in the air. It's still dripping. How deep is it? Is it deep? You have to make this work. 'Where's the key?'

'What? Jessie for God's sake—'

'Where's the key?'

'I don't know.'

'Turn out your pockets.'

He fumbles into his pocket with his left hand and drags stuff out, it spills to the floor. In among the loose change, door keys, penknife, pocket fluff, there are two little silvery keys on a metal ring.

I kick them out of his reach, and step out of the bathroom. He's crouched by the towel rail, supporting the elbow of his right arm with his left hand, staring at me. 'Jess. You don't have to do this. Look, kill me if it makes you feel better. Just don't go back to the clinic.'

'I'll phone a doctor. I'll tell Mum where to find you.' I'm shaking.

'Jessie. Please, Jessie, please don't go . . .' He's crying. My legs are spindly strands of spaghetti. Trust me, this is for the best. This has to end, and I am the one with the power. I am the only one who knows what she must do. Dad's face is bloody where he's wiped his eyes, blood's trickling down his arm, how has it come to this?

'I'm sorry. *I'm sorry*!' I throw down the glass, snatch up my shoes and run down the stairs. I yank back the bolts and undo the Yale before I pause to put my shoes on. He's upstairs. He's not coming after me. He's locked to the towel rail. When my shoes are laced I start to run. His voice trails after me: 'Jessie! Je-e-ess–ieeee!'

I gulp in the cold damp air, and run and run to get away from his calling voice.

Thirty

They have given me and Rosa two rooms up on the third floor. They are where staff can stay overnight if they have late or early shifts. We look into the park, on the other side of the main road. I sat by the window on my first evening and watched it starting to get dark. I felt calm. And grateful I was in a safe harbour after the crazy storm of the last few days. For a long time I just sat enjoying the peace, with my brain disengaged inside my skull, floating there like a tethered boat on a lake. Calmness lapped around me.

Eventually, as dusk fell outside, a question materialised in my head. I watched as the road beneath my window became clogged with rush hour cars. After I'd sat in the darkness watching them for a while, I decided to go and ask Mr Golding. His office is at the end of the corridor past the secretaries. I didn't know if he would still be there because the office staff had all gone home, but I went and knocked. He called to me to come in. His room was dim apart from his desk lamp. I couldn't see his face, only his arm and his hand holding the pen, in the small pool of light.

'Jessie!' he said. 'Come in, come in. What can I do for you?' He tilted the lamp so that the light shone up at the wall behind him. Its soft glow spread over the room, so the desk and chairs and bookcases seemed to be reaching up out of black shadow into the gentle light. He pointed to the leather chair where I could sit.

'How will the embryos know—if they grow up and want to get married—how will they know they're not related?'

'Aha! A young geneticist!' He rubbed his hands in a pleased way, as if I was the cleverest pupil in the class. 'Each embryo has a number—for egg donor—and a colour, for sperm. This record will go to the guardians, and must be made known to the child. So. 2 Blue will know, when he meets 2 Green, that they have the same mother. A 7 Red girl with a 4 Red boy will know they share a father. We will tell guardians when a sibling is born. It will be a support to these children to know a sibling.'

I had a vision of a nursery-full of baby Goldings, all with bald heads and little bow ties. How dim am I? It was only then I realised. 'How many colours are there?' I asked him.

He listed on his fingers, 'Red, yellow, blue, green, purple, brown. Six.'

'Including the technicians?'

He nodded. 'Including Ali and your father.'

We sat looking at each other in the peaceful room.

All around us it seemed as if the building was asleep, as if everyone had gone away.

I wondered if it would make any difference to Dad. 'Would there be anything wrong—?' I asked.

'Of course not. You are the surrogate. The child's genes are from its mother and father, nothing from you.'

'She could be my half-sister. Or brother.'

He nodded.

I thought of the baby two floors below me, in the freezer, silently waiting for her life to begin. My half-sister. Mr Golding passed me a box of tissues from the bookshelf. Then he went over to his window and looked out into the night. When I had blown my nose he turned round and said,

'Jessie. You need to sleep. If you are worried in the morning we talk again, yes?' He picked up the phone and dialled, and I heard him say hello to Rosa. Before I could stop him, he asked her to come and meet me. As I went out of his office I saw her walking towards me along the corridor. 'Goodnight Jessie,' he said quietly, behind me. 'Sleep well.'

Rosa followed me into my room and sat on the chair by the dark window. 'You're not giving up?' she said.

'No. I was asking him about the sperm donors.'

She nodded, staring out into the blackness. I wanted her to go. But she would be hanging around till the very end; we'd been told that after they implant, you have to wait a few days to see if the pregnancy is confirmed. To be certain the embryo has bedded down happily inside you. I would have to spend the last week of my life with Rosa Davis.

'I'm tired,' I told her.

But she wouldn't take the hint. 'Me too. Are you scared?'

Only of other people, I thought. Only of my parents behaving like lunatics. Of Baz, clanging in my head. Of you. 'No. Are you?'

'Not really. It's got to be better than this life, hasn't it?'

'Better?'

'Better than the rubbish you have to put up with day after day.'

I didn't want to tell her anything about myself. 'Like what?'

She glanced at me with her straight eye. 'Not having enough money. Nowhere to live. Everything always turning to shit.'

'I thought you lived with your mum.'

'I can't stay there. Her druggy mates come round and that's that, everything gets nicked.'

I was reminded of Lisa. 'Well you could go and live in one of the Kids' Houses—the *Rising Sun*, or the place in Wales.'

She didn't know anything about them, and I had to explain the whole idea to her. She shook her head when I said she wouldn't need any money.

'You always need money. It wouldn't work anyway. They wouldn't want someone like me messing things up.'

I was about to deny it. But what was the point of meeting that with a lie? 'You're different,' I said.

'Yeah. I'd piss them off. I'd drink all the wine and screw their boyfriends, and forget to feed the chickens.'

I couldn't not ask her. 'Did you sleep with Baz?'

'Sure.'

There was no reason for me to care either way. But tears pierced my eyes.

'You see?' she said, walking heavily to the door. 'Now *you're* pissed off with me.' She pulled the door closed behind her.

I dragged the blankets over me and breathed into the warm darkness underneath them, until my own breath had made it all so hot and damp that I had to stick my head out to gasp lungfuls of proper air. My nose was blocked, I was too hot and then too cold. There was nowhere I could go.

I fell asleep eventually, and when I woke there was a breakfast tray on the table by my bed, with orange juice and bread rolls and dinky individual packets of jam. The tea was cold but I drank it anyway. It was a cloudy windy morning, from my bed I could see big masses of cloud trundling past. It was like my bedroom view at home without the beech tree. I sat back against my pillow and stared at the sky.

It didn't matter about Baz. It mattered, of course it mattered, but only if we were both going to live for eighty years. Then there would be time for everything to change. There would be time to understand. Right now I couldn't know if he really liked her more than me or if he was only sorry for her or if he would still have been going out with either of us in a year. Maybe even he didn't know. I had to rip it out of my head. I wouldn't ask her any more about it.

I kept on staring at the clouds. They were moving across the window from left to right, massive blowsy shapes in different shades of grey, and at different heights in the sky. The closer ones were catching up and sliding in front of others which were further away from the earth. I wanted to volunteer because I wanted to make a difference. That was the thing to hang on to. The coming week would be weird—of course. I would have to say the real goodbye to Mum and Dad, which I dreaded. I would have to talk to Rosa. But the rest of it was my own precious time, and I could use it how I wanted. I put the breakfast tray back on the table and got dressed and went across to the office to ask for some paper.

I decided to finish this. Dad can add it to the pile at Nanna Bessie's.

The history of my decision. For you, my child. I want you to know my story—our story, your beginning. So you understand everything I've thought and felt, and so no one can tell you I was a silly brainwashed girl, or a puppet of Iain's. I don't want anyone trying to claim you for a movement or an idea. You're free, and whatever you want to do with your life, the thought of it makes me glad. Above all I want you to know I'm glad. I'm glad this is happening.

I have been writing and writing, till my fingers ache and my neck is stiff; I am going to write myself all the way to the end of my story, and tell you how things have changed this week, and how I am right now, up to the last possible minute. But now I'm talking to you, I have to give you a name. What can I call you? I don't even know if you're a boy or a girl. I've been thinking about your name for ages and what I came up with was Ray (Rae, if you prefer). A ray of golden sunshine, a ray of hope. But I wonder how old you are as you read this? When I was thirteen something soppy like that would have made me cringe. You could think of the other kind of ray, the fish gliding along the seabed like an arrow. And the mermaid's purses, you'll find those on the beach, where the ray's eggs have floated safely across oceans. Maybe that will seem alright. If not, look, change it. I won't mind!

It's so funny writing to you—I can't believe I won't see you, Rae. You'll see me—Mum and Dad have loads of pictures, plus videos of holidays, you'll be bored to death of seeing me splashing around in the sea and slurping ice-creams. I might look young to you, for a mum. But no—of course, all the mums look young in your world.

I want to tell you one thing I've decided, my darling. If they implant on Monday and it doesn't work—if my pregnancy is not confirmed at the end of the week—I shan't try again. That chance of me not being pregnant, is the last deciding straw. If I am pregnant then you are meant to be. If I'm not, then you're not—well, you won't be! You won't be reading this. And I'll stay alive and go to Eden.

The sirens have been going mad all night. Early this morning lots of police vans drew up on the side road of the park, and police with riot shields ran across the road. The window here won't open but I could hear faint bursts of shouts and chanting. I turned on the little TV in the corner and it was weird seeing the main entrance of this very hospital up there on the screen. There was a massive protest going on. FLAME definitely, and some women with the purple *Mothers for*

Life banners, and a chanting chorus of Noahs. There were Animal Liberation Front kids too, the commentator said the police were taking their threats very seriously. I turned off the sound. I watched the people pushing and struggling and waving their arms at each other, and the police shoving through them, and it made me feel really tired. Let them carry on, I thought. They *will* carry on. They'll carry on like that, thrashing about, hitting each other and smashing things, blindly lashing out at the world—until some way forward becomes clear. Until the new babies are born. I touched the remote and the swirling mass of them disappeared.

Mr Golding came to see me this morning, bringing a consent form for me to sign. He told me that for the time being, no one was going in or out. Staff had slept in the hospital. 'We are under siege!' he joked. There were FLAME activists picketing all the entrances. Some Animal Liberationists had been arrested. He told me the hospital has all essential supplies. 'We hope they will get tired and go home,' he said 'We avoid escalation. But we must explain to your parents.'

I was relieved it was Mum who answered but as soon as she heard my voice she burst into tears. She kept telling me it was too soon. It wasn't a conversation, it was just two people repeating opposite things:

Me—*I'm fine, I'm where I want to be.*

Mum—*You need more time.*

In the end I just had to tell her I'd see her very soon, and put the phone down. I wanted to keep my mind happy and peaceful for you, to stay inside my own calm, and keep floating forward.

I spent the whole day writing, stopping now and then to stare out at the sky, at the slowly, endlessly shifting clouds. Rosa knocked on my door in the afternoon and I told her I would see her later. We had our tea together and sat talking for a long time after it. She was different. I still don't know whether to believe everything she says, but I guess I did believe her when she said, 'Nothing good ever happens to me.' She never knew her dad. Her mum's boyfriend was awful to Rosa and tried to make her have sex with him. There was no one she could tell, there was nowhere she could go. That was when she ran away. She went to London and slept rough and got taken to a hostel. She said she had sex with men to get money. She went back to her mum's flat after her mum kicked the boyfriend out, but she and her Mum fought all the time. Rosa met a drummer at a club and it was love at first sight and she moved in with him. But when he'd been drinking he was violent. He beat her up so she moved back to her mum's again. Her mum was an agency nurse and that's how Rosa found out about the frozen embryos.

Everyone she met seemed to make Rosa's life worse. All the kids at school—like me. Avoiding her, thinking she was weird, hating her for going with Baz. I thought, she's only volunteering because of us. It was almost as if I was her murderer. I wondered about telling Mr Golding. Then I remembered that Baz had said, 'You're both mad.' What would she do if Golding told her she couldn't volunteer? Go back to her mum's? This was the place she wanted to be; like me.

Now we've started telling each other our dreams, and the daft things that pop into our heads. And we've started talking about our babies, and imagining you might be like a sister and brother. She wants her child to be called Zac. I hope the two of you will know each other.

And that is strange. Because you'll know if it's happened, and I won't. Your reality is my dream, and I must lose my reality for you to become real. Then *I* will be just a dream to *you*. Swapping places, either side of the line of being alive. Except you're not dead. You're not alive yet, but I don't have the word for what you are. You're waiting to be alive, they are probably unfreezing you right now, and the whole magic pattern of genes and cells which will grow into you, is triggered. It makes me think of a Chinese shell I got in my Christmas stocking; a dull little grey shell. You drop it into water and slowly the shell opens, and a beautiful pink flower magically spirals out of it. That's you!

The protestors have been going mad and there have been lots of arrests. But anyway, Dad got in to see me. I told Mr Golding I was nervous about seeing him again, so he was escorted to my room by a security guard who waited outside the door. Dad hugged me then he went and sat at the chair by the window. He had a bandage wound round his right hand, with his fingers poking out. I sat on the bed and there was this silence. I tried to think of something to say, then I looked at him and he was crying. I asked him to stop. He got up and turned his back to me, staring out the window and rubbing his eyes. When he was still I crept over to him and he put his arm round my shoulders and we stood looking out the window together at the watery spring sunshine and the buds on the trees in the park.

'Perfect crime,' he said softly.

'Yes?'

'Persuade an innocent, idealistic young girl that the future of the human race depends on her sacrificing her own life. She will come into hospital as trustingly as a lamb to the slaughter. She will welcome the implantation of a baby that will kill her. She'll lie there while her brain is destroyed for nine whole months, and no police will arrest you, no court will judge you, you'll get away scot free. At the end of nine months she'll be taken off life support and she'll be completely dead. And no one will be blamed.'

'Dad,' I said. 'That's wrong.'

He shook his head.

'Listen,' I said. 'You know what was the perfect crime? MDS. Engineer a virus so it's deadly and airborne. You don't even have to be there, it travels all around the world on its own and kills millions of women, and there's nothing to link it to you. Remote mass murder. That's the perfect crime.'

'Well that's true,' he said.

'And what I'm doing is the perfect solution.'

He squeezed my shoulders. 'An answer for everything, my Jess.'

'Well I have got a Father of Wisdom.'

He faced me and I looked for the tiny beginning crinkle of a smile. But what he said was, 'This is wrong, Jess. I wish you wouldn't do it.'

'I know. But I'm going to.'

He let go of me, and sat in the chair again. 'Right. Well what d'you want to talk about?' There was a pause then he said, 'The weather?'

'I want you to promise you and Mum will look after her.'

'Her?'

'Her, him, I don't know. I've been imagining a girl.'

'If I said I wouldn't, would it stop you?'

'No.'

'Cath and I have to give up our own daughter and substitute the child of strangers. We have to go through every step of the past sixteen years that we've loved and lived with you, being reminded every day of what we've lost.'

'She won't be a stranger's child.'

He stared at me.

'The baby will be my half-sister, or brother. Mr Golding said it would be fine.'

There was a little pause. 'That's no reason for you to expect us to agree.'

'It *is* a reason for you to look after the baby.'

'It's no reason. You don't need to do this. There will be other solutions.'

'Dad—'

'There will be, believe me. Please.' He knelt on the floor and put his arms around my legs. There was nothing I could do.

The security guard helped him up and took him away. Then Mum came in the afternoon and it was just as bad. I can't bear it and I can't change it and I can't help it. I'm sorry. I'm sorry. I'm sorry.

Today

Well my dear one, you are implanted. Now it's up to
you, whether to live or not. I've written and written
till my arm aches and a writer's bump has appeared
on my middle finger. And now I've just been sitting by
the window letting my mind go blank. Whatever I
write now is me hanging onto your coat sleeve
because I don't want to part. I should just say
goodbye, shouldn't I? Rosa and I have tried to guess
at what your lives might be like—yours, Rae, and
Zac's. We hope you'll be friends. But what it boils
down to is this: I have to end for you to begin. Your
life is after mine.

Rosa went down to the ward this morning and Dr
Nichol has just told me her pregnancy is confirmed.
They'll test me tomorrow. Now I've said my goodbyes
I don't have to see anyone else. I'm enjoying being
quiet, sitting by the window in my little room, staring
out at the world. I'm enjoying the way it is receding,

all worries becoming flimsy, as easy to brush away as cobwebs.

I like watching the main road from up here. Now they've cleared all the protestors the traffic is flowing again. I think about where the drivers are going. Maybe that one's heading home after working late. He'll open the door and call 'Hello?' and go into the warmth of the kitchen, unbuttoning his coat. 'At last!' his wife will say, 'I'm starving.' She's taking the fish pie out of the oven. 'Did you wait for me? That's nice,' he says, pulling up his chair to the table. 'That smells good.'

Maybe that one is on his way to a meeting to discuss staging the closure of a nursery. When he arrives no one else is there yet, so he moves the chairs into a circle on the blue carpet and sits at one of the little desks to write an agenda. Maybe that one is looking for her lost cat, which is brown and white like an unripe conker. The motorist crawls along slowly, peering into the darkness.

Maybe that one is driving to the airport, meeting nobody, speaking to no one. Silent and deadly, a little cotton-wool wrapped vial in a metal box in his briefcase. A new virus. He hates everyone, he's a perfect criminal. But as he accelerates away from the roundabout, a cat which is brown and white like an unripe conker darts in front of the oncoming car, which brakes and skids and comes crashing into his. His car flips and bursts into flames, killing him on the spot. The intense heat burns through his briefcase and melts the metal box into a sealed black blob, safely entombing that virus forever.

A man who stops to try and help rings the ambulance. As he drives slowly on to the all-night supermarket he is obsessing about the new formula which he and his colleague are convinced may be the first step towards a cure. He puts a jar of damson jam in his basket and has a sudden flash of inspiration. Excitedly he rings his colleague. She thinks he could be right, and they agree to adjust their research first thing in the morning.

Everyone is moving. We each follow our business as importantly as dogs trotting down the street. No one can tell who is special or who is not. All these stories must go on. On and on to their children's children.

Dad talked about fear. He doesn't understand why I'm not afraid. 'Fear is like pain, it's the body's warning system. It teaches us to protect ourselves.' I told him I'm not afraid because I know what's going to happen. I'm going to have an injection and fall asleep. What's to be afraid of? 'When people are executed they know exactly what's going to happen and most of them are terrified,' he replied. I told him, these people weren't choosing to die. Look at suicide bombers, they don't display fear. They have to concentrate on what they're doing, on putting themselves near the enemy and detonating their device without causing suspicion. They *really* have to be brave. All I have to do is be looked after, I don't have to worry about doing it wrong, messing up, getting caught. There's no need for fear.

What I'm doing has made him ill and old, he's gone smaller and the bags under his eyes sag right down his cheeks. And when I saw Mum's white face and red eyes I felt like a torturer. I know I've written bitchy things about them, and stupid kinds of childishness. But it's the only chance now of them ever understanding. So I'm writing them a note to go with this, saying they can read it too. I hope that's alright. Mum? Dad? Hello from Jessie! Imagine me leaning out of a train window, blowing you a great big kiss!

I've been thinking about going. I was thinking about fireworks. After a rocket explodes. What happens to its trajectory? Not the burnt stump and stick that fall to earth, but the trajectory of the rocket's rise? If you could take a pencil and draw a line on from where it explodes, keep going on and up and round, higher and higher, curving out into space. Or what happens at the end of a CD. When you've listened to the music and the music finishes. You know the sound you hear, the recorded silence at the end? Something still going on. Even though it's not the song.

Dearest Rae,

This really is the last, because it's four in the morning and today is my test and they'll keep me on the ward if it's all OK. They'll take me down at eight. I've been sitting here by the window and it's so beautiful, I have to tell you. The sky is clear and the moon is nearly full, just a couple of days off full, I'd guess. In the small hours there was no traffic and everything was perfectly calm and still. You can't see the stars because of the street lamps, but you can see the moon up there alone in the sky. The bright deserted streets look mysterious and welcoming, waiting for everything to start again, waiting for the world to wake up.

I've been thinking about flying. I've moaned about Mum and Dad flying, but I should admit to you, I used to love it! I wonder if there will still be flights in your world? The one I was thinking about was the winter before MDS. I went with Mum and Dad on one of their bargain city breaks.

It was evening, already nearly dark at five o'clock, and there were just a few small clouds in the sky. I was sitting by the window. As we took off and climbed higher I stared down at the lights. We were over the sprawl of greater Manchester, and I could see all the individual lights of houses, rows of lampposts, vertical oblongs of high rise. I could see floodlit football pitches and a glowing misty blue-green rectangle which I thought might be a swimming pool. Then as we went higher the city gave way to country and the lights thinned out into single lines threaded across blackness. When we came to a town again I could make out moving lines of cars along a main road. And then right in the middle of the town's lights there was a sudden patch of blackness. I stared at it, wondering if it was a park, puzzling at the way the lights were not patterned around it but seemed to end all higgledy piggledy. As if there was a yawning black chasm and whole streets had fallen into it.

Then gradually at the top of my porthole there began to be a brightness. And this silvery brightness intensified until I could see it was coming from a great shining balloon a thousand times bigger and brighter than anything on the face of the earth. You know what it was, Rae? The moon! And with moonlight radiating all across the sky, I could see that there were black blobs of cloud hanging here and there, between us and the earth. They were dead patches in the light. As we moved the steady pinprick lights of earth glowed on and on, disappearing as our moving position set a cloud between us and them, and reappearing as we moved on far enough to gain another sightline.

I felt happy then, Ray. Tender towards the innocent, sleeping earth. The dark hills and valleys and reservoirs and seas were all in their positions, keeping the dots of light of one village so many miles from the next, holding each single glowing house steady on its own exact latitude and longitude. And I knew the moonlight was steady too, and the full moon would always rise and roll across the sky every month at the right time. Those clouds were nothing but dark wet air, and finally they would dribble away to nothing.

Then we were descending and my ears were filled by the roaring of the engines, and my eyes with the sudden close ground as we flew over the edge of the airfield, tilting down to landing. And I stopped thinking, because I was there.

I wish everything for you, my Ray, but most of all I wish you might one day feel the peace and happiness I feel now, in sending my love to you.

Xxx, a thousand kisses, Jessie.